Nantucket

Also by Nan Rossiter

Under a Summer Sky
More Than You Know
Words Get in the Way
The Gin & Chowder Club

Nantucket

NAN ROSSITER

KENSINGTON BOOKS
www.kensingtonbooks.com

KENSINGTON BOOKS are published by

Kensington Publishing Corp.
119 West 40th Street
New York, NY 10018

All Kensington titles, imprints, and distributed lines are available at special quantity discounts for bulk purchases for sales promotion, premiums, fund-raising, educational, or institutional use.

Special book excerpts or customized printings can also be created to fit specific needs. For details, write or phone the office of the Kensington Sales Manager: Kensington Publishing Corp., 119 West 40th Street, New York, NY 10018. Attn. Sales Department. Phone: 1-800-221-2647.

Kensington and the K logo Reg. U.S. Pat. & TM Off.

eISBN-13: 978-1-61773-651-3
eISBN-10: 1-61773-651-1
First Kensington Electronic Edition: September 2015

ISBN-13: 978-1-61773-650-6
ISBN-10: 1-61773-650-3
First Kensington Trade Paperback Printing: September 2015

10 9 8 7 6 5 4 3 2 1

Printed in the United States of America

For my dad, the boat builder

WITH HEARTFELT THANKS . . .

To my editor, Esi Sogah, and my agent, Deirdre Mullane, who consistently make thoughtful suggestions and who always have a kind word of encouragement or reassurance ready; to the team at Kensington, who do their very best to make every book a success; to my husband, Bruce, and our boys, Cole and Noah, who inspire me every day and keep me smiling; to my dad—my number one fan—who tells everyone about my latest publishing endeavors; and to all my friends and family, who faithfully read and tell their friends about my books. I am truly blessed!

PART I

*Teach us to number our days, that
we may gain a heart of wisdom.*

—Psalm 90:12

Chapter 1

A sudden gust of wind swept through the weathered boat-house doors, swirling sawdust into the corners and sending papers fluttering to the floor. Forty-three-year-old Liam Tate looked up from the mahogany Gar Wood runabout he was working on, pushed his sun-streaked chestnut brown hair out of his eyes, and realized the late-afternoon sun had disappeared behind an ominously dark cluster of clouds. He brushed the sawdust from his jeans and walked over to stand in the doorway.

As he watched, a hot streak of white light seared the sky, striking the dark gray ocean, and a moment later, angry thunder rumbled across the heavens. Liam felt a warm body pressing against his legs and looked down. "It's okay, Tuck," he consoled, but the big golden retriever just gazed out the doors with worried eyes. "It's only thunder," he added, stroking Tucket's velvet ears, and although the tip of his tail wagged, Liam knew there was no convincing him. Who'd ever believe such a big dog could be so sidelined by thunder?

Liam knelt down and wrapped his arm around him, and

Tuck gave Liam's cheek an anxious lick before turning his attention back to the dark sky. "You're silly, you know that?" Liam whispered, stroking his noble head. "It's just thunder and you'll be happy when things cool off." The last several days had been oppressively hot and humid, and Liam was ready for a change. He didn't mind the heat, but the humidity wore him out. He felt his knee start to ache, kissed Tuck's furrowed brow, got up, and limped stiffly over to pick up the papers. As he did, another gust of wind swept through the doors and pushed several pages of the local newspaper under the workbench. He picked up everything that was within reach and closed the doors.

The boathouse creaked and groaned in the wind, but Liam hardly noticed. The sturdy structure had stood looking out across Nantucket Sound for more than a hundred years, weathering everything nature threw at it—from raging hurricanes and snowy blizzards to blistering heat—and through it all, it had barely lost a shingle.

Liam closed the windows, glanced at his watch, and decided it was time to call it a day anyway—if they left now, they might even make it home before it rained. "Ready to head out?" he asked, looking down at the worried dog glued to his leg. The tip of Tuck's tail wagged tentatively and Liam shook his head. He moved the tools he'd been using from the boat to the workbench, shut off the lights, and pushed open the side door. While he locked up, Tuck hurried over to the old Chevy pickup that was parked in the side yard and sat with his ears back, waiting. When Liam opened the cab door, he soared in like a rocket and plopped down behind the steering wheel.

"Move over, you big lug," Liam said, nudging him. Tuck edged over to the passenger's window, which under normal conditions was his favorite spot, but when a loud clap of thunder split the sky above them, he moved back and tried to sit on Liam's lap. "That's not gonna work," Liam said, gently pushing him off. Tuck gave him a pained look before circling around to lean heavily against him.

Fat raindrops pelted the dusty windshield, and as Liam pulled out of the sandy parking lot, he leaned over to roll up the passenger's window. As he did, the painted wooden sign, swinging precariously in the wind, caught his eye: COOPER'S MARINE RAILWAY—BOAT BUILDING AND RESTORATION. "Ah, Coop, we sure do miss ya, man," he said with a sigh, and at the mention of the familiar name, Tuck wagged his tail. Liam turned on his wipers and looked out through the rain, remembering the day his uncle died.

It had been a sunny summer day like any other: They'd been getting ready to call it quits and Coop had held out a twenty and told him to pick up a couple of six-packs on the way home, but Liam had pushed the twenty away. . . . *It was his turn.* Coop had shrugged and stuffed the bill in his pocket. "Shoot yerself."

Liam had chuckled. "See you in a bit."

"Not if I see yer sorry ass first," he said.

That was it. Those were the last words his uncle ever said to him, and in hindsight, it was fitting.

Winston Ellis Cooper had been named after Winston Churchill, but on the playing fields of his childhood, the other boys had called him Coop, and thankfully, it had stuck. Years later, though, when Liam found out his real name was Winston, he'd teasingly called him Winnie and Coop had chased him out of the boathouse. Oh, how Liam had loved getting him riled!

Cooper had always been bigger than life in Liam's mind: tall, muscular, a Vietnam vet—he'd had SEMPER FI tattooed across one tan, rippling shoulder and a mean-looking bulldog on the other. Liam smiled, remembering how his uncle had always worn a hat—even at the dinner table. In spring, summer, and fall, he'd worn his old Red Sox cap, and in winter, he'd worn the gray wool cap that had been issued to him in the Marines.

But on rare occasions when he forgot his hat, the pale ring that circled his balding head would be visible, and Liam would tease, "I see you're wearing your halo," which made Cooper's cheeks burn bright red.

And that was why, when the undertaker came to take Coop's body, Liam had handed him the tattered, old Red Sox cap and made him promise to put it on Coop's head.

Two years had passed since that summer day and Liam still missed his uncle as much as if it had happened yesterday. "Guess you've got a real halo now, man," he said softly.

He pulled up to the only mailbox on the quiet, dead-end road. The box had seen better days—it was dented and rusty, and two of the letters had faded so much it looked like it said WOOPER instead of W. E. COOPER. Liam had considered getting a new one and changing the name, but somehow it made him feel like he'd be letting Coop go and he just couldn't bring himself to do that. Besides, Mike knew who he was and that was all that mattered. He ducked out into the rain, grabbed the mail, and continued down the driveway to the rambling, weathered beach house his uncle had left him.

Cooper had bought the property when he'd returned from Vietnam. Back then, it had been a run-down, one-bedroom beach cottage on five acres of scraggly, overgrown scrub oak and huckleberry, but Coop hadn't cared. All he'd wanted was a safe haven, a place where no one could find—or bother—him, and all he'd done for the first two weeks was sit on the porch, watch the waves roll in, and drink himself to oblivion—trying to forget the world, the war, and the thankless reception he'd received when he returned home. But when drinking didn't drown out his painful memories, he pulled himself out of his chair, picked up the empty Jack Daniels bottles scattered about, and dug out his tools.

Through the years, he never talked about the war, but he had no problem sharing every detail of the meticulous restoration of the little cottage, telling his young nephew how he'd gutted the entire interior—except for the stone fireplace—rebuilt each window, post, wall, and cabinet; laid down new hardwood flooring; extended the porch; and added on two sunny bedrooms. And as Liam had listened, he'd realized his uncle had poured his heart into the restoration of the little cottage . . . and in return, the cottage had restored his soul.

Liam parked the truck in the side yard and looked over at his nervous copilot. "Ready?" he asked, and Tuck stood, thumping his tail. Liam opened the door and they hopped out, raced through the puddles, and burst into the kitchen, startling the handsome gray tomcat that was curled up on the kitchen chair. Almost immediately, Tuck started to shake, sending a shower in the direction of the cat—who eyed him with dismissive annoyance.

"Sorry, Mobe," Liam said, reaching for a towel. "You should know by now that your pal doesn't share your impeccable sense of decorum."

Liam pulled the anxious retriever back out from under the kitchen table, dried him, threw the towel over the back of the chair, tousled Moby's soft fur, ran his fingers through his own damp hair, and opened the fridge. He reached for a beer, surveyed the fridge's meager contents, and frowned. He hated food shopping and only went when it was absolutely necessary . . . and it was definitely getting to that point. There was one beer left now, along with two eggs, a splash of OJ, and a slice of pizza. But it was the low inventory of beer that would trigger a trip to the market. Liam reached for the pizza, threw it on a piece of foil, and tossed it in the oven. Then he fed his two pals and stood at the back door watching the rain.

Cooper had been the self-proclaimed King of the Crock-Pot, and Liam had always been able to look forward to coming home to a hearty beef stew, a creamy clam chowder, a spicy chili, or an endless array of other original recipes—everything from apricot chicken to mandarin pork—all dishes Coop had created by throwing whatever was on hand into the pot . . . and yet the results were always amazing. Unfortunately, he'd never written anything down, and Liam—who didn't have the same knack for cooking—had lost ten pounds while the Crock-Pot sat on the shelf, gathering dust.

Liam felt a wet nose nudge his hand, pulling him back to the present. The storm was passing, and with his belly full, Tuck was feeling more himself. "Are you reminding me there's a slice of pizza in the oven?" Liam asked, and the big dog wiggled around him, happy to be understood. Liam opened the oven, pulled out the pizza, and sat down at the worn, wooden table. Immediately, Tuck plopped down next to him, trying *not* to look interested, but the long drool hanging from his jowls was a dead giveaway. "You really need to pull yourself together," Liam teased. "And if you lie down, I *might* save a bite."

Reluctantly, Tuck lay down, and while Liam waited for his pizza to cool enough to eat, he sifted through his mail and then dropped it on the table next to the calendar. The calendar, which featured a different classic wooden boat every day, was a gift from John Alden, one of his customers, and although Liam's days all ran together—making any calendar obsolete—he liked this one and tried to stay current. He picked it up, realized he'd fallen behind again, and tore off the pages until he came to Friday and a photograph of a gorgeous Chris-Craft runabout—it was just like the one Coop had helped him restore when he was in high school. Liam studied the boat and then noticed the date—it was July 31—his parents' anniversary. The realization made him pause; then he calculated the years. . . . *It would've been their fiftieth!*

* * *

Winston Ellis Cooper had been born in the early hours of December 7, 1941—just before Japanese bombers reached American shores—but forever after, he'd shared his birthday with the dark anniversary. Three and a half years later, on September 2, 1945—the day Japan formally surrendered—Lillian Venice Cooper, Liam's mother, was born, and the coincidental pairing of dates was never lost on the Cooper children, especially since their father—a navy officer who'd been home on leave in December 1944—always mentioned it on their birthdays. The one thing the Cooper siblings never fully grasped, however, was how the mood of the nation when they were born had affected their childhoods . . . and their personalities.

On the day Cooper was born, the world had been dark with shock and grief, but when Lily was born, it had been full of jubilation, and forever after, their lives—and their individual outlooks on life—reflected the mood of the adults who'd surrounded them during infancy. From the moment Cooper had seen his little sister's blue eyes peering up at him over the soft folds of her pink blanket, he'd been overwhelmed. In his mind, Lily's arrival had made the whole world smile, and at the tender age of three, he took it upon himself to always protect her—in essence, protecting the world—and through the years, he'd done just that.

Liam could still see Coop sitting across the kitchen table, smiling wistfully as he recounted all the times he'd looked out for Lily—the time he'd stood up to Brian Davis because he'd teased her about her freckles; the time he'd shoved Robbie Tyler into the bushes because he'd pulled her pigtails; the time he'd had an all-out brawl with Tommy Wilson because he'd tried to kiss her; and the time, when she'd fallen in love with a soft-spoken boy from Boston named Daniel Tate, he'd "warned Ole Danny-Boy that he'd break both his legs if he broke her heart."

But then his smile faded, because there was nothing he could do the night Daniel lost control of their car on the snowy Massachusetts Turnpike.

Nothing. Except keep the promise he'd made.

Liam held out the last morsel of his pizza and Tuck took it ever so gently. Then Liam balled up the foil, tossed it in the trash, drained his beer, and opened the fridge for another. He pried off the top of the frosty bottle, took a sip, and walked over to the old black and white photo that had hung by the back door for as long as he could remember. The photo was of a young man holding a little boy in his arms . . . and the little boy's head was thrown back in laughter because the woman beside them was tickling him. The woman was beautiful—petite, dark haired, her eyes dancing with light; the man was handsome and tan, and he wore his sunglasses roguishly on top of his head, making him look like he belonged on the pages of an outdoor clothing catalog. They were standing in front of a lighthouse and the playful waves behind them sparkled in the sunlight—it was one of those lovely summer days when the world had seemed so perfect.

Liam studied the photo, trying to remember that day, but then another memory—more haunting and vivid—filled his mind instead. He'd come home late from a cross-country meet and found Cooper sitting at the table with the photo in front of him and a bottle of Jack Daniels beside it. The only light had come from the stovetop, but it was enough to see the tears glistening in his eyes. "What's the matter?" he'd asked, but Coop had looked away, wiping his eyes. Liam had dropped his duffel by the door and sat down across from him. "Coop, what's wrong?"

Finally, Cooper'd looked up and searched Liam's blue eyes. "You have her eyes, you know," he'd said. "You look like your damn father . . . but you have *her* eyes."

Liam had reached for the bottle, but Cooper had grabbed his arm with so much force he'd practically crushed his wrist.

"I don't know why you do this to yourself," Liam said in dismay, pulling his arm away.

Cooper just stared at the photo. "Do you know what your mom asked me that day?" he asked.

Liam shook his head.

"You were just a little tyke and we were walkin' on the beach and she was teasing me about not bein' able to find a girl because I was so damn ornery, and she said I'd never get to have a little fella like you if I didn't get serious and start lookin' for a girl who'd be willing to put up with me. And I said, 'I don't need a girl . . . I'll just borrow you.' And then she stopped, and her eyes got all serious. 'Will you promise me something?' she asked.

" 'Maybe,' I teased, you know . . . trying to lighten the mood.

" 'You have to promise,' she insisted.

"Then I looked straight into those eyes a hers and said, 'Lil, you know I'd do anything for you.'

"She looked down the beach where you and your dad were chasin' the waves, and said, 'If anything happens to me and Danny, I want you to take Liam.'

" 'For Pete's sake, Lil, nothin's gonna happen,' I said."

" 'Maybe . . . but I need to know you'd take him. I need you to *promise*.' " He paused and shook his head. "It was almost as if she knew. . . .

" 'Of course, I'll take him,' I said. 'What d'ya think? I'd let him go to an orphanage?'

"Then she paused. 'There's something else,' she said. 'I want you to promise you'll take him to church.'

" 'Oh, now you're pushin' it,' I said. "You know how I feel 'bout—'

" 'I know how you feel,' she interrupted, 'but I want him to go—I want him to know the Bible stories—just like we did.'

" 'I don't know if I can promise that,' I said.

" 'Promise me,' she insisted, and she was so damn adamant. . . ."

He looked up at Liam. "I guess I wasn't very good about keepin' that one." And then his voice trailed off as he swirled his drink. "I never could get why God took her. . . ."

Liam gazed at the faded photo, smiled sadly, and whispered, "Happy anniversary, Mom and Dad."

Chapter 2

A cool breeze rustled through the open bedroom windows. Liam stirred, and in the half-light of dawn, looked around the room that had been his since he was a boy. He pictured it as it was back then—the shelves lined with books about whales and pirates and shipwrecks; later, they'd been filled with biographies about explorers and aviation. Now the books were mostly about world leaders and world wars, and the only other personal items were photos of Coop in his famous Red Sox cap, and Moby and Tuck curled up together in front of the fireplace.

For years, the room had been painted a soft ocean blue, but the previous winter Liam had painted it tan. Other than that, it was exactly as it had been when Coop first built it. The wainscoting and trim were painted a creamy white, and the four large twelve-over-twelve windows along the back wall—sparkling with a gorgeous view of the ocean—were also white. Liam always thought it was the nicest room in the house and he'd wondered why Coop hadn't kept it for himself. One day, he'd asked him and Coop had said he preferred to sleep in the front of the house . . . so he could hear.

"Hear what?" he'd asked.

Coop had shrugged. "Everythin'."

Liam would never forget the first night he'd slept at his uncle's. At the time, the extra bedrooms were still under construction, so Coop had carried Lily's and Daniel's bags to his room, and although Lily had protested, Coop had insisted, saying he and Liam would be sleeping under the stars anyway, so he wouldn't be needing his room.

That evening, after a cookout—complete with s'mores—and a long walk on the beach, the gorgeous night sky had been so inviting, they'd all ended up sleeping under the stars, and Liam—who must've been around four at the time—had never forgotten it.

Through sleepy eyes, he'd gazed up at the vast, velvet sky, sparkling with diamonds, and listened to the lovely sounds of the adults talking and laughing and sipping their drinks, and when he finally drifted off, he'd felt utterly safe and loved.

Two and a half years later, on a snowy night in December, he'd longed to feel that way again, but when Coop carried his bags to one of the newly finished bedrooms, turned on the light, and said, "This is your room now," he could barely nod. "If there's anything else you need, just holler," he'd added, and Liam had looked around the simply furnished room with its empty bookshelves and nodded again. Then they'd both stood there uncertainly until finally, Coop had wiped his eyes with his thumbs, whispered, "Damn you, Lily," and knelt down to give his six-year-old nephew a hug. "G'night, pal."

Liam had hugged him back, trying ever so hard to be brave, and after his uncle left, he'd tugged his cold pajamas out of his bag, pulled them on, climbed into the stiff, strange bed, and listened to the icy sleet hitting the dark windows. Then with tears streaming down his smooth cheeks, he'd prayed with all his might that his mom and dad would be in the kitchen making pancakes when he woke up . . . just like they had two summers ago.

"Nobody's making pancakes today either," Liam said, playfully pulling on Tuck's ears. The big dog—who was sprawled across the bed next to him—rolled onto his back and stretched his legs up in the air, waiting for a belly rub, and Moby—who was curled up on a pillow—wondered if it was time to find a quieter spot.

Liam scratched Tuck's long belly and the big dog's eyes rolled back in utter contentment. "What *are* we going to have for breakfast?" Liam mused, propping his head up on his free hand and looking out at the sliver of orange peaking over the watery horizon. Hearing the word *breakfast,* Tuck rolled onto his side and leaned over to stuff his nose in Liam's face.

"Nice," Liam said, sitting on the edge of the bed, wiping the wetness and inadvertently touching the scar near his temple.

Half an hour later, after wolfing down their breakfasts, Tuck and Moby were outside, nosing around the yard, when Liam came down the steps with his hair wet from showering. "Let's go, Tuck," he called, and the big golden galloped to the truck. "See you later, Mobe," he said, scratching the cat's ears. "Keep an eye out for moles—they're making a mess of the yard." Moby blinked at him and then hopped up onto one of the sunny Adirondack chairs. "You won't catch moles if you sit in a chair all day," Liam said with a frown.

As soon as he opened the truck door, Tuck hopped in and waited for Liam to roll down his window. Then he pressed his barrel chest against the door and hung his head out as far as he could, his cold, wet nostrils quivering with excitement as he took in all the wonderful scents of the cool, dewy morning.

Ten minutes later, Liam pulled up in front of Cuppa Jo to Go, the local hot spot for breakfast, and got out. "Be right back," he said, coming around the truck. "You stay here," he added, tousling his ears. He climbed the worn, wooden steps of the long gray building and then held the door open for two college girls who were leaving with cups of coffee cradled in their hands.

"Hey, Liam, what can I get ya?"

"Hey, Sally, the usual," Liam said, reaching for a coffeepot.

"Bacon, egg, and cheese?"

"Yes, please ... and could you make one of your famous chicken salad wraps?"

"Thinking ahead for once?" Sally teased, pushing back the silver hair that curled around her kind, seventy-year-old face.

"Yeah," Liam said with a laugh as he filled his cup with steaming black coffee.

"So, where's my pal?"

"Out in the truck."

"How come you didn't bring him in?!"

"Because it's so hard to get him to leave."

"Oh, hogwash! He'll go anywhere for a piece of bacon."

While he waited for his order, Liam looked out the window and watched the two girls who'd been walking out when he was coming in talking to Tuck, and he could tell—by the goofy look on the big golden's face—that he was loving the attention. Liam shook his head, paid for his order, thanked Sally, and went out, but when he got to the truck, the girls were walking away and Tuck was gazing longingly after them. "That's girls for ya," Liam consoled, holding Tuck's chin and looking into his soulful brown eyes. "They love ya and leave ya." Tuck swished his tail in agreement and then, sniffing the bag in Liam's hand, forgot all about his loss. "Fortunately for you," Liam said, "I've got the cure-all—bacon!"

For the rest of the ride, Tuck was back and forth between the lovely smells drifting through the open window and the even lovelier smell drifting from the bag.

As Liam unlocked the boathouse and opened the front carriage doors, Tuck gave the parking lot a quick once-over. Then he charged after Liam, skidded to a stop at his feet, plopped down on his haunches, and gazed at him forlornly.

"You sure know how to work the system," Liam said, unwrapping the sandwich and breaking off a generous piece of bacon. He held it out to him and Tuck took it politely. Liam took a bite and set the rest of the sandwich on the workbench next to his coffee. As he did, a cool breeze rustled through the boathouse, stirring the papers that had blown under the workbench the night before. Liam knelt down, pulled them out, and laid them across the stern of the boat he was working on. Taking another bite, he perused the news. There wasn't much that interested him and he was just about to fold it up to put in the winter burn pile when he noticed an ad for an opening at one of the local art galleries . . . and although it was the gorgeous painting of an island that caught his eye, it was the artist's name that made his heart stop.

Chapter 3

1989

"You're gonna wear the finish right off," Coop said, leaning back in his chair.

"I just want to be able to see your homely reflection from any angle," Liam teased, wiping down the glassy surface of his mahogany runabout for the umpteenth time. He reached for the can of Coke on the workbench, took a sip, and noticed someone walking across the parking lot. "You got yourself a customer, Coop."

"Shit," Coop grumbled, draining his coffee cup and tossing it in the trash. A moment later, a tall man wearing white shorts and a coral linen button-down filled the doorway. "Is Mr. Cooper here?"

"It's *Coop*," the Marine corrected, pushing himself back from his desk.

"Carlton Knox," the man said, walking toward him. Coop extended his hand and then looked past him. Carlton followed his gaze. "And this is my daughter, Acadia."

Hearing the second introduction, Liam looked up, realized there was a girl standing in the doorway, and almost dropped his soda.

"What a beauty," the man said, nodding to the runabout. "What year?"

"1955 Sportsman."

"Is it for sale?"

"Belongs to my nephew," Coop said, nodding to Liam, "and I doubt he'd sell her."

"Is that so?" Carlton said, running his hand along the smooth wood. "And what do *you* say, son? How much would you take for it?"

Liam bristled at being called son . . . *and* at the streak Carlton's hand left on the wood he'd just polished. "My uncle's right," he answered. "*She's* not for sale."

Carlton chuckled. "Every man has a price," he pressed. "I could give you a check right now."

Liam shrugged.

"Maybe you'll change your mind," Carlton added in an amused voice. Then he turned back to Cooper. "Well, how about that forty-foot sloop in the yard? *It* has a 'For Sale" sign on it." Coop nodded and followed Carlton outside to look at the sailboat Clay Mattheson was selling, but Acadia lingered, leaning against the door and taking in every inch of Liam's tall, slender frame.

Liam rubbed out the handprint and pretended not to notice she'd stayed—if there was one thing he'd learned growing up on Nantucket, it was to steer clear of the wealthy families who summered there, and there was no doubt in his mind—from Carlton Knox's appearance and demeanor—his daughter was out of his league.

"Is she *really* yours?" Acadia asked. Liam looked up—impressed that she knew the language of boats—and nodded.

"What's her name?"

"*Tuckernuck II.*"

"That's a funny name."

"She's named after an island."

"Have you been there?"

He nodded.

"Is it far?"

He shook his head.

"Are you always so talkative?"

Liam shrugged—he'd never really thought about how much he talked . . . or didn't. They were both quiet then, and in an effort to prove he was capable of carrying on a conversation, he asked, "Do you have a house out here?"

"No, we're just renting." She walked over to the bow. "My parents want to buy a house, but they haven't found anything expensive enough."

"*Expensive* enough?!"

Acadia laughed. "My father's the type who has to have the best of everything. It's as if he has to prove something, and if he buys a house with a big enough price tag, he'll be able to brag about it at all of his precious cocktail parties."

Liam looked up. Now that Acadia wasn't silhouetted by the sun, he realized how pretty she was—she had long blond hair, Caribbean Sea blue eyes, perfectly straight white teeth, and smooth, tan skin. *She must look like her mother,* he thought, *because she doesn't look anything like her father.* "Where do you live the rest of the time?"

"In the city."

"Boston?"

"No, New York. Actually, we've never lived any one place for very long, but home base has always been our townhouse in New York."

"Where else have you lived?"

"Germany, China, France—my father's job takes him around the world, but now that I'm a senior, my mother wants me to be home to look at colleges. She really wants me to go to Barnard, her alma mater, but my father wants me to look at the Ivy League."

Liam nodded as if he knew all about traveling: In truth, he'd barely been off the island, never mind out of the country. In fact, the only other states he'd been to were New Hampshire and Maine. He and Coop had gone to a stock car race in New Hampshire, and after the race, Liam had had to help Coop, who'd had too much to drink, all the way back to the truck— which they'd parked across the road at a sugarhouse called Sunnyside Maples. Liam, who'd only been fifteen at the time, had then helped him into the passenger's seat and stood there, wondering what to do next. "Jus' drive," Coop had slurred. "Issame's drivin' a boat."

Liam climbed into the driver's seat and looked out at the long line of cars and trucks leaving the race. He pushed in the clutch, jammed the truck into gear, and then tried to slowly let the clutch out while stepping on the gas, but try as he might, he kept stalling, lurching to a stop every time. Finally, after enduring a stream of swears and rude gestures from other race-goers, Coop had had him turn onto a dirt road that didn't look much like a road at all, and they'd ended up coming home through Maine.

As for cities, he'd been to a couple of Red Sox games and he'd gone on a field trip to the aquarium and Faneuil Hall, so he'd been to Boston, but that was the only city he'd visited.

"What colleges are you looking at?" Cadie asked, interrupting his thoughts.

"Me?" Liam looked up in surprise. He'd never heard of Barnard, and although he knew the Ivy League included schools like Harvard and Yale, that was all he knew. He started to answer, "I'm not . . ." but then stopped and casually shrugged. "My uncle wants me to look at Boston. We'll see."

"University or College?"

"Both," he answered, surprised there were two.

Acadia's eyes lit up. "Wow! BU *and* BC—those are great schools. My cousin scored a 1580 on his SATs and he didn't even get into BU. What'd you get on yours?"

"On my . . . ?"

"SATs."

"Oh . . ." Liam suddenly realized he was painting himself into a corner, but oddly, he didn't care. In truth, he hadn't thought about college—in fact, the only thought he'd had on the topic was that he *wasn't* going—and he certainly hadn't taken the SATs. After all, it was a little overzealous to take them your junior year when you could take them your senior year.

"Sixteen forty," he answered nonchalantly.

Acadia looked puzzled, then decided she'd misunderstood. "Well, one of my teachers says anything over 1400 is great, but I only scored a 1320."

"I wouldn't worry about it," Liam consoled. "You can always take 'em again, and I'm sure you'll do better next time."

"I hope so," she said with a sigh. "Enough about school! I get tired just thinking about it."

She watched him polish the chrome around the runabout's glass. "I love Chris-Crafts," she said. "They're so elegant and classy."

Liam wondered how she knew so much about wooden boats, and then, as if she could read his mind, she added, "My grandfather had one on a lake in upstate New York."

"What happened to it?"

"He died and . . ."

"Oh, I'm sorry . . ." Liam said, feeling foolish.

"It's okay," she assured him. "It was a long time ago. Anyway, one of my uncles inherited his boat—which made my father furious. He thought my mother—the only daughter—should've gotten it.

"My grandfather called her *Stardust*—after the song." She

started to hum the old Hoagy Carmichael tune, but then realized Liam was watching her and blushed, laughing. "I know—I'm crazy!"

"No, you're not," he said. "In fact, you're nothing like I expected."

She frowned. "Hmm, I'm not sure if that's a good thing."

"It *is* a good thing."

She blushed again. "Well, I should probably go find my father." She turned. "It's been nice talking to you, Mr. Cooper."

"It's been nice talking to you too," he said, looking after her, "but my last name isn't Cooper."

Acadia looked back. "Oh, I'm sorry. I just called you that because I . . ."

"It's Liam . . . Liam Tate."

"Well, it's nice to meet you, Liam . . . Liam Tate," she teased. "My name is Acadia McCormick Knox, but everyone calls me Cadie . . . *or* Cadie-did. Everyone except my parents, that is. . . ."

"It's nice to meet you, too, Cadie . . . *or* Cadie-did," Liam said with a smile.

Just then, Cooper and Carlton came back in the boathouse, and as Coop walked past Liam, he rolled his eyes, and Liam had to bite his lip to keep from smiling.

"Ready, Acadia?" Carlton asked curtly.

"Yes," she answered, looking back at Liam. "Maybe I'll see you around."

"Maybe," he said with a smile.

After they left, Cooper glanced over and saw the look on Liam's face. "Oh, no ya don't! I know that look—you look like a lovesick puppy! Don't you go gettin' no ideas. I see what's on yer mind. She's pretty . . . but you don't want none a that!"

"You don't see what's on my mind," Liam said with a grin.

"Oh, yes, I do," Coop said, shaking his head, "and that girl's nothin' but trouble."

"How do you know?"

"Cuz I just spent fifteen minutes with her arrogant father—who thinks Clay's asking too much for his sailboat . . . *and* I speak from experience."

"I'd like to hear about your experience," Liam teased.

"Yer not old enough."

"How old were *you?*"

"Old enough to know better!"

Liam laughed, knowing his uncle was never going to share his boyhood escapades.

"A word from the wise, kiddo—the summer girls'll break your heart."

"Maybe," Liam said, sipping his Coke and breathing in the sweet, fresh fragrance that still lingered around him.

Chapter 4

Liam tossed the last bite of his breakfast sandwich to Tuck, who snatched it from the air with the dexterity of an NFL receiver. Then he wiped his hands on his jeans, carefully tore the ad out of the newspaper, and tacked it to the shelf above the workbench. The opening for Levi Knox's art show was Sunday!

"Hey, stranger," a voice bellowed and Liam looked up. Tuck pulled himself off the floor and hurried over to greet the newcomer.

A smile spread across Liam's face. "Oh, man," he said, shaking his head. "If it isn't Jack Regan, legendary leader of Hell's Kitchen platoon!" The two old friends hugged and slapped each other on the back.

"Who's this big fella?" Jack asked, kneeling down.

"That's Tucket—my fearless watchdog."

Jack laughed. "We have a golden too. His name's Boomer, and about the only thing he'd be good at is *watching* while the robbers clean out the house."

"Yep," Liam said with a nod. "That's what Tuck would do

too." He watched as his friend rubbed the big dog's ears. "So what brings you out here?"

"The little missus, of course," Jack said with a grin.

"How *is* Tracey?"

"Oh, she's fine . . . fine."

Liam shook his head again. "I can't believe you're here."

"I can't either," Jack said, standing. "How the hell've ya been?"

Liam smiled. "Oh, you know, same old shit."

Jack looked around. "This place hasn't changed." He turned back. "I was real sorry to hear 'bout Coop."

Liam nodded. "Thanks. It may *look* the same, but it's definitely not."

Jack nodded. "I hear ya. My ole man passed last year and life just isn't the same . . . and we weren't even close like you and Coop."

"So Tracey dragged you out here?"

"Yeah, but she didn't have to drag too hard cuz I knew I'd see you." He paused. "It's been too long."

Liam nodded. "It has."

"On the way over I was trying to remember the last time— it had to be '96 or '7."

"Our tour ended in '94, so that must be about right, but it wasn't the last time we saw each other. I *did* come to your wedding."

"Yeah," Jack teased, "you came all the way to Chatham."

Liam laughed. "It was a stretch . . . but it's not every day you get asked to be someone's best man. How long ago was that?"

Jack squeezed his eyes shut. "Let's see," he said, trying to remember how long he'd been married. "Fourteen years?"

Liam gave a low whistle. "Fourteen! Where'd the time go?"

"I don't know, but it's your fault—we've invited you to Vermont countless times, but you refuse to leave this damn island."

"I know. I know. What can I say? Burlington's a little far."

"Yeah, but it's a great college town with lots of beautiful women."

Liam raised his eyebrows. "You're not supposed to be looking."

"I know, I know, but sometimes a fella can't help it." He laughed amiably. "So, are you seeing anyone . . . or are you still Nantucket's most eligible bachelor?"

Liam shook his head. "Nah."

"Holy crap, Li, don't tell me you're still hung up on . . . on . . . what was her name?"

"No, no," Liam contended, looking away. "I just haven't met anyone."

"You can't meet anyone if you don't try," Jack said, eying him. "And you can't fool me either. I'm the one who propped you up after she swept in here, stole your innocence, and kicked you to the curb . . . but, geez, that was, like, thirty years ago, man. You need to move on."

Liam chuckled. As if that was possible. "How long are you here?" he asked, changing the subject.

"Just the weekend. I've gotta head to L.A. on business tomorrow night and we're going to an art show tomorrow, so I came by to see if you wanted to meet us for dinner. I tried to call, but there was no answer . . . *or* answering machine. Do you have a cell phone?"

"A what?" Liam asked, looking puzzled.

"Oh, man," Jack said, "are you ever gonna engage in this world?"

"I *am* engaged," Liam protested. "I've got my business, my dog . . . I even have a cat."

Jack shook his head. "How about a computer or an e-mail address?"

Liam gave him the same bewildered look.

"You're hopeless, ya know that?"

"I know," Liam agreed with a grin.

"Well, back to dinner—we were thinking of The Brotherhood."

"That'd be great, but it's not the same place, you know. They had a fire and now it's under new ownership. . . . It's fancier, and I actually don't know if they'd let you in," he teased.

Jack grinned. "Well, they'll let Tracey in, and I'll just sneak in behind her."

Liam laughed. "Sounds like a plan. What time?"

"Seven?"

"Seven it is."

"All right, well, I gotta get back—Trace wants to take the kids to the beach."

"Where're you staying?"

"With friends—they have a place out here." He paused, knowing Liam too well. "They're going to be at dinner too . . . I hope that's all right."

"Of course," Liam lied, suddenly wishing he'd declined Jack's invitation—he'd been looking forward to an intimate dinner with old friends, but the unexpected inclusion of strangers changed everything.

"All right. We'll see you later, then."

"Looking forward to it," Liam said, tousling Tuck's ears. He waved as Jack pulled away, and then knelt down and pressed his cheek against Tuck's soft brow. "Oh, well, at least we can put off food shopping for another day," he murmured as Tuck licked his cheek.

He walked back into the boathouse, and although the big golden started to follow, he only made it as far as the doors before he stopped and lay down on the sunny pavement. "Sure," Liam teased, "now that breakfast is over, you're not interested in hangin' with me." Tuck looked up, thumped his tail, and then closed his eyes. Liam shook his head, took a sip of his coffee, and ran his hand over the deck of the runabout.

Three hours later, after polishing the mahogany surface to a warm glow, he walked over to the boathouse doors and pushed a worn metal button on the wall. There was a familiar click of an electrical connection, and a second later, the ancient winch housed under the heavy metal panel in the floor creaked to life and a cable began to creep along the floor, unwinding from a large spool that was also under the panel. Liam pushed the boat, nestled on an old rail-guided marine trolley, out into the sunshine until the cable—straining under the weight of the boat— became taut, and the trolley edged toward the water. When the runabout finally floated free, Liam pushed the bottom button and the winch creaked to a stop.

"Want to go for a ride?" he asked as he walked past his slumbering pup to secure the boat. Tuck sat up, sleepily swishing his tail across the pavement. "C'mon, then," he said, and the big dog pulled himself up, waddled stiffly down to the dock, and waited to be lifted in.

Moments later, after adjusting the engine, Liam backed slowly away from the dock and masterfully spun the boat around. Tuck's muscles tensed as he leaned against the side, his nostrils quivering, and gradually, Liam pushed the throttle forward, picking up speed until Tuck's fur was sparkling with ocean spray.

It had been years—twenty-six, to be exact, *not* thirty like Jack had said—since Liam had taken a ride out to Tuckernuck Island, but as he drew near, he realized it hadn't changed at all.

When he cut the engine and drifted along a secluded stretch of beach, Tuck looked over at him questioningly. "It's okay, pal," he said. The waves lapped gently against the side of the boat, and as he rested his hand on Tuck's head, he gazed at the sandy shoreline and listened to the wind rustle the long, swaying grass, whispering of a summer long ago.

Chapter 5

1989

"Hey, Liam Tate!" a voice called out as Liam ran along Madaket Road. He glanced over his shoulder as two girls sped past him on bikes, waving. He waved back, wondering who they were, and when he rounded the next corner, he realized they'd pulled over.

He glanced down at his body, slick with sweat, and suddenly wished he hadn't thrown his shirt into the bushes five miles back. "Hey," he said, leaning over to catch his breath.

"I didn't know you were a runner," Cadie said, admiringly.

Liam nodded, wiping his dripping brow with his arm.

The other girl, who was also blond and pretty, cleared her throat.

"This is Tess," Cadie said, remembering her friend. "She's on vacation too."

Liam nodded, feeling even more self-conscious.

"We're headed down to the beach for a swim," Tess ventured. "Wanna come?"

Liam shook his head. "No, thanks," and then saw disappointment on Cadie's face.

Tess climbed back on her bike and started to ride away, but Cadie lingered. "I guess I'll see you around, then," she said, stepping on her pedal.

"Wait," Liam said softly, and she looked back questioningly.

"Want to go for a boat ride tomorrow?"

"Sure," she said, glancing over her shoulder. "Should I invite Tess?" she asked, nodding up the road to where her friend was waiting.

Liam hesitated and then shook his head. "Naw . . . just us," he said softly.

"Okay, what time?"

He shrugged. "Early?"

She nodded, suppressing a grin, and then spun her wheels in the sand as she hurried to catch up with her friend. She turned back and waved, and Liam waved back.

When he finally got back to the house, Coop was in the kitchen, stirring a pot of chili. Liam wiped his face with his shirt and turned on the tap, and while he waited for the water to get cold, he eyed the glass in his uncle's hand. "I thought you were stickin' to beer."

"How was yer run?" Coop asked, ignoring him.

"Fine," Liam answered, shaking his head. "Do I have time for a shower?"

"Yep, jus' lettin' 'er simmer."

Liam disappeared down the hall, turned the shower on, stripped off his running shorts, and climbed in. "Damn it, Coop," he muttered, letting the cool water rush over his head and shoulders. "Can't you stick to it for once?"

When Liam had first come to live with his uncle, he'd slowly realized that he acted differently when he had a glass of "Ole No. 7"—as he liked to call it—in his hand. If he'd had a beer or two, he was fine, but if he was drinking the more potent amber whiskey, it was just a matter of time before his mood started to deteriorate. On nights like that, Liam had cleared their plates and watched as his uncle had buried his anguished face in his hands. It frightened Liam to see him acting so strangely and one time, he'd even hidden all the whiskey bottles he could find under his bed so that that Coop would stop drinking, but instead, his uncle had torn the house apart looking for them and then driven to the store—leaving his seven-year-old nephew home alone—to buy more.

Liam hadn't understood the effect alcohol had on people; he only vaguely remembered his parents drinking—they'd had a glass of wine with dinner, or his dad, a beer at a cookout, but they'd never acted the way Coop did. Coop started off with one drink, but never stopped there, and as Liam grew older, he realized drinking made his uncle remember the things he was trying to forget. It was a vicious cycle his mind played on him—he drank to forget the memories of war that drinking dredged to the surface.

Liam turned off the water, toweled dry, pulled on a clean pair of jeans and a T-shirt, and with his hair still damp, went downstairs. "Smells good," he said, reaching for a bowl. He filled it, sprinkled shredded cheddar on top, plopped sour cream on top of that, poured a large glass of milk, and peered under a foil-covered baking pan that was on the counter. "You made cornbread?!"

Coop smiled as Liam cut a huge hunk of the golden bread and sat down hungrily. "You're the best, Coop!" he said, and he meant it. In spite of his uncle's shortcomings, he knew his uncle loved him with all his heart . . . and that was all that mattered.

"Soo . . . is it all right if I take tomorrow off?" Liam ventured, knowing Coop would say yes.

Coop filled a second bowl, piled cheddar and sour cream on top of it, shoed Tom, their old tomcat, off his chair, set a frosty beer on the table, and sat down. "What the hell for?"

"I'm taking the boat out."

"You're gonna let'er get wet?" Coop teased.

Liam grinned, took a long drink, and with a milk moustache, answered, "Yup."

"Must be a special occasion," Coop mused. "Who ya takin'?"

"Nobody."

"Ha! You expectin' me to believe yer takin' yer baby out on her maiden voyage by yerself?"

"It's not her maiden voyage. I took *you* out."

"Yeah, all the way to the first buoy and back."

"We went farther than that," Liam protested.

"Is it Christie?"

Liam shook his head and realized he wasn't going to get away without telling Coop who he was taking. "Cadie," he said casually, dipping his cornbread in his chili.

"Katie?" Cooper asked, looking puzzled as he tried to remember the girls in Liam's class. "Katie Benson?"

"Not *Katie* . . . Cadie . . . with a *C* . . . and a *d*."

Cooper took a long swig of his beer and leaned back in his chair, still puzzled.

"Cadie Knox—she stopped by the boathouse with her father last week."

"You mean the rich girl?" Coop sputtered.

Liam nodded, bracing for a lecture. "She's not what you think. She's different."

Coop rolled his eyes. "Geez, Li, what'd I tell ya? Yer jus' asking fer trouble."

"How do you know that?" Liam asked defensively.

"Cuz even if she takes a shine to ya, her father'll put an end to it like he's stompin' on a bug. I hate to break it to ya, pal, but you come from plain, ole, blue-collar, workin'-class stock . . . and her parents ain't never gonna let her get mixed up with that."

"Why? We have plenty of money, and this house is worth a half a million at least . . . probably more. I've seen the real-estate magazines. I know what beachfront property goes for on Nantucket."

"It doesn't matter, Li. We're not the type a people *they* associate with . . . and there's nothin' that's ever gonna change that."

Liam shook his head. "I'll take my chances."

Coop chuckled. "Well, don't say I didn't warn ya."

Liam finished his chili in silence, devoured a second bowl, and then, as was their routine—Coop cooking, him cleaning up—washed the dishes, all the while stewing over his uncle's callous response to his interest in Cadie.

Chapter 6

Liam had just locked up the boathouse when he heard tires spinning in the sandy parking lot. He looked around the corner of the building, and as the dust settled, he saw John Alden climbing out of his black sedan.

"What's up, John?" he asked.

"Jordy had an accident with *Pride & Joy*—she's hung up on the rocks near our beach."

"Is he okay?"

"He's fine—he and his buddy swam to shore, but *she's* taking on water."

Liam nodded and reached for his launch keys. "We need to get her off the rocks before the tide changes or it'll rip her apart."

The thirty-foot launch, which was kept in a slip next to the railway, was equipped for any emergency—extra batteries, an air compressor, a bilge pump, extra lines, life jackets, and under the foredeck, two large, heavy air bags and two heavy nylon belts—each six inches wide and twenty-four feet long.

John jumped into the boat. "That damn kid," he muttered, shaking his head. "I tell him to be careful, but he thinks he knows everything."

"Most kids *do*," Liam said, turning the key.

Ten minutes later, John's waterfront property—formerly known as the Wellington estate—came into view. Liam glanced up at the stately house as John pointed to the sailboat across the bay. Liam nodded and carefully maneuvered the launch alongside to assess the damage. He suddenly realized the tide was already coming in, so he quickly pulled the two airbags from under the deck, unfolded them, and climbed out onto the rocks submerged just under the surface. Then he and John worked together, belting the airbags to the hull. When they were secure, Liam climbed back in the launch and turned on the compressor. Air began to slowly fill the belts, lifting the damaged boat off the rocks. They waited several more minutes for the tide to rise, too, and when the boat was finally free, Liam gingerly pulled it away from the rocks, its hull groaning.

As they towed it slowly back to the boathouse, Liam looked over his shoulder several times. He and Coop had built the gorgeous eighteen-foot sloop from plans Cooper had drawn. Liam had been in his late twenties at the time, and although he'd grown up with a love for boats that were made by bending wooden planks over wooden frames, his reverence had deepened as he'd worked side by side with his uncle on *Pride & Joy* with her gorgeous, varnished deck and painted white and green hull. "Wooden boats have a way of giving a man's life purpose," Coop had said. "They symbolize things that matter."

Now, as Liam looked back at the wounded sailboat, he shook his head in dismay—if Coop were alive, he'd be crushed . . . but he also knew he would've poured his heart and soul into her repair.

When they finally pulled up to the dock, Liam quickly tied

the launch, hopped out, and maneuvered the damaged sloop, floats and all, onto the marine trolley and set the blocking. Then he started the winch. John watched gloomily as a flood of gray seawater gushed from the hull. Liam stopped the winch halfway up the ramp, removed the floats, and walked around to take a closer look at the ravaged wood.

"Do you think you can fix her?" John asked.

"It looks like her center board's broken—it must've caught the rocks before it could slide into the trunk." He shook his head. "I can fix her, John, but I doubt I'll have her back to you before the season's over. You're welcome to take her to a different shop. I won't charge you for the tow."

John nodded. He knew he could probably take her to a different shop and have her back sooner, but that would be an insult to Liam—who'd helped build her—and whose meticulous craftsmanship, like Cooper's before him, was legendary. "No," he said. "I'm just glad you can fix her. Maybe Jordy'll learn something from not having her around."

"Maybe," Liam said skeptically. He'd known John for years, and although he was a good guy, his parenting skills were definitely lacking, and as a result, his son suffered. Jordy was notoriously spoiled and irresponsible—supporting Liam's long-standing theory that nothing good comes from a kid who has access to too much money. But John wasn't the only one to blame—his wife, Lexi, was a bitch on wheels, as Coop had liked to call any woman he didn't like, and she walked all over John, spoiled Jordy . . . *and* was the undeniable source of the bad seed.

Before he left, John helped Liam un-step and seat the mast. "How much do you think it'll cost?"

Liam shook his head. "I don't know. I'll have to work up an estimate."

John looked glumly at his boat and nodded. "All right, I'll wait to hear from you," he said. Then he shook Liam's hand.

"If you don't hear from me by the middle of next week, give me a call."

John nodded, and as he walked away, Liam stroked Tuck's soft ears, and murmured, "He's got more money than the queen and he's worried about how much it's going to cost."

Chapter 7

1989

A heavy mist was hanging over Nantucket Sound when Liam swung open the carriage doors and hooked them to the outside wall. He stood on the rail tracks, trying to decide if he should wait before pushing out his runabout. The dock—only thirty feet from where he stood—was barely visible, and even though the Cape's most popular radio station, Ocean 104, was assuring listeners the mist would burn off by nine, Liam didn't want the seats to be damp.

He walked to his truck to get the cooler he'd packed that morning with sandwiches, chips, cookies, Cokes . . . and since Cooper had still been asleep, he'd even managed to sneak two beers into the ice. He set the cooler in the back of the boat, threw two beach towels and a blanket on top of it, and began wiping down the glassy surface, whistling softly, and wondering when Cadie would get there. It suddenly dawned on him that his idea of early might be different from hers and he wished they'd settled on a time instead, but as he slipped the Yacht Ensign into the socket in the stern, he heard a soft voice say, "Hey," and looked up. Cadie was straddling her bike with a canvas beach bag over her shoulder. She was wearing a wide-brimmed sun hat with a blue ribbon around it and underneath her snow white tank top he could see the strings of a matching blue bikini.

"Hey," he said with a smile.

"I wasn't sure what you meant by early, so I hope I'm not *too* early."

"Not at all."

She leaned her bike against the wall. "I like to get going in the morning before anyone else is up so I don't have to answer too many questions."

Liam chuckled. "I hear you." He walked over to push the top button next to the boathouse doors and the winch clicked and groaned. "I just have to push her out," he explained, trying not to appear as nervous as he felt. He slowly guided the boat outside and then stood by the door, waiting for the railcar to make its way to the water.

Cadie stood next to him. "It looks like the sun might break through," she said, pointing to a ray of light shimmering through the mist.

"It's supposed to," Liam said, stopping the winch. He walked down to the dock, dropped the fenders over the sides, and se-cured the boat's forward line around a dock cleat.

"Ready?" he asked.

Cadie nodded and Liam helped her in. "I just need to lock up," he said, walking back up to the boathouse, but then he heard his uncle's truck pull in and wished they'd been able to push off before he'd gotten there so he wouldn't have to endure any more questions . . . or warnings. *Oh, well,* he thought, looking up at the boathouse, waiting for Coop to appear, but after several minutes and still no sign of him, he told Cadie he'd be right back. He peered into the boathouse and saw him, sitting at his desk, sipping a cup of coffee.

"Morning," he said.

"Mornin', kid."

"We're heading out."

He looked up and smiled. "Have fun!"

Liam frowned. That's it? No dire warnings or entreaties to behave? No questions about where they were going or when they'd be back? He shrugged. "Okay, see you later."

Coop waved and Liam, still shaking his head, walked back to the boat.

As he untied the lines and climbed in, Cadie searched his face. "Everything okay?"

He nodded and pushed the starter button. The motor rumbled throatily to life, spraying water from its tail pipe.

Liam was seven the first time Coop took him to Tuckernuck Island, and he'd fallen in love with it immediately. It was secluded and beautiful, and even as he'd grown older, he'd never tired of hiking its sandy vistas and bars, digging for quahogs in its shallows, fishing off its shoals, or diving into its clear, cold water. And even though Coop hadn't let him take the boat there alone until he was in his teens—warning him that the tide between the islands was swift and unpredictable—by the time he was sixteen, he'd made the trip so many times, he felt he could do it with his eyes closed.

Tuckernuck Island is a pristine stretch of land two miles west of Nantucket. Its scraggly, low vegetation is similar to that of Cape Cod—scrub oak, pitch pine, bayberry, beach plum, salt-spray roses, and long, swaying beach grass; its wildlife include flocks of terns, piping plover, harbor seals, and the long-tailed duck; it has two salt ponds, each named for their location—North and East ponds; and crisscrossing its pristine landscape are sandy trails and rutted roads that connect neighbor with neighbor and private dock with private beach. There are thirty or so houses—all powered by generators and lit with kerosene lanterns. Stepping onto Tuckernuck is like taking a step back in time . . . and anyone who has had the good fortune of spending an afternoon, a week, a month, a summer, or a lifetime there knows just how blessed they are.

"I still can't believe you own a Chris-Craft!" Cadie said loudly so he could hear her over the motor.

"You should've seen her when we first got her. Coop found her in an old barn on the other side of the island; he paid next to nothing for her. He said she was all mine if I paid for the material to restore her. The body was in really rough shape and the motor was frozen, but she was all there . . . all original. There are before and after pictures in the boathouse. I'll show you when we get back."

Cadie watched Liam steer the boat, his long brown fingers holding the smooth white wheel and controlling the throttle at its center with his thumb. She found his hands mesmerizing and couldn't help but wonder how they'd feel touching her. Liam glanced over and smiled, and she blushed.

He engaged the clutch and pushed the throttle up, and as the runabout picked up speed, slicing through the surf, Cadie's hat soared into the air and landed in the foamy wake behind them. She put her hand on Liam's arm and pointed, and as soon as he saw it bobbing up and down, he swung around to retrieve it. As he slowed down and leaned over to pluck it from the water, his white shirt billowed up, exposing the smooth brown skin of his lower back and the light tan line along the top of his swim trunks. Cadie looked away, surprised at how quickly her mind slipped below that tan line.

By the time the island came into view, the mist was burning off and snowy clouds were floating in the endless blue sky. As they passed the first house, Liam slowed down and the children playing in the yard waved. Liam and Cadie waved back. "I didn't know people *lived* here," Cadie said in surprise. "I thought there was no electricity. . . ."

"There isn't," Liam said, "but just because you can't blow-dry your hair doesn't mean you can't survive."

"That's debatable," Cadie said with a laugh. "Do they live here year-round?"

"Some do."

They circled the island and Liam pulled up to a small white skiff tied to a buoy anchored several yards offshore. He dropped the boat fenders over the side, cut the engine, and tied the Chris-Craft to the buoy too.

"Whose rowboat is this?" Cadie asked uncertainly.

"Ours," Liam replied as he transferred the cooler, towels, and beach blanket to the smaller boat. "There's nowhere to dock, so we have to row to shore."

Cadie stood up and Liam held both boats steady so she could climb from one to the other. Once she was settled, he stepped across too. Then he untied the skiff, pushed off, and sat on the middle seat, facing her. "Want to row?" he teased, holding out the oars.

Without missing a beat, she said, "Sure!"

Liam laughed. "I was only kidding."

"I wasn't."

Liam shook his head, smiling as he started to slip an oar into its lock, and Cadie raised her eyebrows. "Do you think I don't know how?"

"I didn't say th—"

"Switch with me," she demanded, and he suddenly realized she meant business.

They switched seats and Cadie slipped the oars into their locks, plunged one oar straight into the water, and held it against the current. The boat spun around; then she dipped both oars in and pulled back hard. Liam shook his head in surprise as the worn, wooden oars clunked and creaked in their locks, and the waves, lapping against the sides, pushed the boat inland. "This is the easy part, you know. . . ."

"What do you mean?" Cadie asked, eyeing him.

"We have the tide *with* us, but coming back, we'll be fighting it."

"I'm sure I can handle it," Cadie assured him.

"If you say so," he said, lying back casually on the wooden bench seat and putting his hands behind his head.

Cadie looked at his long body stretched out in front of her and sighed.

"What's the matter?" he asked, opening his eyes. "Are you tired?"

"No, it's . . . it's just so beautiful out here," she said.

"It is indeed," Liam agreed, closing his eyes again. "Someday, I'm going to live out here."

"Without electricity?!"

"It's not completely without electricity—most houses have generators."

"And how much energy does a generator . . . generate?"

"It depends on the size, but mine will be big enough to run a small refrigerator and a water pump."

Cadie frowned. "How will you cook?"

"Gas."

"Lights?"

"Kerosene."

"Heat?"

"Wood . . . and a big, cozy quilt," he added with a grin.

"It sounds kind of primitive."

"Primitive?!" he said, opening his eyes. "It doesn't sound *fun?*"

"I don't know," she answered skeptically.

"What if I let you plug your hair dryer into my generator?"

She laughed. "Well, then, I *might* consider it."

"Just think how romantic it would be to have dinner by lantern light every night."

She rolled her eyes. "What about TV?"

He shook his head and closed his eyes again. "Naw . . . just books."

"Your eyes will go bad from the poor lighting."

"I had no idea you were so negative," he teased.

Cadie gave one last pull and the boat slid up onto the beach with a jolt that almost sent Liam into the water. "We're here!" she announced.

"Nice," he said, hopping out to pull the boat higher, and at the same time, splashing her.

"Hey!" Cadie said, laughing good-naturedly. She pulled the oars back into the boat, stood up, handed him the cooler, towels, and blanket, slung her beach bag over her shoulder, and climbed out too.

"Wow," she said, looking up and down the deserted beach. "This *is* beautiful."

Liam grinned. "Welcome to Tuckernuck."

"No wonder you named your boat after it," she exclaimed, watching the only other beachgoers—a flock of piping plovers—chasing the waves.

Liam walked a few yards away, set the cooler down, spread the blanket across the warm sand, and dropped the towels on it.

"Look at these shells," Cadie called, walking along the water's edge. "There are so many . . . *and* they're not broken!"

"That's because Tuckernuck is Nantucket's best-kept secret. Islanders rarely tell vacationers about it. You know the saying: 'It's classified . . . ?' "

"Great!" Cadie said with a laugh as she looked around and realized how vulnerable she was. "And I didn't even tell anyone where I was going."

"Are you nervous?" he teased in an eerie voice.

She searched his tan face and looked into his summer sky blue eyes. "No," she said simply. "I think I could tell if you were crazy."

"Maybe . . ." he said mischievously. Then added, "Would you like to go see an abandoned house with me?"

Cadie laughed. "Why not? Abandoned beach . . . abandoned house—it doesn't matter—either way, they won't find me."

They walked along the water, Cadie picking up shells and Liam skipping smooth stones across the waves. "How come you want to live here?" Cadie asked.

"Wouldn't you?"

"I don't know . . . it's beautiful, but I think it's a little too far from civilization."

"Who needs civilization? Since the beginning of time, civilizations have been nothing but corrupt—they're all about power and war. Man will never learn to get along with his brother—there's always someone who wants *more* power or *more* money."

"That's awfully cynical."

"Cynical, but true. I see it all the time—even living on an island. Nantucket is a microcosm of the world—and it has more than its share of *haves* and *have-nots;* and the ones who *have* only want more."

Cadie nodded. "You don't need to tell *me*—my father is one of them, but there are other *haves* who give away a lot of what they have."

"Not many."

Cadie was quiet, not knowing what to say.

"Living out here would be so simple," Liam continued. "No news, no politics, no rich, no poor, no . . ."

"What would you do all day?"

"Fish, cook, build boats, work on my house, play with my kids. . . ."

"You're going to have kids?"

"Mm-hmm."

"And raise them here?"

"Is there a better place?"

"How many are you going to have?"

"A whole tribe!" he said with a smile. "Being an only child isn't fun."

"So, let me get this straight—you want to escape civilization to get away from everyone . . . but you still want to have a whole bunch of kids?"

"Mm-hmm."

"What if you have a child who can't get along with his or her siblings?"

"That'll never happen. My kids are going to be great; I'll teach them to love nature and to build things with their hands." He stopped abruptly and Cadie, who'd been following him on the narrow path, almost bumped into him.

"Here it is," he said, pointing to a weathered three-quarter Cape with a long thicket of roses climbing over its roof.

"Oh, my," she whispered softly.

Liam pushed open the rickety gate. "I'm going to buy this place someday."

Cadie followed him up the overgrown path and Liam lifted the train of tiny pink roses that hung over the house and jiggled the wooden door open. They stepped into a room that was bare of furnishings but filled with light. Cadie looked around at the wide board flooring, covered with sand, and at the broken panes in the windows. "It sure needs work!"

"It does," Liam agreed, surveying the little house as if he already owned it. "But it'll be beautiful when it's done. Just look at these fireplaces," he said, motioning to the tremendous stone chimney dividing the main level into three rooms—each with its own hearth.

"I can definitely see its potential," Cadie said as she followed him through the kitchen and out into the yard. The heady aroma of lilacs filled the air as she gazed at the overgrown gardens.

"There's an herb garden over here," Liam said, kneeling

down next to a small raised bed. He brushed off the faded wooden markers. "Basil, chives, thyme . . ."

"Do you know who owns it?" Cadie asked.

Liam shook his head. "It's been like this since I was a little kid and it just gets more overgrown every year."

"Maybe the person's too old to take care of it."

"Maybe."

"I can picture a woman coming out here to snip herbs for her dinner or lilacs for her table."

Liam nodded. "Whoever it is, I hope they don't put it on the market before I have enough money to buy it."

They walked back through the house and Liam closed the doors.

"It's beautiful," Cadie said as she followed him back along the path. "Thank you for showing it to me."

When they got back to the beach, Liam pulled off his shirt. "Going in?"

Cadie watched him straighten out the corners of the blanket. "I *am*," she said, "but I need some sunscreen on my back." She held out a bottle of Coppertone and pulled her tank top over her head. "Would you mind?"

Mind?! Liam shook the bottle, poured a generous puddle into the palm of his hand, smeared it across her shoulders and felt her shiver. "What's the matter?"

"It's chilly."

"Oh, don't be a wimp," he teased, rubbing the cream under the strings of her bikini. "Want help on the front too?"

"I think I can handle the front," she said, taking the bottle back from him.

"Well, let me know if you change your mind," he said with a grin as he rubbed the extra sunscreen on his nose.

Cadie watched him walk to the water. She'd never met anyone like Liam before. Most of the boys in her circle of friends were more concerned about the cars they drove and the girls they'd been with than they were with the state of the world; and even though Liam owned a boat that would be the envy of every boy she knew, he loved it for its beauty, not its value.

He turned back. "Coming?"

"Yup," she said, stepping out of her shorts and following him.

Chapter 8

Liam was surprised to find a parking spot on Broad Street on a Saturday night. He backed into it and climbed out, glancing at his watch as he hurried across the street—he hadn't realized how late it had gotten after he'd towed John Alden's boat back to the boathouse. He ran his hand through his damp hair and looked up at the beautifully restored New England building. It wasn't his first time at The Brotherhood of the Thieves. In the off-season, he often stopped by the old whaling bar to have a beer with the old salts, but he avoided going out in the summer months, and he'd never been to the restaurant.

He stepped inside and was immediately greeted by a friendly hostess who showed him to the patio where the Regan party was already getting started. Tracey stood up as soon as she saw him. "Hey," she said, giving him a warm hug. Liam smiled and kissed her lightly on the cheek; then he shook Jack's hand and nodded politely to their friends. "This is Chase Travis," Jack said, motioning to a handsome, blond-haired man wearing round, tortoise shell glasses. "And this is Devon Travis," he said, motioning to the slender Asian man sitting next to him. Both Chase and Devon stood to shake hands and Liam realized that, although they shared a last name, they couldn't possibly be brothers—unless one was adopted. He glanced at Jack for a sign, but his face was unrevealing. "Chase and Devon own The Painted Parrot."

"I've heard of it," Liam said, not missing a beat. He had an open mind—*to each his own,* he'd always believed. "Over on Old South Wharf. It's new . . ."

"Yes," Chase said, sipping his martini. "We just opened this summer and it's been a huge success—bigger than we ever dreamed." He looked over at his partner for confirmation and Devon nodded. "We're featuring an up-and-coming new artist in our next show," Chase continued. "Levi Knox—his work is amazing. In fact, we've already sold a piece!"

"The opening is tomorrow," Devon added.

Liam nodded. "I saw an ad in the paper."

"I told you the newspaper was worth it," Devon said, smiling victoriously.

Chase rolled his eyes. "We're still trying to figure out the best venues for ads—I think magazines, but Devon insists vacationers read the local paper too."

"Well, I'm not a vacationer, but that's where I saw it," Liam confirmed as their waitress came over to take his drink order. He quickly glanced at the list of beers and then eyed Jack's glass.

"Whale's Tale," Jack said.

"I'll just have what he's having."

The waitress nodded. "Are you ready to order dinner or should I come back?"

"Come back," they all said, and Liam, who was still trying to catch up, opened his menu. He glanced down, but out of the corner of his eye he saw Tracey looking at him.

"What?" he asked with a boyish grin. She laughed and he felt his heart skip. *Yep, nothing's changed,* he thought. If there was any other girl on earth, besides Cadie, whom Liam felt he could've spent his life with, it was Tracey, and the funny thing was, the two weren't anything alike. Tracey had dark, wavy hair—which he now noticed had silver strands weaving through it—and jade green eyes, and because she was Greek and had olive oil running through her veins, she was perpetually tan. But the biggest difference between them was that Cadie had come from a wealthy family who vacationed on Nantucket, and Tracey—the youngest daughter of a lobsterman and a waitress—was a native islander who was well acquainted with hard times. Unfortunately, she was also the childhood sweetheart of his best friend.

Tracey looked up and smiled, her green eyes seeing right through him. "What what?" she said flirtatiously.

"You're lookin' as fine as ever, woman. Are you sure you're with the right man?"

Jack laughed. "Wow! You *do* have a line or two!"

Liam grinned at his old friend. "I'm *not* a virgin, ya know."

"I'm glad to hear it," Jack said, "although thirty years of celibacy is nothing to cheer about."

"Who said anything about celibacy?"

Tracey listened to their banter and laughed. She loved Liam—she always had. In fact, if Jack hadn't asked her out first, her life might've been very different.

"How're the kids?" Liam asked.

"Getting big!" Tracey said, reaching for her phone and showing him the most recent pictures of T. J., their ten-year-old son, and Olivia, his seven-year-old sister.

Liam leaned closer to get a better look, and Tracey murmured, "Mmm, *you* smell good!"

"I showered just for you," he teased, admiring the pictures. "Man, the apple doesn't fall far from the tree, does it?" he said, eyeing Jack. "Look how blond they are!"

"What can I say?" Jack said with a shrug. "It's those stubborn Norwegian genes."

"Stubborn is right," Tracey said with a laugh, showing Chase and Devon the pictures too.

"How are your parents?" Liam asked.

"Fine. They're living in Florida now."

"I know. Your dad didn't want to leave Nantucket."

"He didn't—in fact, he still refuses to sell the house, so it just sits here empty. But they're getting older, and after his heart attack, they really needed to move closer to one of us. Vermont was definitely out of the question since they'd had enough of winter, so they're down in Palm Beach near Elisa—who's only five minutes away. It worked out . . . although I miss them."

"Your dad's a character," Liam said, his voice filled with obvious affection for Dimitri Elias.

She laughed. "He is indeed . . . and he thought the world of Coop," she said, smiling sadly. "You must miss him."

"I do. Thanks for the card, by the way. . . ."

"You're welcome. I wish we could've come."

Liam nodded. "Your dad spoke at the funeral. . . ."

"I know."

"The two of them always had such a good time when they were together," Liam said, smiling. "Good ole Dimitri. I can remember watching them walk down the street"—he motioned in the direction of Broad Street—"holding each other up. Talk about a pair of drunken sailors! And your mom would always call me to see if I would go round them up."

Tracey laughed. Just then, their waitress came back with Liam's beer. "Ready?" she asked, and they all smiled sheepishly and looked back at their menus. "Okay, I'll come back," she said with a laugh.

"Just a couple more minutes," Jack called after her. "Damn, she's a looker," he murmured, and Liam looked up in surprise . . . and then realized Tracey had heard too.

After they finally ordered, the evening flew by, and Liam discovered that sharing his old friends with strangers wasn't as bad as he'd expected. Chase and Devon were both funny and cheerful . . . *and* they were obviously in love. Liam also learned that Tracey—an art history professor at UVM—had been Chase's advisor, which explained their lasting friendship.

"Are you still teaching?" Liam asked.

"No, I'm home with the kids. It was too hard to juggle teaching and being a mom—our schedules are different and Jack travels so much, plus both kids play sports, and then there's the inevitable sick day. It's just easier being home."

Liam nodded and then noticed Jack eyeing the waitress again. "How's work for you?" he asked, trying to draw his attention back to the table.

Jack looked back, startled. "Me?! Oh, fine. Same old shit, ya know—lots of traveling, but the money's good and that's what matters, right, hon?" he asked, smiling at Tracey.

"If you say so," she said in a resigned voice.

Liam frowned, sensing discord between them.

As the evening wound down and they stood to leave, Liam realized he'd had a little too much to drink, and as he steadied himself, Chase turned to shake hands and almost fell over. "You should come to the opening tomorrow," he slurred.

"Yes, you *should* come!" Tracey chimed, wrapping him in a hug. "Then we'll see you again . . . *and* you can see the kids."

"I was actually thinking of coming," Liam said with a smile. Then he turned to shake Jack's hand. "Then you and I can have a talk. . . ."

Jack nodded and slapped him on the back. "We'll see . . ."

Chapter 9

1989

"I can't believe you brought beer!" Cadie said as she wrapped a towel around her shivering body and sat on the blanket next to Liam. Her lips were blue and goose bumps covered her arms and legs. "I thought you were an innocent island boy. . . ." she chattered.

"What makes you think island boys are innocent?" he teased, handing her the frosty bottle.

"Oh, my goodness!" she said, holding it. "What I really need is a cup of hot cocoa."

"You'll warm up," he promised, rubbing her back through the towel. "Anyway, you didn't answer my question."

"That's because my brain is frozen—what was it?"

"What makes you think island boys are innocent?"

"Oh!" she said with a laugh. "I don't know . . . you just have this sweet, innocent look about you. I would've never guessed you drank."

"I don't know if I should take that as a compliment," he

mused, opening his beer. "Sometimes I drink. Not often. But I figured you did—being a rich kid with rich friends and all. That's why I brought 'em."

"I don't know if I should take *that* as a compliment or not," she teased.

"Don't take it the wrong way," he said. "I just meant . . ."

"I know what you meant. You're quick to criticize—*and* assume—stuff about rich people, and then you assume those same people make assumptions about *you*."

Liam shrugged and took a sip of his beer. "You're right," he admitted sheepishly. "I guess I do have a little bit of a chip on my shoulder." He paused. "It probably comes from living with Coop, but then again, I've never met anyone with money who acts like you." He reached into the cooler. "Ham or turkey?"

"I can't believe you packed lunch too."

"I always pack lunch. If I don't eat, I get crankery."

"Is that a combination of hungry and cranky?"

"It *is*—my mom used to say it when I was little."

Cadie smiled and peered into the cooler. "I'll have whatever you don't want."

"It doesn't matter . . . you pick."

"Turkey."

"It has cheese on it—is that okay?"

"I don't mind—I'm just *so* impressed."

"It's not a big deal," Liam said, handing the turkey sandwich wrapped neatly in wax paper to her. "I've been packing my own lunch since I was seven."

"That's kind of young to be making your own lunch."

"Well, it was either that or be crankery."

"Coop didn't make your lunch?"

"Sometimes he did, but sometimes he wasn't up yet," Liam said, taking a bite of his sandwich.

Cadie slowly unwrapped her sandwich. "How come you live with him?"

Liam swallowed the bite he'd taken and took a sip of his beer. "Because my parents died in a car accident."

"Oh, no!" Cadie said. "I'm so sorry." She put her hand on his arm and her touch went right through him.

"It's okay," Liam said, looking over. "It was a long time ago."

"How did it happen?"

"They were coming home from a Christmas party in a snowstorm and a tractor trailer lost control and hit them head-on."

Cadie shook her head in horror. "That's awful."

Liam nodded. "A state trooper came to our house, but Jess, my babysitter, and I were the only ones home. I was in bed, but I heard the knock on the door and then I heard Jess crying, so I went to see what was wrong. I saw the trooper standing by the door and I saw Jess on the phone. She pulled me into a hug, and I stood there listening to her as she told her mom what happened . . . and I thought she was talking about someone else. I had no idea she was talking about *my* parents.

"She still sends me Christmas cards. She used to send a regular card—you know, with just a Christmas scene, but the last few years, she's sent one of those photo cards of her family— she has kids of her own now." He paused. "Sometimes I wish she'd just stop sending cards . . . it always reminds me of that night."

"How old were you?"

"Six."

"That must've been so hard."

Liam looked out at the waves. "It was. I couldn't wrap my mind around the fact that I'd never see them again—that they were just . . . gone." He paused. "At their service, I heard people say it was good thing I was so young because I wouldn't remember them, but I remembered everything—I remembered how my mom's hair smelled and the way her eyes sparkled when she looked at me; how my dad always said she could give hugs with her eyes . . . and how soft-spoken and patient he was.

One time, he was helping me with a Lego model of a plane and he just watched, waiting for me to figure it out. 'You got this, Li,' he'd say. 'You got this.' "

He turned and smiled at her. "And *you* said I wasn't talkative. Look how you've gotten me to do *all* the talking!"

Cadie smiled. "Well, thank you for telling me about it. I didn't know you had so much happen." She paused. "Is Coop your mom's brother or your dad's?"

"My mom's."

"Do you have other family?"

"I have a grandfather on my mom's side—Coop's father— but he and Coop don't get along, and my grandparents on my dad's side live in California. I only met them once—at my parents' service. At the time, there was a bit of a debate about who was going to get me, but my mom had left a note saying she wanted Coop to be my guardian . . . and that was that."

Cadie nodded thoughtfully. "Have you liked living with him?"

Liam nodded. "For the most part—he's a veteran and he struggles with his memories of Vietnam, but he's a good guy." He took a sip of his beer and looked over at her again. "Enough about me. What about you and your family? Do you have brothers and sisters?"

Cadie shook her head as she swallowed the last bite of her sandwich. "No, I'm an only child too."

"Are your parents from New York?"

She nodded. "My parents are from Montauk. We have a house there too."

Liam offered her a chocolate-chip cookie. "Is that in New York?"

She nodded and smiled as she reached for a cookie—the fact that Liam hadn't heard of one of the wealthiest towns in New York made him all the more perfect.

"Are you warming up?" he asked, sealing the ziplock bag.

"Yup, I'm ready to go back in."

"You are not," he said with a laugh; then he turned to her, searching her eyes. He gently touched her cheek, and then, to his own surprise, leaned over and kissed her. She kissed him back, tasting his sweet lips.

Liam's eyes grew solemn and his voice was husky as he spoke. "I've never felt this way before."

"I haven't either," she said softly.

Liam kissed her again and then pulled away. "I'm ready to go in again," he said with a smile, and Cadie watched in surprise as he got up and trotted toward the water.

Liam plunged headfirst through the waves and swam underwater for as long as he could, the cold, clear water cooling his body and clearing his mind. He really *hadn't* felt this way before—his heart was pounding, his head was spinning, and the rest of his body, well . . . it was as if everything was suddenly spiraling out of control and he really needed it to slow down.

Moments later, he walked back toward the blanket and reached down for his towel.

"Feel better?" Cadie asked.

"Much," he said with a grin; then he shook his head, sending beads of cold water in her direction.

"Hey!" she said, laughing and pulling her towel around her.

Chapter 10

Liam felt a cold, wet nose nudging his hand and opened his eyes. He saw a pair of soft brown eyes peering at him. "Hello," he murmured, and Tuck, happy to find evidence of life, wiggled happily. Liam looked at the clock on the bedside table and groaned. "Eight o'clock! How the heck did that happen?!" Tuck licked his face and wagged his whole hind end, knocking the clock to the floor. Liam leaned over to retrieve it, and as he sat up, felt his head start to pound. "Damn," he muttered, rubbing his temples.

He shuffled to the bathroom, relieved himself, splashed water on his face, and looked in the mirror. "Man, you have *definitely* seen better days . . ." he mumbled, and Tuck, who'd followed him into the bathroom, continued to wag his tail. "No comments from the peanut gallery either," Liam said, eyeing him. He opened the medicine cabinet, reached for the aspirin bottle, popped four in his mouth, put his head under the faucet, and swallowed. "Remind me," he grumbled as Tuck followed him to the kitchen, "never again."

He let Tuck out and Moby in. "Sorry you got left out,

Mobe," he said apologetically as he scooped kibble into their bowls and put on a pot of coffee. When the coffee was done, he propped open the door, eased into one of the Adirondack chairs on the back porch, and took a sip, hoping his hangover wouldn't last all day.

The night before, they'd started off with a couple of beers, but then Jack had ordered a round of tequila shots—which had been fun, so they'd ordered more . . . until they'd each ordered a round and it had come around to Jack again. Eventually, Liam had lost track of how many they'd had, but when he stood up, he knew it was too many.

Now, as he listened to the waves, he recalled the bizarre conversation he'd had with Jack as they'd stood in front of the urinals in the men's room. Liam blinked at the bright morning sunlight. Had Jack really talked about an encounter he'd had with the wife of a friend in the men's room of an Outback Steakhouse while Tracey and the friend waited for their table?

"In the Bloke's Room!" Jack had said as he relieved himself. "Damn, she was hot, and I pushed her up against the wall of the stall, pulled down her panties, and gave her all I had. Afterward, I went to find our table while she waited. But before the evening was over, I said I had to use the men's room again . . . and damn, if she didn't follow me . . . and when I pulled her skirt up, I realized she never put her panties back on. All through dinner, she'd been sitting next to me with no panties on. Man, I thought I was gonna explode."

Liam had leaned against the cool bathroom wall, trying to comprehend what Jack was saying. "You cheated on Tracey?" he asked in a voice that was barely audible.

"Li, I've been with Tracey since high school. Don't get me wrong . . . I love her . . . but I can't imagine going through life screwing only one woman . . ."

Liam had felt his fists clench . . . and if he hadn't been so drunk . . . and Tracey hadn't been waiting, he would've clocked him.

* * *

"Damn," he mumbled now, opening his eyes. "What an ass. I can't believe my best friend is such an ass." Tuck rested his head on Liam's lap and he stroked his soft ears. *Whatever happened to the honor code that was drilled into our heads when we enlisted? Did Jack forget everything they'd learned? Or had the boy he'd known in high school never really changed?* Liam would never forget the time Tracey had tearfully told him she'd seen Jack kissing Diane Hollis, a girl from Martha's Vineyard High School, behind the football bleachers after the Island Cup game . . . and she hadn't been the only one who saw them—when Jack had boarded the ferry back to Nantucket, the whole football team had started singing "Jack and Diane."

Thinking back, Liam realized Diane was probably just the first of Jack's indiscretions, and he couldn't help but wonder if Tracey knew about others. Maybe she'd known all along—and just lived with it. But if she didn't know, someone should tell her.

He watched the waves, wondering if he should skip the art show—he would certainly be avoiding a lot of trouble if he did. He looked into Tuck's soulful eyes, and whispered, "There's a lot to be said for keeping things simple, ole pal." Tuck thumped his tail in agreement.

Chapter 11

1989

"I told Mrs. Wellington you'd be at the party tonight," Libby Knox said in an annoyed voice. "They're having a clambake and fireworks. Everyone's going, so I don't know what friends of yours are going to the movies . . ."

"I told you, Mother. I met them at the beach."

"I hope that boy from the boatyard isn't one of them," Carlton said, peering over his newspaper. "I don't want you hanging out with him."

"Why not?" Cadie asked, her voice edged with anger.

"Because he has no future."

"How do you know? It just so happens he's applying to BU *and* BC."

"Yeah, let me know how that turns out," Carlton scoffed sarcastically.

Cadie stared angrily at the newspaper blocking her view of her father. "I'll do what I want," she said softly.

"What did you say?" Carlton asked, his voice rising as he lowered his paper.

"Nothing," she muttered.

"Well, I want you to reconsider," her mother said.

"I'm *not* reconsidering. I don't care about the Wellingtons' party . . . *or* any of the stupid people who will be there." And before her parents could say anything more, she walked out, slamming the door behind her.

"I know she's been spending time with that boy," Carlton said angrily. "I've heard his truck on the road. He's nothing but trouble."

"Well, we can't very well forbid her. . . ."

"We certainly can!"

"I heard the Walshes will be there tonight," Libby said. "They're flying out to the island this afternoon and Taylor is coming too."

"Now there's someone with whom she should be spending some time," Carlton said, folding the newspaper. "Taylor Walsh is a sophomore at Yale—pre-law, and he has an internship at Franklin and Collins this summer."

"Well, it's a shame Acadia made other plans," Libby said with a sigh. "Maybe she'll change her mind."

Cadie stood in the driveway, listening to her parents. "It's a shame *you* don't know that Taylor Walsh is the reason Lila Jacobson had to have an abortion," she muttered. "If Taylor was the last person on earth, I wouldn't spend time with him."

She walked around the house, brushing away angry tears. She'd seen Liam several times since he'd taken her to Tuckernuck Island, and every time, she'd had to lie about where she was going. She knew all too well that her parents' plan for her included getting a degree from highly selective college and marrying well . . . and a boy like Liam—who worked in a boat repair shop—had no chance of fitting into that plan, but she didn't care—she'd be an old maid before she married for money.

She walked down to the beach and looked out at the waves. She'd only known Liam for two weeks—hardly long enough to be in love . . . or was it? She'd never met anyone like him—he was soft-spoken and gentle and sure of himself, and when she was with him, she felt happier than she'd ever been. He could make her heart race *and* ache all at the same time . . . and if that wasn't love, she didn't know what was.

The last two times they'd been alone, they'd come so close to making love that she didn't know how he'd stopped. On Sunday night, when she knew he'd be locking up the boathouse, she'd come up behind him and put her hands over his eyes. He'd turned around, pushed the door open again, and pulled her inside. The late-day sun had streamed through the windows, casting golden light across the floor, but Liam had pulled her into the shadows, kissing her softly, and when he pressed against her, she could feel how aroused he was. She'd unbuttoned his jeans and he'd slid his hands under her skirt . . . and then he'd knelt down . . .

Cadie closed her eyes, remembering his sweet touch and the pleasure he'd given her . . . and the way he'd tasted when he kissed her again.

"Acadia!" a sharp voice called, interrupting her thoughts. Cadie turned and saw her father standing in the doorway. "Come up here, please!"

Obediently, Acadia trudged to the house. "Your mother and I have decided that it would be impolite if you don't make an appearance at the party."

"I already have plans," Cadie said defiantly.

"Cancel them."

Cadie felt hot tears stinging her eyes again and she quickly looked away—there was no way she was going to let him see her cry.

* * *

An hour later, Acadia stepped into the spacious circular entrance of the Wellington estate and smiled when she replied to
Mrs. Wellington's question about how her summer was going.

"The kids are down on the beach."

"Thank you," she said politely. "May I use your bathroom
to change?"

"Of course. There's one right off the kitchen," Mrs. Wellington said, pointing, "and there's another down that hall on the
left . . . and that hall on the right," she added, motioning to the
two ends of the stately home.

As Cadie walked back through the tiled entrance, she looked
out through the floor-to-ceiling windows along the back wall
and saw her parents being greeted by the other adults who were
already chatting and drinking while two busy bartenders wearing vests and bow ties tried to keep up with their orders.

"They must hate their jobs," she muttered. "*I* would hate
their job."

As she walked down the hallway with her beach bag over
her shoulder, she saw a phone on a small table in the hallway . . .
and stared at it as if it were a foreign object. She glanced over
her shoulder, picked up the receiver, and dialed the number
she'd memorized the very first time Liam said it.

When she returned to the party ten minutes later, her smile
was genuine; and when her mother—forgetting she already knew
Taylor—introduced them, she nodded politely; and when her
father peppered him with questions about Yale and his internship, she even managed to look impressed. Afterward, at her
mother's suggestion, she followed Taylor down to the beach,
listening as he bragged about the parties his frat house had
hosted that year. "It was totally out of hand," he said, laughing.

As soon as they reached the beach, a bunch of boys playing
volleyball good-naturedly jeered Taylor's arrival. He smiled
and high-fived them and then opened a large cooler, pulled out

a beer, and let the lid drop. Then, he remembered his manners. "Wanna beer?"

"Sure," Cadie said. She had a little over an hour to kill, so she may as well make the most of it.

"Don't let him get you drunk, Cadie," one of the boys teased, spiking the volleyball. "He's a total predator."

Cadie nodded as she walked over to join the girls. "Thanks for the tip," she called back. "You don't need to worry."

"Ahh, Taylor, she's got your number," all the boys teased, but Taylor just shrugged and gulped his beer.

"Hey, Cadie-did!" Tess called. "I thought you weren't coming."

Cadie shook her head. "I wasn't, but my father insisted—he thinks I should spend more time with Taylor," she said, rolling her eyes.

"You're kidding!" Tess exclaimed. "Doesn't he know he's just one step up from being a serial rapist?"

"No . . . he thinks he's quite the catch!"

Tess shook her head. "Our parents live in a world of their own."

"That's for sure. Anyway, if my parents are looking for me later, cover for me, will you?"

Tess raised her eyebrows. "Hmm . . . got a hot date? Actually, don't tell me—if I don't know, I won't be lying," she said with a laugh.

Cadie laughed, too, and sipped her beer.

The caterers were just setting up the dessert table when they finally went back up to the house to fix their plates. Cadie walked past it, adding a lemon square and a cream puff to her plate before walking over to join Tess, who was already perusing the dinner buffet. There was corn on the cob, clams on the half shell, steamers, filet mignon, coconut shrimp, bacon-wrapped scallops, and a wide variety of salads. Cadie looked at all the offerings, but there wasn't anything that appealed to her—ever since she'd started seeing Liam, she hadn't had much of an appetite, so the plate she fixed was with him in mind—and when her plate was full, she made sure her parents saw her, nodded discreetly to Tess, and walked leisurely around the house as if she was looking for a place to sit. She glanced over her shoulder to make sure no one had followed her and then wandered through the gardens and out onto the quiet road . . . *Freedom!*

She walked in the direction from which she knew Liam would come, rounded the bend in the road, and saw him leaning against the hood of his truck, wearing his favorite torn jeans and a T-shirt. Her heart sang at the sight of him and she walked faster, her white skirt billowing around her slender waist.

"Hey," he said with a slow smile.

"Hey."

"What's this?" he asked, nodding to the plate.

"Dinner . . . for you."

"What about you?"

"I'm not hungry. . . ."

He reached for a coconut shrimp, squeezed the tail, and popped it in his mouth. "Mmm . . . how come you're not hungry?" he asked, tossing the tail into the pine trees along the side of the road.

"I think it has something to do with you," she said with a smile, reaching into her beach bag for the plastic ware she'd grabbed. Her hand touched something cold and after she handed him the napkin she reached back in and produced two frosty bottles.

"Nice!" Liam said with a grin. "So, where are we going?"

"I don't know," she said, glancing over her shoulder, "but we should go soon."

Liam tossed another shrimp tail into the woods and opened

the door for her. Then, giving her the plate to hold, he climbed in and started the truck. Suddenly, a black Mercedes came down the road from the direction of the party and Cadie ducked. Liam waited for it to pass and looked over at her. "What? Are you not supposed to be seen with me?"

"No," she lied. "I'm supposed to be at the party."

"Well, maybe you should stay. There's no point in getting in trouble."

"I won't get in trouble—there're so many people, my parents won't even notice. I just need to be back as soon as the fireworks end."

"Then we shouldn't go far," he said, driving past the black iron gates of the Wellington property and turning onto a long, sandy road that ended abruptly at a secluded beach.

"How do you know all these places?" Cadie asked, looking around. "From taking your other girlfriends?"

Liam laughed. "Yup, all my other girlfriends have been here," he teased. "Actually, it's from riding my bike everywhere when I was a kid. I know every inch of this island."

"Is that the Wellingtons'?" Cadie asked in surprise, pointing across the water.

"It is."

"Hey, I think I see my parents!"

He laughed as Cadie handed the plate back to him and opened her beer. "I've already had two," she confessed, taking a sip.

"You have?! *And* you haven't eaten?"

"I don't need to eat."

He looked at her eyes. "Yes, you do. You probably have a buzz right now."

"No, I don't."

"Yes, you do!" he said with a laugh. "Eat something," he commanded, holding out the plate.

Cadie picked up the cream puff. "You know what I love about cream puffs?" she asked, seductively licking the chocolate.

"I can't imagine," he said, suddenly feeling aroused.

She closed her eyes and put the whole thing in her mouth. "Mmm," she murmured, "the cream."

Liam smiled. "You're killing me, you know that?" he said, putting the plate on the dashboard.

"I'm sorry," she teased with a mischievous gleam in her eyes.

"No, you're not," he said, sipping his beer.

"Mm-hmm," she countered.

"Prove it," he said, searching her eyes.

"All right," she said, moving closer and unbuttoning the top of his jeans. Liam watched her and then leaned back against the door and closed his eyes.

Ten minutes later, he pulled her onto his chest, kissed the top of her head, and tried to wrap his mind around what she'd just done. "Damn, Cadie," he whispered. "You sure know what you're doing. . . ."

She leaned against him. "No, I don't. . . ."

"Yes, you do," he said softly, kissing her cheek and searching for her soft lips. "My uncle's right," he whispered. "You *are* trouble."

She laughed. "That's funny . . . that's what my father says about *you*."

"He does?" Liam asked, pulling back to search her face. "Why?"

"I don't know," she lied.

He lifted her chin to look at him. "Yes, you do."

"Why does your uncle think *I'm* trouble?" she asked, changing the subject.

" 'Cause you'll break my heart."

"No, I won't."

Liam searched her eyes. "You won't?"

Cadie shook her head. "Never," she said, laying her head against his chest and feeling his heartbeat. They were both quiet as they watched the fireflies blinking in the woods.

And then the first fireworks screamed into the sky.

Chapter 12

"Oh, to be a dog," Liam mused softly as he got up from his chair. "At least you have the sense to not drink stuff that'll make you feel like crap the next day," he said, bending down to scratch Tuck's silky ears. "I think the only way I'm gonna feel better is to sweat this stuff right out of my system. What do you think—want to go for a run?" Tuck blinked at him, considering the invitation, then yawned, stretched his legs, and closed his eyes again. "I'll take that as a 'no,'" Liam said with a half smile.

One of the hardest parts of running, Liam knew, was the first few steps, but he also knew—from years of running—that once he reached the half-mile mark, his body would fall into an easy rhythm and the fog would clear from his mind.

It was still early when he set out, and as he trotted along the quiet road, he was still trying to decide if he should go to the art show. After hearing Jack brag callously about his extramarital relations, he didn't know if he wanted to see him again. And how could he look Tracey in the eye, knowing what he knew? He felt miserable and he wasn't even the one who had cheated!

And then there was Cadie—was it crazy to think she might be related to the artist whose show it was . . . just because they shared a last name? And even if she was related, what were the chances she'd be there? Liam ran his fingers through his hair and wondered if she'd recognize him.

Chapter 13

1989

"Did you get caught?" Liam asked as he watched Cadie lean her bike against the boathouse.

"No," she said, following him down to the dock. "I told you they wouldn't notice. In fact, my father was so drunk my mother had to drive home."

Liam shook his head, picturing an inebriated Carlton Knox. "Will they miss you today?" he asked, climbing into the boat to give the chrome a quick polish.

"No, my mother's getting her hair done and going to a luncheon, and my father's golfing all day."

Liam nodded thoughtfully.

She watched him, and teased, "Don't you worry you're gonna wipe the finish right off?"

Liam stepped back onto the dock. "Nooo, I don't," he said, rolling his eyes. Then he wrapped his arms around her and moved to the edge of the dock as if he was going to throw her in.

"Hey!" she said, squirming and giggling. "You'll be sorry."
"Will I?"
"Mm-hmm! Men have died for less than that!"
"They have?" he said, laughing.
"Yes," she nodded, holding his arms.
"I probably shouldn't, then," he teased, edging closer.
"Besides, I'm sure you don't want me to get your seats wet."
He nodded thoughtfully. "That's true . . . but they'll dry—
after all, it *is* a boat. It's made to get wet."
"Well, if I go in, you're coming with me. . . ." she said, still
laughing and holding his arms.
"Hmm . . . sounds like a threat," he mused.
"Not a threat. A *fact.*"
"Is that so?" Liam said, stepping to the edge. Suddenly, Cadie
squirmed free, causing him to lose his balance. The look on his
face was priceless as he realized he had no chance of saving
himself, and the next second, he splashed headlong into the
water, sputtering and laughing at the sudden reversal of fortune.
Cadie was laughing so hard she had to hold her sides.
"Very funny," Liam teased good-naturedly as he pulled
himself up on the dock.
"Mm-hmm," she giggled, backing away, but before she
knew it, he had his dripping arms around her again, and she
could feel his cold, wet clothes soaking hers.
"Ready?" he teased, and even though she knew what was
coming, it was shocking to tumble into the frigid New England
water. A moment later, they both came up, face-to-face, laughing, and Liam pulled her toward him and pressed his lips
against her full mouth, tasting the salty water. "I love you," he
whispered.
"I love you too," she said softly.

He looked down at her wet tank top and, with a mischievous grin, traced his fingers over her breasts, lightly making circles around her erect nipples. "What's going on here?" he teased.

"They're saluting you," she said with a laugh, "which is the opposite of what's going on down here," she said, pressing against him.

Liam laughed. "Ahh, no, he doesn't like the cold."

"Well, maybe you should let him warm up. . . ." she said with a slow smile.

"Right here?!"

She laughed, looking around. "Well, maybe not *right* here. . . ."

"Hmm," he murmured, kissing her again. "Maybe I will. . . ."

Suddenly, they heard voices in the parking lot and they looked up to see Cooper and another man walking toward the boathouse. Cadie ducked behind Liam. "That's Taylor's father," she whispered.

"Taylor who?" Liam asked.

"Walsh," she whispered. "He's friends with my father."

"Oh," Liam said, trying to figure out how they could get in the boat without being seen. "Go around," he said softly, motioning, and Cadie made her way around to the other side of the boat as Liam untied the line and pushed the boat away. Waves from the wake of a passing boat lapped quietly against the sides, rocking the boat up and down, and Liam could see Cadie half-swimming half-pulling, trying to help, and he prayed that Coop—who he knew had seen them—was keeping Mr. Walsh occupied. Finally, when they were about a hundred yards out, Cadie climbed up the ladder on the back and Liam followed. He slid into the seat and pushed the starter and the old runabout rumbled to life. Then he slowly turned around and, without looking back, headed out to sea.

"Wow! That was close!" Cadie said with a grin as she pulled a towel around her.

Liam, who'd pulled off his wet T-shirt, nodded but didn't smile.

"What's the matter?" she called over the rumble of the motor.

"Nothing. . . ."

"Something," she said, putting her hand on his thigh.

He looked over with a sad smile and shook his head again, and since the only way to communicate was to shout, Cadie waited, watching his handsome profile and windswept hair. Finally, just as Tuckernuck came into view, he pointed to two whales breeching above the blue-gray water. "Want to get closer?" he called. Cadie nodded enthusiastically and Liam changed course, slowing down as they drew near to the spot where they'd seen the whales go down. Hungry seagulls skimmed the water all around them, but there wasn't any sign of the gigantic mammals—in fact, the water was calm. Then, suddenly, out of nowhere, one of the whales breeched thirty feet from the stern. They watched in amazement as it slapped the water, and even though the runabout was seventeen feet long, it was no match for the tremendous whale whose wake rocked the boat back and forth like a toy. Liam started to pull forward, but the second whale breeched right in front of them. "Too close!" he shouted, backing up and turning at the same time. Finally, they were able to move away and watch from a safer distance.

"That was amazing!" Cadie said when they finally pulled up alongside the skiff. "I've never seen a whale before."

"You haven't?!"

She shook her head.

"I've seen tons . . . pardon the pun," he added with a grin.

"Pun pardoned," she said with a laugh, handing him the cooler and beach bag.

He held his hand out to her. "Are you rowing?"

"Sure," she said with a smile.

"Great!" he said, untying the line.

Cadie slid the oars into their locks while Liam stretched out on the bench seat across from her. She eyed his shirtless, tan body. "Lovin' the view," she said with a grin.

"No staring," Liam teased. "Just rowing."

"Aye, aye, Captain," she said with a salute.

Liam shook his head and closed his eyes. "So, are you hung over?"

"Pshaw! Three beers . . . noo," Cadie said, pulling on the oars.

"Not a lightweight?"

"No, I can handle my liquor."

"Good . . . because I brought wine."

"Good . . . because there's truth in wine."

Liam opened one eye and peered at her. "Is someone not telling the truth?"

"You."

"Me?! How?"

"I asked you what was wrong before and you said 'nothing.'"

"Nothing *is* wrong."

"Then why did you look so unhappy back at the boat-house?"

Liam looked up at the blue sky. "Because I can't figure out why you hide every time we see someone you know. Are you embarrassed to be seen with me?"

Cadie stopped rowing. "I'm not embarrassed," she began slowly. "I just . . ." She hesitated, not knowing what to say. "I just don't want anyone to talk about us. I don't want anything to happen that will jeopardize being able to see each other."

"Do your parents know you're seeing me?" Liam asked, sitting up.

"No."

"Why not? Am I *not* good enough?"

Cadie could see the hurt in his eyes. "Not at all," she lied. "It's my father." She shook her head. "You . . . you wouldn't understand," she stammered.

"Try me."

Tears welled up in her eyes. "Liam, please don't do this—don't ruin our day. *I* want to spend time with you. . . . *I* want to *be* with you. . . . It doesn't matter what my parents think."

Liam shook his head—her tears felt like knives to his heart. "Cooper was right—your parents will *never* let you be with a lowlife like me. Is that it?"

"You're not a lowlife," Cadie said angrily. "Don't say that."

"Yeah, well, why can't you tell them? If you can't tell them, what future do we have?"

Cadie shook her head. "I don't know. I haven't thought about it. I just want to spend time with you *now.*"

"We can't just think about now. We have to think about tomorrow. What if they find out and make you stop seeing me?"

"That won't happen."

"It might. And eventually your vacation's going to end—what happens then?"

"I don't know—we'll figure it out when that happens. Why can't we just enjoy the time we have?"

Liam shook his head. "I don't know, Cadie. I guess I feel like one of us is going to get hurt."

"I told you I'd never hurt you."

He searched her eyes. "I want to believe you. . . ."

"Then do it," she said, pulling the oars again.

As they neared shore, Liam hopped into the water and pulled the skiff high up onto the beach, reached for the cooler and blanket, and then held out his hand. Cadie took it and as they walked along the beach, they were both quiet, lost in their own thoughts. When they reached the house, Liam pushed the door open and held back the curtain of wild roses for her to walk under. "Did you clean?!" she asked in surprise, looking around at the swept floor and noticing a bouquet of blue hydrangeas on the mantel. Liam tried to suppress a smile as he spread a blanket across the hardwood floor and lit candles that were on either side of the bouquet. He reached up to turn on a radio and Don Henley's "The End of the Innocence" drifted through the room. "When did you do all this?" she asked in amazement.

"This morning," he said, opening the wine.

"You've already been here today?!"

He nodded as he filled two cups.

"Well, it looks very nice."

"Thanks," he said, handing a cup to her. "I don't know much about wine—just that white is supposed to be chilled and red isn't."

"That's more than most people know." She took a sip and licked her lips. "It's good. Where'd you get it?"

"Coop's liquor cabinet."

"Won't he miss it?"

"The only thing he'd miss is his beloved *Ole No. 7*."

Cadie gave him a puzzled look.

"Jack Daniels."

"That's what my father drinks!"

"Maybe if they knew that about each other, they'd act differently. Maybe they'd have a drink together."

"Maybe," Cadie said doubtfully. Then she smiled and held her cup up in a toast. "To your future home!"

"Thanks," he said, tapping her cup and taking a sip. "Are you hungry?"

Cadie shook her head, and then, hearing the unmistakable, slow whistle at the beginning of Guns N' Roses's "Patience," smiled. "I love this song."

"I planned it."

"You did not," she said with laugh.

"Mm-hmm," he said, taking her cup and setting it on the mantel next to his. Then he put his hands on her hips and gently pulled her against him and swayed slowly to the song. Cadie could feel how aroused he was, and with a mischievous smile, she moved her hips.

"What are you trying to do to me, girl?" he whispered.

"Nothin'," she teased.

"If that's nothin'," he murmured, "I can only imagine what something's like."

"Somethin's much better."

"Is it?"

"Mm-hmm."

Liam gently kissed the top of her head and slowly made his way down to her lips. "Mmm . . . you taste like sweet wine," he said softly, "and you smell good too."

"Baby Soft."

"Baby soft?"

"Mm-hmm," she said, unbuttoning the top of his jeans.

As she slipped her hands inside his boxers, he closed his eyes, but when she slid his jeans down and knelt in front of him, he put his hands on her shoulders and opened his eyes to watch. Finally, barely able to hold on, he pulled her tank top over her head and knelt next to her, his heart pounding. She slid off the bottom of her bikini and lay back across the blanket, and Liam, leaning on one elbow, lightly traced his fingers along her smooth skin. "You're so beautiful," he said softly.

Moments later, she gently pulled him on top of her, and he slowly pushed himself deep and hard inside.

Chapter 14

Liam sprinted along the beach, dove into the surf, and swam underwater until his lungs felt like they'd explode. His record for holding his breath was a minute and fifty-six seconds. When he was a boy, he'd always wanted to break two minutes, but every time he'd almost made it, the water had grown dark and he'd felt Jack pulling him up.

"Sheesh, Li, you're gonna freakin' kill yourself," Jack shouted.

And Liam sputtered, "Just leave me alone. I could do it if you didn't pull me up!"

"You'll die!"

"No, I won't . . . and if I do, who cares?" But what he never said was: *If I die, I'd get to see them again—if I just stayed down a little longer, I'd get to see my mom and dad again!*

Then, one time, Jack hadn't been there. No one was. He'd sucked in as much air as his lungs could hold, ducked under, opened his eyes, and silently counted as the second hand on his watch ticked slowly around . . . once . . . twice. His lungs had ached and he'd closed his eyes, hoping time would go faster. When he'd opened them again, the second hand was at fifty-six. Immediately, everything went black, and when he came to, he was facedown in the sand, waves gently lapping over his legs. He'd picked up his pounding head and spit up a mouthful of gray seawater. That was the last time he tried.

Liam couldn't remember ever being afraid of dying. His grandma had died when he was little, and his mom had assured him that she was in heaven, where, yes, they served spaghetti and chocolate cake; but when he asked her when she'd be back, his mom had said she was in heaven *for eternity.* Liam had frowned, trying to grasp this new concept. Eternity was a long time. In fact, trying to wrap his mind around its actual length made him feel overwhelmed and sad. To think that, after you died, you just floated around heaven for *ever,* with never any other options, was the gloomiest thought he'd ever had. Time just went on and on and on . . . *endlessly.*

One time, he and Jack had talked about reincarnation and Jack had said he thought it was hogwash. "What are you going to come back as?" he'd teased. "A dog?" Liam had laughed, but the idea of coming back as someone . . . or something . . . was definitely better than being stuck in heaven forever.

Liam wiped his face and pushed back his wet hair. The run had definitely helped—he felt better, but he still wasn't in the mood to see Jack. As he walked toward the house, Tuck trotted down the path toward him and dropped a tennis ball at his feet.

"Sure, now you want to play," he teased, picking up the ball. Tuck jumped back, barking excitedly, and Liam threw it as far as he could. Tuck charged after it, his barrel chest plowing through the waves. Moments later, he came back, shaking water everywhere, and dropped the ball at Liam's feet again, and before Liam could pick up the ball again, he was racing back toward the water. "I wish I had half your enthusiasm," Liam said with a laugh as the dog plunged into the water after the bobbing green ball.

Maybe coming back as a dog wasn't such a bad idea!

Chapter 15

1989

"Oh, no! I forgot to take pictures," Cadie said, remembering her camera, and after they moved everything from the skiff to the runabout, she pulled it out and focused it on the island. The sun was setting and golden light was streaming through the trees. "It's beautiful," she murmured, taking several shots. Finally, they turned and headed back, flushed, tired, and sunburned. They'd swum naked, laid in the sun, made love again, hungrily ate the chicken salad sandwiches they'd brought, drank the wine, went back to the house . . . and made love one last time.

Liam wished the day would never end, and as the runabout skipped across the waves, he pulled Cadie close and prayed no one would find out. He didn't care if she didn't tell her parents. They'd find a way to be together—they *had* to.

As the boathouse came into view, he slowed down and glanced at his watch—it was almost nine o'clock—Coop should've been long gone by now, but the doors were still open and a figure was standing outside. "Damn," Liam muttered, shaking his head.

"What?" Cadie asked, following his gaze. "Oh, no," she murmured, her heart racing, and as they reached the dock, Carlton Knox strode toward them.

"Where the hell've you been?"

"Liam took me for a ride."

"A ride?! That must have been some ride—you've been gone *all* afternoon."

Liam stared at him defiantly, wanting to say: *Actually, it was some ride. Your daughter is quite the cowgirl!* But he bit his tongue, looked up at the boathouse, and realized Cooper was standing in the doorway.

"Get in the car!" Carlton barked.

Tears filled Cadie's eyes as she reached for her bag, and when she looked up and tried to give Liam a smile, Carlton growled, "Now!" She silently got out of the boat and walked up the ramp. Cooper offered Cadie's bike to Carlton as he stalked by, but he bristled. "She won't need it anymore." Then he thought better of it, took it roughly from Cooper, and heaved it into the Dumpster.

Liam watched in dismay, his heart breaking, and as their SUV pulled away, hot tears spilled down his cheeks.

"What an ass," Cooper said, shaking his head. "From the very first day I met him I knew he was an A-hole." Liam didn't say anything as he set the rest of their things on the dock, and when Coop asked, "Are ya bringin'er in?" he just shook his head and walked toward his truck.

"Hey, Li . . ."

Liam stopped but didn't turn around.

"It's not the end of the world. It may seem like it now, but it's not. You have to trust me on this . . ."

Liam continued walking, out of the warm light shining through the boathouse windows and out into the shadows.

Chapter 16

The bittersweet memory of that summer haunted Liam for years—Cadie had left without saying good-bye, and as the gentle summer breeze had turned to an autumn wind, he was reminded of her at every turn, his heart aching for their paths to cross again. By November, his classmates were gathering letters of recommendation and applying to colleges, but he was barely passing his classes, and although he knew college would be a way off the island—a way to escape his memories—he had no idea where he'd go. So, on a December evening just before Christmas, he walked home through sleeting rain and told Cooper his plans.

"There's *no* way you're enlisting," Coop railed. "Your mother would never forgive me!"

"I already did," Liam said.

"Damn that girl!" Coop swore, slamming the table. "I told you not to get involved with her!"

"It has nothing to do with her," Liam said defiantly. "Jack enlisted too."

Coop rubbed his temples as if his head might explode. "Is that why you did this? Because of Jack?!"

"What's wrong with Jack?" Liam asked defensively.

"Everything!" Cooper said in an exasperated voice. "Why don't you see him for who he really is?"

"I *do* see him for who he really is. When I was in second grade, he was the only one who wasn't afraid to talk to the *orphan*. He listened to me . . . and he's always been there for me."

Coop's voice softened. "That may be true, Li, but there's something about that kid that I just don't trust. And I can't believe you let him talk you into this."

"He didn't talk me into it—I talked *him* into it."

"Right," Cooper said, his voice edged with sarcasm.

Liam shook his head and started to walk away.

"Liam, wait."

He stopped but didn't turn around.

"Joining the Marines may seem like an honorable thing to do," Coop continued, "but I've been there. I know the horrors of war . . . and I don't want you to ever have to see what I—"

"You don't need to worry," Liam interrupted. "We're not even *at* war."

"We're not *now*," Coop said, "but in this crazy world things can change in a heartbeat."

"Maybe," Liam shrugged. "I really don't care . . ."

"Well, I care," Coop said, clenching his jaw. "And your parents would care."

"Well, if I die, they can tell me themselves how much they care."

Coop stared at his nephew as if he was seeing him for the first time, and then turned away so Liam wouldn't see the pain in his eyes.

For the next several months, it had felt like there was an impenetrable wall between them, and then, on July 5, 1990—two weeks after graduation—Liam and Jack left for Parris Island. One month later, Iraqi troops invaded Kuwait, and five months after that, Liam and Jack were deployed to Saudi Arabia as part of the first allied infantry group supporting Operation Desert Storm.

Liam stood in the shower as cool water rushed over his shoulders. "Damn, it, Jack! Why'd you have to tell me?" he muttered. His mind drifted to the night before their battalion was set to enter Kuwait. Jack had appeared out of the darkness with a pair of newly issued desert boots and dropped them next to Liam. "Size ten, right?" he asked. Liam nodded and Jack sat down next to him. "Why so glum, mate? We'll be fine—I've got your back," Jack assured him cheerfully.

Liam looked over, mustering a smile. "And I've got yours."

For the next eight days, their small band of brothers trudged over rocks and deep desert sand, carrying more than a hundred pounds of equipment, weapons, and personal gear on their backs. Their mission, after blasting through two minefields, was to take Al Jaber Air Base—thought to be the primary command post for enemy forces—but as they made their approach, plumes of black smoke from burning oil fields filled the air, stopping them in their tracks . . . and when they were finally able to continue, under the cover of darkness, everything went wrong.

Almost immediately, they came under fire and Liam heard Jack shouting, "Get down! Get down!" Then he felt a hot-white burning sensation in his knee and another as a bullet grazed his temple below his helmet. A second later, he was pushed to the ground as more artillery fire whizzed past his head. "Are you okay?" Jack shouted.

"I'm fine . . . except my knee . . . and my head." And then he'd looked over and saw blood trickling down the side of Jack's face. "Oh, shit, man, are *you* okay!?"

Jack laughed. "I'm fine, buddy. If *you're* fine—I'm fine."

But Jack wasn't fine. He'd covered Liam's body with his own and was hit in the shoulder, chest, and face. They were both medevaced out as soon as it was light.

Liam touched the scar near his temple—it didn't hurt like the scar on his knee—which still ached at times, especially when he kneeled, but he was alive, and there was no doubt in his mind it was because of Jack. How do you turn your back on a friend who has put his life on the line for you? No matter what he's done, you can't just give up on him.

Liam pushed the shower knob in hard, and a piece of plastic broke off and fell in the tub. "Damn it," he grumbled, picking it up and throwing it in the trash.

He dried off, wrapped a towel around his waist, and looked in the mirror—at least he didn't look as tired as he had that morning. He shaved, pulled on a clean T-shirt and jeans, and wondered if he should wear a button-down. He'd never been to an art show—what *did* people wear? He looked in his closet and then in his dresser drawer and finally pulled out a blue polo—not too casual but still comfortable.

He went downstairs, opened the fridge, and groaned, realizing he still hadn't been to the store. He rummaged around in a drawer for a notepad and pen, and jotted down a short list of things he needed to pick up on the way home. On the top of the list he scrawled *"BEER."* Then he stuffed the list in his pocket, fried the last two eggs, finished the OJ, gave Tuck a treat, and promised to be back soon.

Chapter 17

As Liam looked for a parking spot near Old South Wharf, he wondered why he was setting himself up for more trouble. Common sense was telling him he should leave his past where it belonged and let Jack and Tracey solve their own problems. In fact, if he was smart, he'd just go to the boathouse and get started on John Alden's boat. "I guess I'm not that smart," he muttered, looking at all the people milling around the entrance to the gallery.

Liam crossed the street, made his way through the crowd, and stepped into the bright, airy space. He quickly scanned the room and immediately saw Tracey talking to Devon. She was holding a glass of wine and her arm was draped over the shoulders of a boy who looked just like Jack. Liam smiled, realized she hadn't noticed him, and took advantage of the chance to look at the paintings alone.

The artist's work was reminiscent of Andrew Wyeth's— rustic, simple, and earthy. Some paintings were of old New England barns and sheds, but others were of wooden skiffs, lobsterpots, and lighthouses—perfect for the Nantucket crowd. It was an impressive body of work for an artist who'd only been out of college a couple of years.

Liam reached the back of the room, turned, and saw the painting that had been used in the newspaper ad—it was breathtaking! He stared at the sunlight peeking through the trees and then looked at the card. It was simply titled, *The Island,* but Liam knew immediately it was Tuckernuck. As he stood still, studying the painting, he felt someone standing next to him and turned to see Tracey. "I'm so glad you came," she said.

"Me too."

She looked around and motioned for the two kids—who were standing near the crudités table—to come over, and the little girl elbowed the boy to get his attention and then nodded to her. They shuffled over and Tracey put her arm around the boy's shoulder. "This is T. J.," she said, "and this is Olivia," she added, pulling her daughter against her other side.

Liam reached out to shake their hands. "It's nice to meet you."

"It's nice to meet you too," they said shyly before whispering a request to go outside.

"Okay," Tracey said, "as long as you stay together. . . . T. J., you take care of Olivia."

They both nodded and skipped out, relieved to be free of the stuffy art show.

"Cute," Liam said as he watched them go.

"Thanks," she said. "They're good kids."

She took a sip of her wine and motioned to the paintings. "His work is beautiful, isn't it?"

Liam nodded. "It's gorgeous."

"He even painted your island," she added with a smile.

"I see that," he said, then pointed to the card next to it. "What does the red dot mean?"

"It means someone bought it."

"Oh," Liam said, sounding disappointed.

"That's why you have to get here early."

"I would've been here early," he said, eyeing her, "but I was feeling a little hung over."

"You were?" she teased. "I can't imagine why."

"You mustn't be, though," he said, nodding to her glass.

"Oh, no . . . this is called hair of the dog," she said with a laugh. "You should try it."

He shook his head. "I've sworn off drinking."

Tracey laughed. "I know all about swearing off drinking—especially Peachtree!"

Liam smiled. "I remember that night . . . some of it anyway."

"I remember it very well," Tracey said, searching his eyes.

"I remember the important part," Liam said with a slow smile.

"You mean the part where you got me drunk and took advantage of me?"

"I think it was the other way around," he teased, recalling the night after their high-school graduation.

Almost everyone had been at a party at Josh Abram's house and Jack had shown up with Ally Calder, a junior, and even though Tracey had broken up with Jack several weeks earlier at their prom, she still wasn't ready to see him with someone else, so she'd grabbed Liam's arm and pulled him away. "Let's go," she'd whispered, and somehow they'd ended up at the beach with a six-pack of beer and a pint of Peachtree.

"So, Liam Tate," she'd teased as they'd sat on the beach, "how come you never asked me out?"

"Because you're Jack's girl," he'd answered, taking a sip of the sweet brandy.

"Not anymore," she'd said, reaching across him for the bottle, but he'd teasingly held it away from her and then, as she'd leaned over him, laughing, their lips had met. "Mmm, you taste peachy," she'd murmured.

"If I remember correctly," Tracey said with a smile, "you were the one who held the bottle out of my reach."

"That's because I thought you'd had enough."

"You were also the one who suggested going swimming."

"I was just trying to cool things down," Liam said innocently. "I planned on leaving my boxers *on*. You were the one who thought we should skinny-dip."

"Are you sure it was me?" she teased.

"Positive."

"Well, you have to admit—it *was* fun."

"It was," Liam said, his eyes sparkling. And then his eyes grew solemn. "And yet, you still went back to him."

"I did," Tracey said with a sigh.

"I never understood why," Liam said. "I thought we . . ."

She shook her head. "Taking Jack back was the biggest mistake of my life, but at the time, he was having second thoughts about enlisting and he begged me to wait for him . . . and then Desert Storm happened." She paused. "I thought I was going to lose both the boys I loved."

Liam shook his head. "Meanwhile, I get slammed twice in one year."

Tracey searched his eyes. "I've always loved you, Li. I still do—we were so close—as thick as thieves, but you were still hung up on Cadie . . . and that night, we were so drunk . . . I guess I felt like we were both on the rebound . . . and I didn't know if you were really interested in being with me."

"You could've asked. . . ."

"I *should've* asked," she said, searching his face. "I never regretted that night, though," she said with a slow smile. "It's one of my fondest memories."

Liam half-smiled and looked around at the crowd. "Where *is* Jack?"

"He was feeling a little hung over too."

"He didn't come?"

She shook her head. "No . . . so who knows what he's up to."

Liam frowned, seeing sadness in her eyes.

"Things aren't that great between us, Li."

"You seemed fine last night."

She took a deep breath and let it out slowly. "He'd kill me if he knew I was telling you this, but we've been having trouble for years. I've tried everything—we've been to counselors and he's been to a therapist, but it's like the promise to be faithful has no meaning for him. I've threatened to leave him and he promises he'll change, and he does . . . for a while, but then he always goes back to his old ways."

"How'd you find out?" Liam asked, relieved that he didn't have to tell her.

"Oh, an endless breadcrumb trail of the usual clues—late nights when he's not where he's supposed to be, text messages, e-mails, photos . . . and the original clue—lipstick on the collar."

"I'm sorry, Trace," Liam said.

She nodded. "I've never told anyone this, Li, but he has two other kids about whom I'm not supposed to know."

"No way," Liam said, staring at her in disbelief.

She nodded. "He has a daughter who's three years older than T. J.—which means he's basically been cheating on me our whole married life. And I just found out he has a three-year-old son, so it's never stopped. T. J. and Olivia have no idea they have other siblings."

Liam shook his head. "Why do you stay with him?"

"For the kids—I want them to have a full-time dad."

"What about you? What about *your* life?"

Tracey shook her head. "The kids would be crushed. I just

can't do that to them . . . at least, not now. If you had kids, you wouldn't let them be hurt either—I know *you.*"

Just then, Devon walked over with a huge smile on his face. "I finally pulled him away," he said cheerily, gesturing to the young man beside him. "Tracey, Liam, this is our famous artist."

Levi Knox looked like he was about nineteen—he was tan and slim and his chestnut brown hair was streaked from the sun. "Congratulations on your show," Tracey said, enchanted by his ocean blue eyes. "It's beautiful! Your artwork, that is . . ." she clarified, blushing.

Devon watched their exchange and then looked at Liam as if he were seeing him for the first time. "Oh, my goodness," he exclaimed in surprise. "I knew you reminded me of someone, Liam . . . and now I know who—you could so easily be Levi's older brother."

Tracey nodded, realizing how much Levi looked like the Liam she'd loved in high school, but Liam laughed and shrugged. "I don't think so," he said, "Levi's much better looking." Then he turned to shake his hand. "Congratulations."

Levi thanked them both and they were able to talk for a few minutes, but then Chase collected Levi to meet a potential buyer, and as they walked away, Tracey nudged Liam. "Why didn't you ask him?"

"Ask him what?"

"You know *what*—if he's related to Cadie."

Liam shrugged, looking around. "If he was, she'd be here. Besides, if he was her son, he'd have a different last name."

"Maybe he's her nephew."

"That would be a little tough—she was an only child."

"Have you tried searching for her?"

"I went to New York. I walked around in the pouring rain. . . ."

"I don't mean in person," Tracey said, shaking her head. "I mean on the computer."

"On the *what?*" Liam said, feigning confusion.

Tracey laughed. "Jack's right—you *are* impossible!"

"Not as impossible as *he* is," Liam said.

"I'll drink to that," she said, finishing her wine. Then she eyed him. "Have a drink with me. It's no fun alone."

"Yes, it is. I do it all the time," Liam said as she pulled him toward the bar. She asked for two more glasses and then they went outside.

"Are you driving back to Vermont tonight?"

"Yes . . . well, the kids and I are . . . we have to drop Jack off at Logan on the way. Supposedly, he has a business trip, but he could be going to Bermuda for all I know," she added, taking a sip of her wine.

Liam watched the people walking in and out of shops. "I'm sorry things have turned out the way they have."

Tracey smiled. "Nobody's life turns out the way they hope it will, Li. Look at your life—you lost your parents, the girl you loved, and then Coop—you certainly haven't had it easy." She turned to him. "You know that old saying: 'Life sucks, and then you die'? Well, it's true."

"Sheesh," he said, draping his arm along the bench behind her. "You're even more pessimistic than me."

Tracey laughed, glanced at her phone, and swore softly. "I didn't realize it had gotten so late," she said, draining her glass. "I have to find the kids or we're going to miss the ferry. Will you tell Devon and Chase I said good-bye?"

Liam took her glass. "Of course," he said, searching her eyes. "If you need anything, Trace—day or night—just call."

She nodded, her eyes glistening. "Thanks, Li," she said, hugging him. "It's nice to know I have *someone* I can count on."

"Safe trip home."

She nodded, mustering a smile and kissing him lightly on the cheek. "Thanks . . . and don't worry—I'm tough . . . I'm Dimitri's girl, remember?" He watched her walk away, and moments later saw T. J. and Olivia skip out of a store. Tracey pulled them close, kissed the tops of their heads, and then turned to wave.

Liam went back into the gallery, set their glasses on the bar, and glanced around for Devon and Chase. He started to walk toward them, but then heard someone calling his name.

Chapter 18

Cadie could hardly believe her eyes when Liam turned around. He ran his long, tan fingers through his sun-streaked chestnut brown hair and she realized that the years had been kind to him—although his shoulders were broader and there were wisps of gray hair around his ears, his faded jeans still hung casually off his slender hips the way they had that summer, and his ocean blue eyes still sparkled with light.

"It's *so* good to see you," she said.

Liam swallowed, his heart racing—he'd been waiting his whole life for this moment, and now that it was here, he didn't know what to say. Cadie wasn't the same youthful girl he'd so carefully preserved in his mind—in fact, he almost hadn't recognized her. She looked older—tired and thin—and her hair was darker.

"Are you always so talkative?" she teased, and Liam smiled, remembering the first time she'd asked him that question.

"It's . . . it's good to see you too," he stammered.

"I wondered if you'd come."

"I saw an ad in the paper and the artist's name caught my eye. Is he a relative?"

Cadie nodded. "He's my . . ." Just then, a little towheaded boy who looked to be around six or seven barreled into her and wrapped his arms around her waist.

"He's my son," she said. "I actually have *two* sons," she added. "This is Aidan."

The little boy studied Liam with eyes that were the same stunning Caribbean blue as his mother's and then hid behind her.

"He looks like you," Liam said with a smile.

Cadie nodded, putting her arm around him.

"Are you still in New York?"

"No, I'm renting an apartment in Boston."

Liam frowned. "No townhouse?"

She shook her head. "Liam, I . . ." she began, but then stopped. "Are you in a hurry?

"No," Liam said, his heart pounding.

"Aid, why don't you go find Levi," she whispered, and the little boy nodded and ran to his brother's side.

Feeling a small hand slip into his, Levi looked up, saw his mom standing with Liam, and nodded.

"Let's go outside," Cadie suggested.

Liam followed her out the door he'd just come in and waited for her to continue.

"I don't even know where to begin. . . ." she said with a sad smile.

Suddenly, their past washed over Liam like a tidal wave. "Cadie . . . I tried to find you. I went to New York. I looked everywhere."

"My father," she said. "He made it so you *couldn't* find me. He told me you used me. He said you didn't love me."

"That's not true," Liam said.

"At first, I didn't believe him, but as time went on, and I didn't hear from you, I started to believe him."

"He lied." Liam said, his voice choked with emotion. "I didn't know how to reach you. I didn't know where you lived or where to write. I checked the mail every day, though, hoping to hear from you."

"I couldn't write. My life was a mess."

"You couldn't find time to write a quick note?" he asked, incredulously.

"I was pregnant and my father made me marry a boy I didn't love. He said if I didn't marry him, I'd have to give up our baby."

Liam shook his head—he'd heard enough. Obviously, she'd gotten over him more easily than he'd gotten over her. "You don't need to explain."

"I *do* need to explain because . . ." She bit her lip, fighting back tears. "Because the child I was carrying was *ours.*"

Liam stared at her in disbelief, trying to wrap his mind around what she was saying; then he looked at the young man standing near the paintings—so poised and soft-spoken.

"Don't you see?" Cadie asked. "He looks just like you . . . and he has your quiet, easy ways."

Liam searched her eyes. "Why didn't you tell me? Didn't you think this was something I would want to know?"

"With all my heart I wanted to tell you, but I was young and scared and my father controlled my life. He said if I tried to contact you, he'd disinherit me. I wasn't strong enough to break free. My marriage was failing. I had no money, no income—my father paid for everything—our home, Levi's education. *Everything.* As the years went by, it became harder to tell you because so much time had passed . . . and because my father had convinced me you didn't loved me."

"What's different *now?*" Liam asked, his voice edged with anger and confusion.

"Now, I owe it to you and I owe it to Levi. He's on his own," she said, "and although I have Aidan, I can't live that way anymore. My whole life has been a lie. And now, I have ca—I mean, I'm . . ." she stopped. "Liam, a day hasn't gone by when I haven't thought of you. All these years, if it wasn't for Levi, I don't know what I would've done. Having him was like having part of you with me."

"Does he know?" Liam asked.

She nodded. "He started asking questions years ago. I had to tell him. He wanted to come out here then and find you, but I put him off. Liam, he never stopped asking. I think that's why he pursued this show . . . so I'd finally *have* to come."

Liam looked up and saw Levi walking toward them. He had a huge smile spreading across his handsome face, and Liam shook his head in disbelief. . . . He had a son!

PART II

When you pass through the waters, I will be with you; and when you pass through the rivers, they will not sweep over you.

—Isaiah 43:2

Chapter 19

Liam was still in a state of shock as he and Cadie walked along the water. "When do you have to be back?"

"Tomorrow—I have an appointment."

"Are the boys going with you?"

"Yes," Cadie said, swinging Aidan's hand. "Levi helps out with Aidan. I honestly don't know how I'd manage without him. Aidan's father has been out of the picture since before he was born, and even though Levi was away at R.I.S.D. the first few years, he always helped out when he was home . . . and now, well, I need him more than ever. It's not fair, though, because he has his own life."

"Do you think they'd like to stay here while you go to your appointment? You could come back after."

Cadie hesitated. "What about Cooper?"

Liam took a deep breath. "Coop died two years ago."

"Oh, Liam, I'm so sorry," she said. "What happened?"

"He had a heart attack. We were closing up and he asked me to run an errand on my way home—which I did, so I thought he'd beat me home, but then he never came home. At first, I wasn't worried—it wasn't unusual for a customer to stop by at the end of the day, get talking, and lose track of time—but when it started to get dark and he still wasn't home, I went back to look for him. I found him on the boathouse floor in the dark. I think it must've happened right after I left."

"That's awful," Cadie said, putting her hand on his arm, and he felt her touch go right through him.

He shook his head. "I know he lived life on his own terms— doing what he loved, and even though he struggled with his memories of Vietnam, and never stopped being *on watch,* he had a good life. In the end, it was the hard living . . . and never going to the doctor that did him in."

"Well, it was good that he had you in his life. He would've had a lonely life if you hadn't come along."

"I guess," Liam agreed. "I never thought about it that way."

"It must've been part of God's plan—bringing you into his life. God's always making plans we humans have trouble understanding," she said with a smile.

"That's for sure," Liam said with a laugh. "I don't think I'll ever understand the plan He has for me. Every day, I try to find some meaning in the things that have happened, but so far, it's just been one loss after another . . . and for no reason I can fathom."

"That's not true," Cadie said with a smile. "You gained something today."

"You're right," he said with a nod, "*and* I still can't believe it," he added softly. Then he looked over at Cadie. "Tell me everything."

She raised her eyebrows. "*Everything?*" she asked.

"Everything."

"That would take all night."

"I *have* all night," he said with a smile.

"Where should I start?"

"At the beginning—when you realized you were pregnant."

Cadie squeezed her eyes shut and laughed. "That is *not* a fun memory," she began, "but, okay. Well, I'm sure you remember how angry my father was—especially that night."

Liam nodded, remembering how Carlton Knox had loomed over them when they'd gotten back to the boathouse.

"Well, it didn't get any better. We left Nantucket the next morning . . . on the earliest ferry. My father wasn't taking any chances. Unfortunately, it was already too late."

"Damn, I wish I could've been there!"

"No, you don't," Cadie said, eyeing him. "By the end of August, I was praying for a red spot on my underwear every time I pulled them down . . . but I always ended up staring at snow white cotton fabric in disbelief and thinking *this* cannot *be happening.* And then I started getting sick—and it wasn't just a queasy stomach . . . and it wasn't only in the morning—I couldn't keep *anything* down . . . ever! At this point, my mother began to get suspicious and insisted I go to the doctor—*her* doctor." Cadie looked over at Liam. "And sure enough—I was knocked up," she said with a half smile. "It's funny, I'm able to laugh about it now, but back then, I was panic-stricken."

Liam shook his head regretfully. "How come we didn't use birth control?"

"Because we were young and foolish and didn't think anything would happen. Anyway, this was before the HIPAA law, so my mother's doctor was on the phone with *her* before I even knew. My parents were livid—this was uncharted territory for them, especially since they were, and still are, devout Catholics. Needless to say, abortion was out of the question, and the two alternatives were adoption or marriage.

"At the time, my father's 'dream' son-in-law was Taylor Walsh—a boy whose reputation would've put Warren Beatty to shame . . . and every other girl's father seemed to know it except mine. He thought Taylor—a Yale law student who came from old money—was a perfect match, and somehow he struck a deal with Taylor's father. Unfortunately—*and* unbelievably—it included a prenup. The rest is history. Literally."

"How long did it last?"

"On paper, twenty years, but we were separated for most of it—which was fine with me. Taylor was a playboy."

"Maybe I'm naïve," Liam said, shaking his head, "but I don't get why men who have everything in a marriage still cheat."

Cadie shook her head. "I don't either, but in fairness to Taylor, he didn't have everything. It was an arranged marriage and we both knew it. I didn't love him."

"Maybe so, but if he tried harder, you might've."

Cadie shook her head and looked into Liam's eyes. "Not when I was in love with someone else."

Liam realized what she was saying. "I never stopped loving you," he said, reaching for her hand.

"I never stopped loving *you* either," she said, her eyes filling with tears.

Chapter 20

"I have to stop at the store," Liam said as Cadie came down the path from the Nantucket Inn after checking out. "I'm a little low on food," he explained, taking her luggage and setting it in the back of the truck.

"Are you sure you want us to stay over?" she asked.

"Yes, why pay for a hotel when you can stay at a five-star beach cottage for free?"

"I don't know. Because it's an imposition?"

"It's not an imposition," he assured her. "Besides, Levi and I have a lot of catching up to do." He looked over and smiled. "And so do we."

"Devon said he'd drop Levi off after they do a little celebrating."

"Did you want to go with them?"

"No," she said with a tired smile.

"Well, I can drop you off at the house if you want to take a nap, and Aidan and I can run my errands."

"No, no," she said, waving him off. "I'm too tired to *celebrate,* but not to stop at the store."

"That makes sense," he teased. "I hope you don't mind the mess or the welcoming committee."

Aidan, who was sitting between them in the truck, looked puzzled. "Who's the welcoming committee?"

"The welcoming committee is Tucket, my golden retriever, and Moby, my old gray cat."

"You have a dog *and* a cat?!" Aidan asked, wide-eyed.

"Yep," Liam said with a nod. "Moby is a little aloof, but Tucket will be absolutely beside himself."

Aidan frowned. "What's aloof and how will Tucket be *beside* himself?"

Liam looked down. "Aloof is how Moby acts when he's pretending he doesn't notice me . . . and being 'beside yourself' is just a saying—it means he'll be very excited to meet you."

"Well, I'll be beside myself too," Aidan said, looking up at his mom with a grin.

Cadie laughed. Both of her boys had always wanted a dog, but she'd told them that their lives were too busy and it wouldn't be fair to the dog. The truth was her father hated dogs and he'd never pay for the expenses one would incur.

Liam pulled into the Stop & Shop parking lot. "Coming in?"

"Sure," Cadie said. "Do they have coffee?"

"I think so," Liam said, rounding up a cart.

"Do you want one?" she asked.

"No, thanks," he said, pulling his list out of his wallet and studying it. Beer was still first, but now he needed a bit more—something for supper *and* breakfast, so while Cadie headed off to find the coffee, he and Aidan wheeled through the produce.

"Do you like blueberry pancakes?" Liam asked.

Aidan nodded happily, deciding this trip was definitely taking a turn for the better.

"Salad?"

He shrugged.

"Hamburgers and hot dogs?"

He nodded and smiled.

"Cat food?"

"Nooo."

"How 'bout s'mores?"

"What's a *sumore?*" he asked with a frown.

Liam stopped the cart and looked at Aidan as if he had two heads. "You've never had a s'more?!"

Aidan giggled and shook his head.

"Where's your mother? We need to talk!"

Aidan swung around, looking for Cadie, but she hadn't caught up with them yet.

When she finally did, they were in the beer aisle and she was happily sipping her coffee. "Mmm, this hits the spot."

Liam eyed her. "You have failed as a mother," he said dramatically.

Cadie looked alarmed. "I'm sure you're right, but what happened since I went to find coffee?"

Liam nodded to Aidan, who, with his arms full of marshmallows, chocolate, and graham crackers, smiled brightly. "I've never had a s'more."

"Oh!" Cadie said with a laugh. "A minor infraction. I'm sure I've done worse."

Liam looked up. "Does Levi like beer?"

"Doesn't every college kid?"

"I don't know—I never went to college."

"I thought you were going to go to Boston College or Boston University."

"I enlisted instead."

"You did?!" Cadie said, frowning and trying to remember the state of the world back then. "Did you see combat?"

"Desert Storm."

"Were you okay?"

"I was hit in the knee and the head," he said, rubbing his temple, "but I survived. Did you go to college?"

She shook her head. "It's funny neither of us went when that was one of the first things we talked about."

Liam looked back at the beer case. "Do you know what he likes?"

"I'm sure he'll drink whatever you have."

Liam plunked a case of Whale's Tale heavily into the cart and then looked down at Aidan. "Should we get ice cream?"

"Yes!" Aidan said with a grin.

"What flavor?"

"Strawberry."

"A man after my own heart," Liam said, tousling his hair.

Ten minutes later, they pulled into the driveway and Tuck trotted over to the truck with his tail wagging, but when he realized there was someone in the truck besides Liam, his enthusiasm tripled, and when Aidan climbed down, he wiggled all around him, licking his cheeks and almost knocking him over. Aidan grinned and put his hands on Tuck's head. "Hey, boy," he said softly, as if he'd owned a dog all his life.

"Oh, my goodness," Cadie exclaimed, "he's so handsome!" And Tuck obliged by giving her a wet, sloppy kiss too. "How old is he?"

"Six."

"He's the same age as me!" Aidan exclaimed in happy surprise.

Liam nodded. "Coop brought him home when he was just eight weeks old. One of his customers had a litter, and Tuck was the only one left. No one wanted him because he was the smallest, but as you can see, he's filled out."

"How could no one want *you?*" Cadie said, holding Tuck's big head in her hands and looking into his soulful brown eyes.

Liam nodded. "Coop was his true love—I was just second fiddle, but when Coop died, we got pretty close—we helped each other through it. I don't know who was sadder."

"He must have been part of the plan for *your* life," Cadie said with a smile as she looked up at the weathered gray cottage, trimmed with white and surrounded by beds of pink beach roses, purple and blue hydrangeas, scarlet bee balm, and golden black-eyed Susans. "It's beautiful here!"

Liam smiled as he lifted out their bags, and Aidan ran to the edge of the yard with Tuck at his heels. "Mom, come see the ocean!"

Chapter 21

Liam lit two old red lanterns, stoked the hot embers in the stone fire pit, and added more wood. "Are you ready to make s'mores?" he asked, eyeing Aidan, whose eyelids were getting heavy and who had Moby curled up on his lap.

Aidan perked up. "I'm ready!" he said, and Liam pulled open the bag of marshmallows and tossed one to Tuck, who caught it and gulped it down all in one fell swoop.

"He likes marshmallows?!"

"He likes everything. Everything except mushrooms and broccoli."

"I don't like mushrooms or broccoli either," Aidan said, putting his hand on Tuck's head. "We must be related."

"You must be," Cadie said with a laugh.

Liam opened the graham crackers and chocolate, slid three long crackers out of one of the packages, carefully broke them in half, broke the chocolate, set it on the crackers, and then handed out long roasting forks and showed Aidan how to plunge the fork into the soft, puffy marshmallow. "You have to find some hot embers and hold the marshmallow close enough so it toasts but doesn't burn." Just as he said this, Cadie's marshmallow burst into flames. "Your mother is a beginner. She's showing you how *not* to do it."

Cadie held up her marshmallow torch and laughed. "I'm just trying to give this party more light," she said, trying to blow it out, but when the flame grew bigger, she shook it and the fiery marshmallow flew across the yard like a meteor . . . and Tuck, seeing its low trajectory, raced after it.

"It's hot!" Liam called, but the hapless dog scoffed it down in one warm bite.

"Tuck, you're so silly," Aidan said, laughing. Then, holding up his golden brown marshmallow, he asked, "How's this?"

"Perfect! If I didn't know better, I'd think you were a professional," Liam said approvingly. "Now put it on top of the chocolate and put the other graham cracker on top of that and squeeze them together so the hot marshmallow melts the chocolate."

Aidan squished the marshmallow sandwich together and took a big bite. "Mmm, this is good," he said with white fluff and crumbs sticking to his cheeks. "Can I have another?"

"You're supposed to say, 'Can I have s'more?' " Liam corrected.

"Ohh," Aidan said with a grin. "Can I have *s'more?*"

"One more," Cadie said, keeping a careful eye on her marshmallow, "and then it's time for bed."

"Mom, it's one *s'more*," Aidan corrected, putting another marshmallow on his fork and holding it over the fire. Then he looked up at the stars. "This is the best night ever," he said softly.

Liam looked up too. "It sure is."

Ten minutes later, while Cadie was tucking Aidan into bed, her phone, which she'd left on the table, hummed. Liam glanced at it and saw there was a message from Levi. When she came back out, he pointed to it. "Your wayward son is making one more stop."

"*Our* wayward son," she corrected, "and he deserves to celebrate," she added with a smile. "He's worked hard for this and he sold four paintings today!"

"Just as long as Devon and Chase don't have too much influence over him. . . ."

"No worries there," Cadie assured as she texted back. "Levi has a girlfriend."

"He does?!"

Cadie nodded. "Yes—her name is Emma and they've been going together since college."

"Was she at the show?"

"No, she couldn't come. She is visiting her family in England. Levi was supposed to go with her, but that was before the opportunity for this show came up."

"She's British?"

"Yes," Cadie said. "I think her accent is what really got him—plus, she looks like Emma Watson . . ."

"Who's Emma Watson?"

Cadie eyed him. "She's the actress who plays Hermione in the *Harry Potter* movies." She paused. "Please tell me you've heard of Harry Potter. . . ."

Liam shrugged, looking puzzled, and Cadie laughed. "You're still keeping the world at arm's length, aren't you?"

Liam smiled. "It's safer that way."

"Did you ever buy that little house on Tuckernuck Island?"

"I did."

"Did you restore it?"

"No, I haven't been back."

"You bought it and you haven't been back?!"

Liam nodded and took a sip of his beer. Then he stirred the

embers and tiny sparks of light flew up into the night sky. "Tell me more about Levi."

Cadie took a deep breath and smiled. "He's a love—he always has been. He was a happy baby, never cried, slept through the night almost immediately—in fact, I think my father was disappointed he didn't give me more trouble—just to add to my misery, but he was so good . . . and he was the light of my life. He still is!

"I wish I'd had the courage to leave home and come back to you," she said sadly. "You deserved to be a part of his life."

"I wish you had too," Liam said, leaning back in his chair. "To think that I've had a son all these years and never had the chance to spend time with him." He shook his head sadly and Cadie felt tears stinging her eyes again. Liam smiled wistfully. "You can still *tell* me about him, though."

"What else do you want to know?"

Liam looked thoughtful and then his face lit up. "When did he start walking?"

"Ten months," she said with a proud smile. "He reached all the big milestones early—he was potty trained by two and a half, riding a two-wheeler by three and a half, reading before kindergarten."

Liam laughed. "Well, he didn't get the overachiever trait from me."

"We spent a lot of time together," Cadie recalled. "I didn't work and Taylor was never around, so it was just Levi and me. We went to the park, to the museum, to the library."

"Sounds like you're a good mom."

"She's a *great* mom!" Levi said, strolling down the path. Tuck struggled sleepily to his feet and wiggled over to greet him. "Hey! Who's this?" he asked.

"That's Tuck," Cadie said.

"Hey there, Tuckaroo," Levi said, kneeling down and tousling Tuck's ears as he wiggled all around him.

Finally, he stood up and sat in one of the chairs. "This is really nice," he said, admiring the fire pit.

"Thanks," Liam said, leaning back. "My uncle and I built it a long time ago."

"Very cool," Levi confirmed with an approving nod. "By the way, I'm sorry I'm so late."

"Not a problem," Cadie said. "How was your evening?"

"It was fun. Boy, can those two drink. I had to drive Devon's car here; then he insisted he could drive back, but I don't know if it was such a good idea."

"You should've texted me," Cadie said, frowning. "We could've picked you up."

"It's fine," Levi assured her. "You don't need to worry."

Cadie shook her head. "It's my job to worry."

"Well, worrying isn't good for your health."

"It's too late for that."

Liam listened to them bicker and shook his head. "I guess I didn't miss the arguing."

"We don't argue," Cadie insisted.

"Yes, we do," Levi said with a grin.

"Oh, I give up," Cadie said wearily as she stood, "and as wonderful as this evening has been, I think I'm going to head to bed—I can hardly keep my eyes open . . . and then you two can get to know each other."

"Good night, Mom," Levi said, standing up to give her a hug. "Thank you for everything—especially making the trip out here."

"You're welcome, hon. I'm glad it went so well."

"Me too," he said, stuffing his hands in his pockets.

"I'll come in and make sure you have everything you need," Liam said, picking up his empty bottle. "Want a beer?" he asked, looking at Levi.

"Sure, what's one more?" Levi said, reaching for a marsh-mallow and a fork.

Liam eyed him. "I hope *you* know how to make a s'more. . . ."

Levi frowned. "What's a s'more?"

Liam rolled his eyes and Cadie laughed. "He knows what a s'more is. I told you he's like you—he even has your sense of humor."

Liam followed Cadie inside, rinsed out his bottle, put it in the dish drain, took two more out of the fridge, and set them on the table. "Did I put out a towel and washcloth?" he called.

"You did," she said. "And you really don't have to give the boys your room."

"Yes, I do," he said, peering around the doorway of the spare bedroom. "This bed and Coop's are full-size. Mine is a king, so they'll have plenty of room."

"I hate to displace you."

"You're not displacing me," Liam assured.

"Mmm," she said, sounding skeptical.

He smiled, lingering, but the years—and something else he couldn't quite put his finger on—seemed to be standing be-tween them. "Good night," he said.

"Good night. Thank you for everything—that was, *by far,* the best cheeseburger I've ever had."

Chapter 22

"Guess you found a new friend," Liam said, eyeing Tuck's head on Levi's lap as he handed him a beer.

Levi stroked Tuck's smooth ears and smiled. "What a great dog."

Liam took a sip of his beer. "He *is* a good dog . . . and he's good company."

"When I was growing up, I begged my mom for a dog, but she always said we were too busy and it wouldn't be fair to the dog, but I think it was really because my grandfather hates dogs."

Liam studied him. "Do you get along with him—your grandfather?"

"No," Levi answered bluntly. "We hardly speak. I hate the way he treats Mom, and he doesn't give me the time of day. He's completely different with Aidan—scoops him up, swings him around, showers him with gifts."

"I'm sorry to hear that—I'm sure it has everything to do with me."

"Well, he should've gotten over that by now."

Liam took a sip of his beer. "So, tell me how you came to be an artist."

Levi smiled. "I don't know. I just always loved to draw—even when I was little. If I had a book report to do, I'd spend more time drawing the cover of the book report than I did writing about the book, and when I was in high school, I drew all the posters for the school plays and most of the illustrations for the yearbook—I even designed the cover my senior year." He paused. "I guess it was my way to escape—I'd get so caught up in a drawing, I'd lose track of time. I'd just listen to music and draw, and by the time I looked up, it would be dark outside."

"That happens when I'm working on a boat sometimes," Liam said. "I get so caught up in what I'm doing, I lose track of time."

"What kind of boats do you work on?"

"Wooden boats—old runabouts, canoes, sailboats—anything made from trees! No fiberglass or plastic. When I was in high school, Coop and I restored an old Chris-Craft, and right now, I'm repairing an eighteen-foot sloop that we built twenty years ago."

"What happened to her?"

"The owner's son ran her up on some rocks."

Levi nodded. "That's a cool job. How'd you learn how to do it?"

"From helping Coop," Liam answered. "He was my mom's brother—he raised me after my parents died."

Levi nodded. "My mom told me about that. It must've been hard to lose your parents at such a young age."

"It was. I used to pray every night that they'd be there when I woke up."

"God must've had other plans for you," Levi said with a smile.

Liam laughed. "You sound like your mom."

"Did she say that too?"

"She *did.*"

Levi smiled. "I'm not surprised. She has a pretty strong faith—it's gotten her through some tough times . . . and I guess it's rubbed off on me."

"It's a good thing to have rubbed off on you," Liam said. "My mom was the same way—Bible stories, Sunday school, bedtime prayers . . . and even though I was little, I can still remember standing with my hands on her shoulders while she helped me pull on the warm, stiff pants and shirt she'd ironed for church."

"It's funny how stuff like that stays with you."

Liam nodded. "She used to wear a perfume called patchouli— it had a very unique scent, and after she died, if I was walking through a department store and happened to see it, I'd stop and smell it—just to remember her, and other times, I'd put a dab on my shirt so I could remember her all day." He looked up at the stars. "Anyway, Coop was supposed to take me to church, but he wasn't much of a churchgoer. He always said he found God in nature. Needless to say, we didn't go very often, but he did make sure I knew my Bible stories—David and Goliath, Daniel in the Den of Lions, Noah's Ark." Liam smiled. "So I'm not completely biblically illiterate."

"He sounds like he was a great guy."

"He was," Liam said wistfully. "I wish he was still around so you could meet him . . . and he you. He'd definitely get a kick out of all this. I bet he's having a good laugh about now."

Levi smiled and then his eyes grew solemn. "She didn't tell you, did she?"

Liam took a sip of his beer. "Tell me what?"

"She has cancer."

Liam almost choked on the sip he'd just taken. "She does?! What kind?"

"Pancreatic. She was diagnosed two years ago, so it's a miracle she's still alive. She gets tired easily and she almost didn't come this weekend, but she really wanted to see the show . . . and *you*."

"Is she being treated?"

Levi nodded. "She was having chemo—that's why she wears a wig, but the treatments were making her sick, and the medicine they give people to help them *not* get sick hasn't helped at all. Two weeks ago, she told her doctor she couldn't take it anymore and he stopped her treatments. Almost immediately, she started to feel better, but he warned her that the cancer would spread, without treatment. Her appointment tomorrow is to find out if there's anything else they can do, but I know they've reached the point where they're more concerned about her quality of life."

"I'm *so* sorry, Levi," Liam said, shaking his head in disbelief. "I thought she looked tired and her hair looked darker . . . but it's been so long since I've seen her."

Levi nodded. "Aidan doesn't know, and neither do my grandparents . . . or if they *do* know, they haven't said anything. I haven't told anyone except Emma—who I only told recently because she was going away. Other than that, there's been no one *to* tell, and I've been going crazy keeping it all inside. That's how I got so much work done these last two years— it was my escape." His voice was choked with emotion as the feelings he'd been keeping bottled up inside finally spilled out. "I don't know what I'll do if she dies. . . ." he said, his eyes glistening.

I don't know what I'll do either, Liam thought. *I just got her back. . . .*

Chapter 23

Liam was stirring blueberries into the pancake batter when Cadie appeared in the doorway. He looked up. "Morning."

"Mornin'," she replied sleepily.

"Coffee?"

"Mmm."

"How'd you sleep?"

"Good," she said, pulling her robe around her thin frame and settling into one of the kitchen chairs. Tuck got up off the old gray mat in front of the door and moseyed over to say hello. "Hello, honey," she said softly, gazing into his eyes and making his whole hind end wiggle. "You should be a therapy dog, you know that?" she added, and Tuck's tail swished in agreement.

"He *would* be a good therapy dog," Liam said. "He can always tell when someone's feeling blue or under the weather." He set two steaming cups of black coffee on the table. "Cream and sugar?"

"No, thanks."

Liam sat down across from her and smiled. "I always *knew* you were my kind of girl."

Cadie cradled the cup in her hands, peered at him over the rim, and saw sadness in his eyes. "Levi told you, didn't he?"

Liam nodded.

"I thought he would."

"He's taking it pretty hard. He needed to tell someone."

"I know," Cadie said softly. "He tries so hard to stay positive . . . and strong for me. He's always saying, 'We're gonna beat this, Mom,' but I know, deep down, his heart is breaking."

"Well, you're his mom and he's worried he's going to lose you."

"That's why I came here, Li—because he's going to need his dad. He's going to need *you.*"

Liam took a deep breath and let it out slowly. He could almost hear Coop's voice: *Be careful what you wish for!* Two days earlier his life had been simple. He'd gotten up, gone to work, played with his dog, weeded his garden, had a beer and something to eat, and gone to bed . . . and he'd fully expected the remainder of his days to be much the same—give or take the order of events—until finally, his days ended and his ashes were scattered across Nantucket Sound. And that would be the proverbial that.

At least, that had been the plan.

"It's amazing how your life can change in a heartbeat," Cadie mused as if she could read his mind. "I'd just moved to Boston when all this began. I'd finally broken free from my parents and had a job for the first time in my life . . . and then, all of a sudden, I started to lose weight—which, initially, was a good thing because I hadn't lost the weight I'd gained with Aidan, but then I started having these intense pains in my stomach and back." She paused, seeing the look on Liam's face. "I know—hard to believe, right? The two times you've known me—years ago and now—I was either girlishly slender or sickly thin. You never saw me when I was tipping the scale at a hundred and sixty!

"Anyway, one day, I'm starting a new life and a new job—*with* health insurance, thank goodness—enjoying my boys . . . and the next day, my doctor is telling me I have cancer. I was stunned. I kept thinking, *This can't be happening . . . this cannot be happening . . . someone must've mixed up the test results.* But then they were giving me prescriptions and a schedule for chemo and I felt like I was being whisked off into a nightmare where I was a spectator watching my life unravel.

"I began to watch other people—total strangers—walking down the street, shopping at the store, running through the park, and my heart ached because all I wanted was for my life to be like theirs—it didn't matter what problems they had. All I wanted was to go back to the day before I found out. I wanted to be able to enjoy the simple things again—like going for a hike with my boys, watching the sun set, reading a good book— all without the dark specter of cancer hanging over me.

"I prayed constantly, begging God to make it go away and promising to never ask for anything else again." She searched Liam's face and then smiled sadly. "But that wasn't His plan, because my cancer didn't just miraculously disappear . . . and I fully expected it to!

"Finally, I decided I wasn't going down without a fight. I went from denial to envy to resolve. And I *did* fight—I did everything they asked—I had chemo and radiation; I lost my hair; I was sick all the time until I just couldn't take it anymore and I wondered if it would be better to die; I tried tofu and miso soup, Chinese remedies, Reiki—you name it!"

Liam suddenly realized the chasm between the life changes they were each facing. "Levi told me you have a strong faith," he said, "but how can you *not* be angry at God? How can you not blame Him?"

"I *am* angry . . . and I *do* blame Him . . . but that doesn't mean I've stopped believing. I wouldn't have made it this far without Him, and I've come to learn that I have to wake up each day with a new resolve . . . ready to take on what that day will bring, knowing that, no matter what happens, He's by my side." She searched Liam's eyes. "Cancer changes people, Liam . . . it's changed *me*. I don't look at life the same way. Being sick makes you realize just how precious each moment is . . . and it makes you want to live each day as if it's your last . . . because it very well might be."

Just then, Aidan shuffled sleepily into the kitchen. "I'm hungry."

"You are?" Liam asked, tousling his hair.

"Mm-hmm. What's for breakfast?"

"Pancakes," Liam said.

"Blueberry?" he asked, leaning against Cadie and putting his hands on Tuck's head.

"Yup," Liam said, standing up. Then he looked at Cadie. "What time is your ferry?"

"Ten thirty-five."

"We're leaving?" Aidan moaned. "But we just got here."

"I'm sorry, hon," Cadie said, putting her arms around him, "but I have an appointment."

"You *always* have an appointment," Aidan said gloomily.

Liam looked up from ladling batter onto the griddle and saw the disappointment on Aidan's face. Then he pictured John Alden's boat waiting for his attention . . . and he suddenly found himself weighing the two options. "Hey, pal," he began, "if it's okay with your mom," he continued, "maybe you can stay with me while she goes to her appointment."

Aidan's face lit up. "Can I, Mom?" he asked excitedly.

"I don't know, hon," she said, looking up at Liam in surprise. "Don't you have work to do?"

"This is more important. Plus, he can come with me to work."

"Please, Mom!" Aidan pleaded. "Then you can come back tomorrow."

"That's just it, hon. I don't know if I *can* come back tomorrow—it's a long trip and you know how tired I get."

"You can do it—it's not hard."

Cadie smiled, brushing back his hair. Then she looked at Liam again. "Are you sure?"

He nodded as he flipped the pancakes. "I'm sure," he said, although he really wasn't sure at all.

"Do you want Levi to stay too?"

Liam shook his head. "No, I think he should go with you."

"Well, if you're absolutely sure . . ."

"I'm absolutely sure," Liam said, hiding his uncertainty with a smile. He smoothed melting butter over the steaming pancakes, oozing with juicy blueberries, and set them on the table.

Cadie put two on a plate for Aidan and one on a plate for herself and then drizzled maple syrup over them. She cut a small piece with her fork and put it in her mouth. "Mmm, I thought you didn't know how to cook."

"I *don't* know how to cook . . . but I *do* know how to make pancakes—a man can't survive without pancakes."

"That's right," Aidan agreed with his mouth full of the buttery, syrupy cakes. "A man can't survive!"

Just then, Levi came in, wearing boxers and a T-shirt. "Barely surviving here," he said, sitting down at the table.

Chapter 24

Aidan leaned against Liam and watched as Cadie and Levi became specks of bright color. Then Liam put his hands on his shoulders. "Ready?"

He nodded. "C'mon, Tuck," he called, and the big golden trotted along beside him. "What are we doing today?" Aidan asked as he scooted over to the middle so Tuck could sit next to the window.

"Well, I thought we'd pick up something for lunch and then head over to the boathouse."

Aidan nodded. "What are we going to do there?"

"We're going to work on a sailboat that has a hole in it."

"How did it get a hole?"

"A boy ran it up on the rocks."

"Why?"

"Because he wasn't being careful."

"My mom always tells me to be careful."

Liam smiled. "That's because she doesn't want anything to happen to you."

Aidan nodded and then grew quiet. "I don't want anything to happen to her either."

Liam looked over and watched Aidan rest his head on Tuck's back. He felt tears sting his eyes, but he didn't say anything—he didn't know what *to* say.

Twenty minutes later, after introducing his new helper to a very surprised Sally, they left Cuppa Jo to Go with one chicken salad wrap, one peanut butter and jelly sandwich, and two Cokes, and when they got to the boathouse, Aidan hopped out into the sunny August morning and looked around while Liam unlocked the big carriage doors.

"Wow," Aidan whispered softly when he saw the hole in the side of the sailboat. "That's awful . . . it looks so sad."

Liam looked up from putting their lunch in the fridge. "It *does* look sad," he agreed.

"What are the train tracks for?" Aidan asked, sliding his sneaker along one of the worn metal rails.

"That's the marine railway—it's how we pull boats out of the water."

Aidan nodded thoughtfully, studying the rail car cradling the sailboat. "And what's that?" he asked, pointing to a second track running perpendicular to the first.

"That's the transverse track—it's used to move the boats over to the shop."

Aidan wandered over to the workbench. "You sure have a lot of old tools!"

Liam nodded. "They're old, but they still work. This was my uncle's first chisel." He held up the sharp tool and traced his finger along the smooth, wooden handle. "And this was his first hand plane," he added, pointing to the plane.

"What's this?" Aiden asked, twirling the handle of the clamp that was bolted to the bench.

"That's a vice," Liam said, showing Aidan how to crank it

tightly against a piece of wood. "It acts like a second set of hands."

Aidan nodded and followed Liam over to the shop. "And these are the big tools," Liam said, gesturing to the machinery around the workshop. "This is a table saw, and this is band saw—they're used to cut boards; and this is a jointer—it's used to make the face of a warped or bowed board flat, and then, after the board is flat, it can be used to straighten and square the edges too; and this is a planer—it's used to make a board that's been jointed a flat, equal thickness from end to end; and this is a lathe—it's used to make masts and booms, like those," he explained, pointing to the back wall lined with long, cylindrical pieces of wood. "And *this* is the steam box—this is where planks are steamed so they can be bent to fit the frame."

"You can bend wood?!"

"Yup . . . after it's been steamed."

"And what are those?" Aidan asked, pointing to a pile of white nylon cloth neatly folded and piled on the floor.

"Old sails."

"And that?"

"A wood stove."

"Do you use it?"

"In the winter."

"And what's that?" Aidan asked with a mischievous grin, pointing to a tired silver box with two round speakers.

"That's my radio, silly," Liam said, tousling his hair. Then he looked back at the sailboat and Aidan followed his gaze.

"Can I help?" he asked brightly.

Liam hesitated, remembering all the times he'd asked Coop the same question . . . and Cooper had always found something for him to do. "The first thing we need to do is move the boat to the shop, so I need you to push that button," he said, pointing to the metal button next to the workbench. Aidan stood on his tiptoes and pushed, and the ancient winch creaked to life and the rail car began to move. Liam guided it, and when the boat was in place, he told Aidan to push the lower button. Liam turned on the lights in the shop and ran his hand lightly over the sailboat. Then, he removed the broken centerboard pieces and, with a small pry bar, began to gingerly pry off the damaged planks, mentally noting the thickness of the wood he'd need. "Try to lay them on the floor in order," he said, showing Aidan exactly what he meant.

Aidan took his job seriously, carefully laying each piece of broken wood on the concrete floor in the order they were handed to him, and by lunchtime, all of the damaged planks and frames, lying side by side, looked like the pieces of a giant jigsaw puzzle.

Aidan scratched his head. "What's next?"

Liam stood beside him, surveying the wood. "Next, we use the broken pieces for templates . . . to make new ones. We'll use white oak for the frame," he added, thinking out loud, "and then we'll turn her upside down and fit new mahogany planks to the frame and screw them into place. Then the entire bottom will be sanded and repainted. Finally, we'll turn her back over and sand and varnish her deck so she looks like new."

"That's a lot of work," Aidan said with a groan.

"It is," Liam agreed, "but we're not doing it all today. It'll take weeks."

"Then can we take it for a ride?"

"Yes, then we can take *her* for a ride," Liam corrected.

"Her?"

"Yes, boats are always referred to in the feminine."

"Why?"

"Because in the old languages, like Latin, objects were assigned gender—boy and girl—and the gender of boats has always been feminine."

"Oh," Aidan said, looking confused.

"And, on top of that, it's believed that sailors loved their boats almost as much as their moms and girlfriends. Sometimes, they even named them after them."

"I don't know if I could love anything more than mine!" Aidan said.

"I know what you mean," Liam agreed. And then paused. "Ready for lunch?"

"Yes, I'm starving!"

Tuck suddenly appeared at their side, his copper fur warm from the sun. "You heard one of your favorite words, didn't you?" Liam teased.

"What word is that?" Aidan asked, stroking Tuck's smooth head.

"Lunch!" Liam whispered, and Tuck wagged his tail.

Chapter 25

All the seats in the waiting room were taken when Cadie turned around from signing in, but an older gentleman saw her and immediately stood up and motioned for her to take his. At first, Cadie shook her head, but he nodded insistently, and since she really didn't feel very well after making the long trip, she thanked him and gratefully sat down. The woman who'd been dozing next to him felt him move, opened her eyes, and smiled, her kind face crinkling with friendly wrinkles. "It's no fun, is it?" she whispered conspiratorially.

Cadie smiled and shook her head, wishing with all her heart she would live long enough to have smile lines.

The woman reached up and touched the brightly colored kerchief on her head. "You won't believe this," she said, "but I used to have beautiful red hair . . . and it stayed red well into my sixties. Redheads keep their color longer—did you know that?"

"No, I didn't."

The woman looked up at Levi. "Is he your son?"

"Yes," Cadie said with a proud smile.

"He's very handsome," she whispered.

"Thank you. He's a good guy—he keeps me going."

The woman nodded. "My Ed keeps me going too. He was in the navy during the war—he's as tough as nails, but he's as soft as a teddy bear too. I'm not sure how he's going to manage when I'm gone."

"I worry about the same thing," Cadie said with a sad smile. "I have a younger son too—he's only six."

The woman nodded. "You've been blessed."

"I have, but sometimes I can't help but wonder why God wants to take it all away."

The woman studied Cadie, her kind blue eyes sparkling with light. "It may seem like He's taking it away, but He's not. Your job, dear, is to keep the faith. God will take care of your boys . . . just like He'll take care of my Ed."

"Mary?" a voice called, and the woman looked up. A nurse was standing by the door, holding an iPad. She smiled and Ed reached out to help her up, but before she did, she gave Cadie a hug. "Remember what I said," she whispered, and as she let go, Cadie felt an odd sense of peace washing over her.

Moments later, a different nurse stood by the door, calling Cadie's name, and as they were ushered down the hall, Cadie turned to Levi and smiled. "I wonder if St. Peter stands by the pearly gates with an iPad too."

Levi rolled his eyes. "Let's not find out, okay?"

Chapter 26

Liam's phone often didn't ring for weeks on end. Sometimes, he even picked it up to make sure it still had a dial tone, so when he climbed out of the truck that afternoon and heard it ringing insistently, his heart started to pound.

"Hello?" he said, picking it up.

"Dad?"

"No, I'm sorry. You must have the wrong num—"

"Dad, it's *me,* Levi."

"Oh! I'm sorry, I . . ."

"I've been trying to reach you all afternoon."

Liam could hear the tremor in his son's voice and his heart began to race. "Why? What's the matter?"

"Mom's in the hospital."

"She is?! What happened?"

"We went to her appointment," Levi explained, "and just like I expected, her doctor told her there was nothing more they can do. He said her quality of life was the most important thing, and although he was reluctant to tell her how much time she had, she insisted on knowing and . . ." Levi's voice broke. "He said a month . . . maybe two."

Liam stared blindly out the window, tears springing to his eyes as he tried to wrap his mind around the frailty of life—*of Cadie's life*. "Is that why she's in the hospital?"

"No," Levi said tearfully. "When we were walking out, she started to lose her balance and then she started to slump and slide along the wall. I reached out to steady her, but she collapsed in my arms. They rushed her to Mass General and now she's in ICU. They think she might've had a stroke." There was a muffled sound on the other end of the line and Liam pictured the young man he'd just met—*his son*—bearing the weight of the world on his shoulders . . . and his heart broke for him.

"Levi, are you okay?"

"Dad, can you . . . can you come?"

"Of course," Liam said, tears sliding down his cheeks. "I'll come right away. Give me your number so I can reach you." Levi gave him his cell phone number and Liam jotted it on the back of the shopping list he'd made the day before. "Sit tight and we'll be there as soon as we can, okay?"

"Okay," Levi said.

Liam hung up the phone, turned the scrap of paper over, and gazed at it. How was it possible that just yesterday his biggest concern had been remembering to get beer?

He watched Aidan throwing a tennis ball for Tuck in the late-day sunlight, and for the first time since Cooper died, whispered a simple prayer: "Please hold Cadie and Levi close." Then, his mind started to spin with the complicated logistics of getting to Boston as quickly as possible. He glanced at his watch—it was seven-thirty . . . *and* it was Monday, which meant there wouldn't be many people leaving the island with vehicles that night, so hopefully there would be room for them on the ferry. If not, he could take the launch to Hyannis . . . but then he'd have to take a taxi all the way to Boston or rent a car . . . or he could just take the launch all the way to Boston—he'd never done that before, but it had to be possible. Just then, Moby swished through his legs, reminding him it was suppertime. He looked down and groaned. "And then there's you guys . . ."

He picked up the phone again, looked for Sally's number, and dialed.

"Hey, Sal, it's Liam. Listen, I have to go to Boston . . . Yes, I remember how to get there. I'm calling to see if you'd be able to look after Tuck and Moby while I'm gone? . . . Yeah, I'll leave Moby here if you could just swing by and feed him once in a while and I'll drop Tuck off . . . is that okay? I know, it does take a lot to get me off the island. . . . Yeah, a friend . . . Yeah, me too . . . Thanks, Sally. . . . I'll be by in a bit."

Liam pushed the hook switch down, released it, and dialed another number to see if it was possible to reserve a spot for the truck on the ten o'clock ferry.

Half an hour later, after a light supper of grilled cheese sandwiches and tomato soup, Liam loaded Tuck's food, bowls, and leash in the back of the truck along with his duffel bag and Aidan's backpack. "Have we got everything?" he asked, mentally running through the list in his head.

"Do you have your toothbrush?" Aidan offered.

Liam nodded.

"Clean underwear?"

"Yes."

"Then you have everything you need," Aidan said matter-of-factly.

"I hope so," Liam said with a smile. He scratched Moby's ears. "We'll be back, pal." Moby pushed his head into Liam's hand. "Maybe you could catch a mole while we're gone." But Moby just stretched out along the soft, worn couch and blinked at him, as if to say, *doubtful.* Liam turned on the stove light and locked the door.

When they pulled up in front of Sally's cottage, Tuck climbed over Liam's lap, leaped to the ground, and raced to the door, tail wagging. He barked twice, announcing his arrival, and when Sally opened the door in her bathrobe, he practically knocked her over. "Hullo, sweetheart," she said as he bathed her face with kisses. "My goodness! Did you miss me?"

Liam shook his head. "Are you sure he's not *your* dog?!"

"He could be," Sally said with a smile as she took the bowls from his hands. "I wouldn't mind one bit . . . but I honestly think he likes me because I'm usually wearing his favorite fragrance."

"What's that?"

"Bacon."

Liam laughed. "Well, maybe I'll just have to leave him with you permanently. . . ."

"No, you won't," she teased.

"I might," he said, setting the food on the porch. "By the way, he's already eaten, so don't let him fool you." He looked around. "Where'd he go anyway?"

Sally pointed, and Liam peered into the brightly lit living room and saw Tuck sprawled out on Sally's couch. "I'm sorry he doesn't have better manners."

"Not to worry—he's fine."

"I don't know how long I'll be gone, but I'll call as soon as I have an idea."

Sally waved to Aidan who was waiting in the truck and Aidan waved back. "Is everything okay?" she asked.

Liam shook his head. "I don't know . . . it doesn't sound good."

She put her hand on his shoulder. "Well, take as long as you need. Tuck will be fine and I'll go see Mr. Moby tomorrow. You could've brought him over, too, you know."

"I know, but he hates riding in the truck. I can't thank you enough. When I have more time, I'll explain."

Sally nodded. "I would love to hear it. Who would think that *you*—of all people—would have a past! I bet it would make a good book."

Liam shook his head as he climbed in the truck. "I doubt it." Then he smiled. "But maybe you could tell me about you and Cooper sometime. . . ."

Sally shook her head, feigning innocence. "There's nothing to tell."

"Yeah," he said, nodding knowingly. "I'm sure *that* would make a good book too."

Sally shook her head and waved, but as he pulled away, she laughed. "It might make a good book . . . it just might."

Chapter 27

Levi sat up with a start and looked at his phone—it was ten-thirty! He rubbed his neck and gazed at the web of tubes and monitors crisscrossing his mom's frail body, and then he noticed there was a soft pink hat on her head and he remembered how, during the commotion of being rushed to the ER, her wig had fallen off and been lost. He was glad—he hated that wig! He'd never forget the first time she'd modeled it for him, waiting hopefully for his approval. "I thought I'd see what it's like to be a brunette."

"It looks nice," he'd said, even though it made her look completely different. "You can't even tell it's a wig."

She'd looked in the mirror uncertainly. "Do you really think so?"

He'd nodded, fully believing no one else would know, but as time went on, he'd wished she'd found a baseball cap or a bandana to wear instead . . . anything but that wig! He'd never tell her though—it broke his heart to see her fighting so hard . . . and he'd do anything to protect her dignity.

He felt someone touch his shoulder and turned to see the same nurse who'd gently slipped the pink hat onto his mom's head smiling at him. "Are there any other family members coming?" she whispered.

"Yes," he answered with a nod, "but I'm not sure when they'll get here."

"Well, she's not going to wake up for some time, so why don't you go down to the cafeteria and get a bite to eat, and if they come while you're gone, I'll tell them where you are." Levi nodded, but then lingered, watching her check Cadie's vitals. Finally, he turned and walked slowly down the long, quiet hallway.

The only people in the cafeteria were two young doctors. They were talking quietly at a corner table, but when he walked in, they looked up. Levi looked around to see what was available—the hot food line was closed, but there were still a variety of sandwiches in the refrigerated section. Levi reached for an egg salad sandwich, and while he filled a cup with steaming coffee, he looked around for a cashier. Moments later, a heavy-set woman with copper-colored skin appeared from the back and Levi reached into his back pocket for his wallet.

"Coffee's free after ten," she said with a soothing Jamaican lilt; then she studied his face and frowned. "You're lookin' mighty sad, child," she added softly, "in fact, if I knew you better, I'd give you a hug."

Levi smiled.

"That's better, now . . . and that ole sandwich's free too." Levi started to protest, but she shook her head. "Whatever your troubles are, child, the Good Lord's lookin' out for you—don't you forget that . . . and you need anything else, you just ask for Ruby."

Levi nodded. "Thanks, Ruby."

Ruby smiled. "Go eat."

Levi hadn't realized how hungry he was, but when he sat down, he found himself devouring the sandwich and deciding it was *the* best egg salad sandwich he'd ever had. Between huge bites, he sipped the coffee and realized he hadn't eaten anything since he'd had pancakes that morning.

Five minutes later, he put the top back on the coffee, threw out his trash, and hurried back to his mom's room. As he turned down her hallway, he saw three figures standing outside her door—one was the nurse, but he couldn't make out the other two. As he drew near, though, the nurse saw him and smiled and the two figures turned.

"Hello, Levi," Carlton Knox said.

"Hello, Grandfather . . . Grandmother," he said with a polite nod.

Then his grandfather looked around and frowned. "Where's Aidan?"

Chapter 28

Aidan was sound asleep inside the ferry's cabin when it docked in Hyannis, but when Liam gently lifted him and carried him down to the truck, he murmured, "Are we there?"

"Not yet," Liam said softly. "You can keep sleeping." He opened the truck door, set him in the passenger's seat, and slipped the seatbelt around him. Then he climbed in the driver's side, turned the key, switched on his headlights, opened his window, and waited for his turn to bump down the ramp. He followed the line of traffic winding off the ferry, down Ocean Street to Bay Street and onto Old Colony Road, but when most of the line turned right onto Main, he turned left onto Center and followed it out to Barnstable Road. "Just like riding a bike," he murmured as he circled the rotary and merged onto Route 132 toward Route 6.

Traffic was light as he crossed the Sagamore Bridge and tried to remember the last time he'd been off the Cape. After his time in the marines, the only other time he'd been off the island—besides when he went to Chatham for Jack and Tracey's wedding—was for a Patriots game, and that had been at least twelve years ago. One of Coop's clients had given him tickets to a playoff game and it turned out to be *the* coldest game in Patriots history—four degrees with a negative twelve wind chill! They'd frozen . . . or at least *he* had frozen; Coop, as usual, had plenty to drink, so the temperature hadn't fazed him one bit, but Liam had shivered all the way back to Hyannis, and then they'd ended up missing the ferry. After staying in a motel that night, Liam decided that leaving the island was more trouble than it was worth, and he'd never left again . . . until tonight.

The old truck wasn't used to highway speeds, and as they rumbled up Route 3 to Route 1, cars zipped by on both sides of them, and Liam hoped it wouldn't fall apart. He looked out the window at the Boston skyline blinking in the distance and it dawned on him that he didn't know where the hospital was. He glanced over at Aidan—still sound asleep—and tried to prop him up, but he just slumped over again. "Oh, well, pal," he said softly, "I wish I could take your shoulder strap off so you could lie down, but there's probably a law against that. I wonder if they'd believe me if I said I didn't know."

Liam clicked the radio on low and a country song about a boy whose life changed after he got a girl pregnant drifted through the cab. Liam had heard the Kenny Chesney song hundreds of times, but he'd never really listened to the story it told. "I guess it's kind of fitting," he mused softly.

As they neared the city, he started to keep an eye on the signs. Finally, recognizing Storrow Drive, he got off, but then it took him a half hour to actually find the hospital—which turned out to be on Fruit Street. As he parked the truck near the emergency room, he glanced at his watch—it was almost twelve-thirty! He scooped Aidan into his arms and walked past several emergency vehicles with their lights flashing eerily across the night sky. Aidan looked around. "What happened?" he asked in a worried voice.

"Nothing," Liam assured him. "It's just the emergency room."

They hurried inside, but it was total chaos and several minutes passed before Liam was able to get the attention of the receptionist and ask what floor ICU was on. She frowned. "Fourth, but you can't take children up there," she said, nodding to Aidan.

Liam nodded as if he knew that, but as soon as another emergency demanded her attention, he disappeared down the hall. "We'll find it on our own."

They ducked into an elevator and Liam pushed the button for the fourth floor. A moment later, the doors opened up to an entirely different world. Liam stepped out into the silent hallway with Aidan in his arms.

"Where're we going?" Aidan whispered.

"We're looking for Levi."

"Oh," Aidan said with a smile.

Just then, a nurse came out of one of the rooms and saw them. "I'm sorry, sir, but children aren't allowed in ICU."

"Yes, I know, but his mom is a patient, and we've just come all the way from Nantucket. I'm actually looking for my son, Levi Knox—who is here alone."

At the mention of Levi's name, the nurse smiled. "If you'll have a seat right over there," she said, motioning to the waiting area, "I'll get him."

"Thank you," Liam said as he set Aidan down in a chair and sat next to him.

Moments later, Levi appeared, looking disheveled and exhausted. Aidan rushed over and Levi scooped him up. "Hey, pal, how're you doin'?" he asked, mustering a smile.

"Good," Aidan said, squeezing him with all his might.

"Easy, there," Levi laughed. "I *do* need to breathe."

Aidan grinned and slid down from his arms; then Levi turned to Liam, and immediately, his eyes filled with tears. "I can't believe this is happening."

Liam nodded and put his arm around him. "How's she doing?"

"She's still sleeping. Do you want to see her?"

"Yes, but Aidan has to stay here."

"Okay, I'll stay with him. It's the first room on the left."

As he walked into the room, Liam brushed back his own tears. Cadie was behind a clear partition; she looked fragile and thin, and her head looked small under her new hat. He pulled a chair up next to her bed and Levi's words echoed in his mind . . . *I can't believe this is happening.*

"Oh, Cadie," he whispered. "How *did* all this happen?" he whispered, touching her smooth cheek. "All I've ever thought about was seeing you again. I know it sounds crazy . . . but all my memories of being with you are what's kept me going." Liam slipped his hand into hers—it was cold and he rubbed it, trying to warm it up. Suddenly, the monitor next to her bed came on, startling him, and he watched as it went through its battery of tests. When it stopped, he watched the blue line that monitored her steady heartbeat. "Please don't take her from me again," he whispered.

Finally, he got up and walked back to the waiting area. Aidan was curled up on a small couch, asleep again, and Levi was sitting in a nearby chair with his head in his hands.

"Hey," Liam said, sitting across from him.

Levi looked up. "Is she still asleep?"

Liam nodded. "They've probably given her something, so why don't you and Aidan go home for a bit, get some rest, and take a shower. I'll stay here until you come back. Is there someone who can stay with Aidan?"

Levi shook his head. "If Emma was here, she would . . . but my mom never used a sitter—he's always been with one of us. Oh! By the way, my grandparents were here and they said they'd be coming back in the morning."

Liam frowned. "I thought you said they didn't know."

"I didn't think they did, but my grandfather has all kinds of connections. Anyway, they're staying in town. I don't know why they care now—they never cared before. In fact, the first thing he asked me was '*Where's Aidan?*' He never even asked how she was doing."

Liam frowned. The last person on earth he wanted to see was Carlton Knox, but if he was coming back in the morning, it seemed unavoidable. "All right," Liam said with a sigh. "Whatever. We'll deal with it when it happens. In the meantime, why don't you two head home?"

Levi nodded gratefully—he was physically and emotionally drained, and the idea of crawling into his own bed and leaving the world and all its worries behind was more than a little enticing. He scooped Aidan into his arms and then remembered he had Cadie's phone in his pocket. "Here, take this so I can call you."

Liam looked at the phone as if it was a foreign object and shook his head. "I won't even know how to use it."

"It's easy," Levi assured. "If it rings, the screen will light up and tell you what to do—it's a touch screen, so you just use your finger and then hold it against your ear like a regular phone." Liam looked doubtful, but Levi smiled. "If Aidan can do it, so can you."

"I'm not so sure about that."

"Do you want me to call you now so you can try it?"

Liam shook his head. "No, but don't be disappointed if I don't answer."

Levi smiled. "Okay, I won't." Then he hugged him and walk down the long hallway with his little brother's head on his shoulder.

Chapter 29

When Liam opened his eyes, a sliver of sunlight was streaming through a small opening at the top of the curtain. He looked over at Cadie—she was still asleep, but her cheeks had a little more color than they'd had the night before. He stood up and looked out at the blue sky and tall buildings. *This is such a far cry from the world I know.* He pictured Tuck, at that very moment, nosing around Sally's shop, looking for crumbs and hoping for handouts; then he pictured Moby, lazing in the morning sunshine; and finally, he pictured the boathouse, locked up and silent, waiting for him to get back to work. He couldn't remember a summer day when the boathouse hadn't opened—even on the day of Coop's funeral, he'd stopped by, sat outside, and drank a couple beers in his honor.

His thoughts were suddenly interrupted by music and he looked around, searching for the source. Then he realized it was coming from his pocket. He pulled Cadie's phone out and looked at the screen; just as Levi said, there was a bar across the bottom that said SLIDE TO ANSWER. He slid his finger lightly across the surface, looked at the screen again, and then held the phone to his ear. "Hello?"

"I knew you could do it," Levi said.

Liam smiled. "Well, don't expect me to call *you*. . . ."

Levi chuckled. "We'll have that lesson later." He paused. "How is she?"

"Still asleep."

Just then, a nurse came into the room, and when she adjusted the intravenous tube taped to Cadie's arm, she stirred. The nurse hurried out. "I'll be right back."

"Hang on," Liam told Levi. "I think she might be waking up."

"Okay," Levi said. "We'll be right over." And then he was gone.

Liam looked at the screen; it said CALL ENDED. He slipped the phone back in his pocket. Gently, he touched Cadie's hand and she moaned and moved her head; then her eyes opened and she looked around.

"Hey," Liam said softly.

"Hey," she replied with a weak smile. "What happened?"

"You had a stroke."

"I did?"

Liam nodded.

"Where are the boys?"

"They went home to get some sleep, but they're on their way back."

Cadie nodded, looking around again.

"What are you looking for?"

"Water."

"I'll get the nurse," Liam said, standing up, but when he turned to walk out the door, he almost bumped into Carlton Knox.

Despite the years, the two men immediately recognized each

other. "Great!" Carlton Knox growled. "What the hell are *you* doing here?"

Liam swallowed. "It's nice to see you too," he said, biting his tongue before he used the word *asshole.*

The nurse reappeared with a doctor in tow, but when she saw how many people were in the room, she immediately frowned. "I'm sorry, but there's only one visitor at a time allowed in ICU . . . and right now, you *all* need to step out."

Liam nodded. "I was just coming to tell you she was thirsty."

"I'll take care of it," the nurse assured him as the doctor walked over to the side of the bed. "In a few minutes, one of you may come back . . . but as I said, only one at a time."

Liam smiled at Cadie as he walked out, but as he passed the Knoxes, he felt his heart pound—the last thing he wanted was a confrontation—so as soon as he got outside, he headed down the hall and, without looking back, took the elevator down to the main entrance, hoping it would be the way Levi would come in. He paced back and forth, glancing at his watch, and then remembered he had Cadie's phone. He pulled it from his pocket and looked at the black screen. . . . *How the hell do you turn this damn thing on?* On a whim, he pushed the button at the bottom and the words SLIDE TO UNLOCK appeared. He slid his finger across the screen and stared at all of the icons before noticing a small green phone. He touched it, and a list of recent calls appeared—all from Levi. He tapped one of the calls and the words CALLING LEVI appeared. He put the phone to his ear and Levi answered almost immediately. "Wow! I'm impressed!"

"Thanks," Liam said with a smile. "I guess I'm not as dumb as I look."

"I guess not."

"Listen, your grandparents are here, so I came down to the main entrance. Which way are you coming in?"

There was a pause. "I must've just missed you because we just got off the elevator."

"Damn," Liam said, shaking his head. "Well, consider yourself warned."

"Thanks. I see my grandmother now; my grandfather must be in the room."

"Do you want me to come up and get Aidan?"

"No, I can handle it," Levi assured him.

"Okay," Liam said. "Well, I don't want to upset your mom, so just call me when they leave."

"Sounds good."

Liam looked at the screen as it went black, felt his stomach grumble, and looked around for the cafeteria. He saw a sign for it and the restroom—both of which he needed.

Chapter 30

Liam had just devoured a breakfast wrap and was taking the top off his coffee when he heard music again. He looked around the cafeteria and then remembered it was coming from his pocket. He pulled out Cadie's cell phone and smiled sheepishly at everyone who was looking to see who had "Love Shack" for their ringtone.

Liam lightly swiped his finger across the screen, and answered, "They left already?"

"Yes," Levi said angrily. "But not without upsetting her first."

"Why? What happened?"

Levi was so angry all he could do was sputter something incoherent.

"I'll be right up," Liam said, putting the lid on his coffee. He threw out his trash, and as he pushed the button for the elevator, shook his head—he definitely wasn't used to being caught up in this much drama.

Liam came around the corner and saw Levi sitting in the

waiting area while Aidan drove a toy John Deere tractor across the windowsill, but as soon as he saw Liam, he got up and walked toward him. "You aren't going to believe this. My grandparents are filing for custody of Aidan."

"What?!" Liam said. "That's crazy! What right do they have?"

"They tried to sugarcoat it—they said they could give him a better home, and that I was too young to be tied down."

Liam raised his eyebrows. "Your mom will never go for that."

"I know," Levi said, shaking his head. "She was so upset, I thought she was going to have another stroke, and then the nurse came in . . . and she was livid. She told them to leave and not come back, but as my grandfather was walking out, he said his attorney would be in touch."

Liam took a deep breath and let it out slowly. "Why don't you go in and see her and I'll stay with Aidan."

Levi nodded and Liam sat down. Carlton Knox was an even bigger ass than he thought—his daughter was dying of cancer and he was more concerned about who was going to get custody of her little boy. Liam watched Aidan playing quietly—he was such a sweet little kid . . . and smart, too—it would be tragic if the Knoxes won custody.

"She wants to talk to you," Levi said, coming back.

Liam walked toward Cadie's room, his heart pounding. "Hi," he said, peering around the clear partition.

"Hi," she said with a tired smile. "I'm *so* sorry I dragged you into all this. I bet you wish you'd never gone to that art show."

"You didn't know," Liam said with a sympathetic smile.

Cadie sighed. "You're right, I didn't know what a mess it would be . . . and how everything would turn out and I *never* expected my parents to show up." She shook her head. "My father is so well connected—he has friends in low *and* high places. I should've known he'd be keeping tabs on me." Her eyes glistened. "He does have a point, though—it's not fair for me to burden Levi with Aidan, and I certainly can't afford a lawyer to fight him."

Liam swallowed, not knowing what to say.

Finally, Cadie broke the silence. "Liam, I'm not winning this battle."

"You don't know that, Cadie. You can't just give up."

"It won't help denying it," she said resignedly. "I'm going to die and someone else is going to raise Aidan."

Liam looked out the window.

"I'm glad I got to see you again, though," she said with a smile, "and I'm glad you finally know about Levi."

Liam nodded, tears filling his eyes. "I'm glad too."

"It's funny, the first night I found out I had cancer, I couldn't fall asleep . . . and when I finally did fall asleep, I had this crazy dream that I was walking across a frozen pond, and all of a sudden, I fell through the ice. I was frantic—I kept pushing on the underside of the ice, but it was pitch-black and freezing cold and I was being pulled along by a current. I woke up crying, and every night after that, I had the same dream. It was so real I became afraid to fall asleep."

"Do you still have that dream?"

"No, my doctor gave me a prescription to sleep and it broke the cycle. But now I'm afraid to fall asleep because I might not wake up." She looked around the room. "I wish I wasn't going to die in a hospital."

"You don't have to," Liam said softly.

Cadie shook her head. "The only alternative is my tiny apartment, and I can't expect Levi to take care of me."

"It's not the only alternative," Liam said. "You and the boys can stay with me . . . and Levi doesn't even have to stay the whole time—he can come and go."

Cadie looked shocked and shook her head. "That's crazy! You can't just put *your* life on hold."

"I don't have anything pressing going on," he said, searching her face. "Cadie, don't you see? I've spent most of my life thinking about you and wanting to be with you again . . . and I never had the chance. Now I have that chance, and I want to make the most of it."

Cadie eyed him skeptically. "Do you realize how hard this will be . . . waiting for me to die?"

"Honestly, I think it might be the only meaningful thing I do in my life."

"That's not true," she said, shaking her head. "I'm sure you've brought light to many lives. You just don't realize it. Look at all the boats you've built and restored for people . . . not to mention all the lives you've touched by just being a good guy."

Liam laughed. "That's very kind of you, but I honestly don't think I've touched that many lives . . . *and* this isn't a pity party for me!"

Cadie smiled. "Well, it's not going to be a pity party for me either! If you really want to do this, I don't want sad, gloomy men tiptoeing around me."

Liam nodded. "Deal."

Chapter 31

"They're here!" Aidan hollered at the top of his lungs as Tuck hurried over to the car.

Cadie opened her door and the big dog put his paws on the edge of the seat and slobbered her with wet kisses while Aidan stood behind him, smiling. "C'mere, Tuck," he said, pulling on his collar so he could give her a hug too.

"Missed you, sweetie," she murmured, breathing in his lovely little-boy scent.

"Missed you, too, Mom. Wait 'til you see your new bed— Liam put it in *his* room."

"I can't wait," she said as Levi reached into the back for her bags.

"Where do you want to be?" Liam asked, helping her out of the car. "Would you like to sit out on the porch for a while?"

"I think I better just lie down for a while," Cadie said, leaning on him.

Liam nodded, realizing how featherlight she felt. He guided her to his room and she looked around at the new arrangement— Liam's bed was up against the wall and a hospital bed was near the windows so she could look out over the yard and see the ocean. Levi pulled down the covers and Liam propped up the pillows behind her. "How's that?" he asked, opening one of the windows.

"It's perfect," Cadie said, wincing as she tried to get comfortable.

Liam frowned. "What hurts?"

"Nothing," she lied. "I'm fine."

"Can I get you anything?"

She leaned back wearily against the soft pillows. "Nope, I'm all set."

"Okay, well, the bathroom's in there when you need it—equipped with railings and such, and I found out that Nantucket actually has hospice care—who knew?" he said with a smile. "So a nurse will be coming to check on you."

Cadie smiled weakly. "You probably never heard of hospice before this week," she teased.

"You're right," he said with a grin. "But I know *now*."

Cadie looked out the window and saw Aidan throwing a tennis ball for Tuck. "Aidan has a new friend," she said.

"He does," Liam said. "Tuck's never really been around little people before, but he loves Aidan—he's even been sleeping on his bed."

She smiled. "That's so great—he needs that."

Cadie didn't remember falling asleep—the only thing she remembered was watching Aidan throwing the ball—but when she woke up, there were streaks of pink across the dark blue sky. She shivered and reached up to shut the window. "Need help?" Liam asked, appearing in the doorway, drying his hands on a dish towel.

"I was just trying to . . ."

"If you need anything, call me," he instructed, shutting the window. "That's what I'm here for. How about a blanket?"

"That would be great."

Liam reached into the top of his closet, pulled out a soft, blue fleece blanket, and as he did, a stuffed animal tumbled to the floor.

"What's that?" Cadie asked.

"That's Teddy," he said, picking up his old bear.

"What an original name," Cadie teased.

"I know," Liam laughed, looking at it. "Would you like him to keep you company?"

"Sure," Cadie said with a laugh. "Where'd you get him?"

Liam sat on the bed and propped Teddy up against the pillow next to her and she lightly touched his frayed fur and worn pads. "My goodness, he looks like he's been through the war."

"He has," Liam confirmed. "He was the only Christmas present my parents had bought for me before they died. Cooper found him when he was going through their things."

"That explains his much-loved appearance," Cadie said with an understanding nod.

"I don't hold on to many things, but somehow, I could never let Teddy go."

Cadie nodded, trying to picture Liam when he was younger. "Do you have any old photographs?"

"Some . . . not many."

"I'd love to see them."

"Well, first, I need to know if you'd like some supper—we had spaghetti, and I managed to save some before your boys ate it all."

Cadie smiled. "Okay," she said with a nod. "I'll have a little . . . not too much."

"Something to drink?"

"Tea?"

"With milk?"

"A little."

"You got it."

"Mommy, you're awake!" Aidan said, running into the room with Tuck at his heels and hopping onto the bed. "Did you know there's no TV here?"

"There isn't?" she said. "How're you going to manage without *SpongeBob*?"

He shrugged. "I don't know, but there're lots of books about shipwrecks and pirates and he's"—he pointed to Liam—"going to find them for me."

"That sounds wonderful."

Aidan nodded and then looked up as Levi appeared with a tray.

"That was quick," Cadie said.

"The water's still heating," Levi explained. Then he looked at his brother. "Hop off, Aid, so Mom doesn't spill."

Aidan moved to Liam's bed while Tuck sniffed the air and edged closer to Cadie. "That's not for you, Tuck," Aidan said, tugging on his collar.

Tuck backed away reluctantly and then climbed up on Liam's bed next to Aidan and put his head on his paws. Levi sat next to him and scratched his ears. "You already had some spaghetti," he consoled softly, but Tuck just sighed.

"Sheesh, it's a regular party in here," Liam said, coming into the room and carefully setting the tea on Cadie's tray. "I didn't make it too full," he said. "There's more in the pot."

Cadie looked at each of them. "Boy," she said, smiling. "If I knew I'd be taken care of by so many handsome men, I'd've gotten cancer sooner."

"Yeah, that's a good reason," Levi said, rolling his eyes.

Chapter 32

The next few days slipped by—each much like the ones before—and despite Liam's promise to not tiptoe, they all ended up trying to be quiet so Cadie could rest. On the days when she had more energy, she took short walks in the gardens or along the beach or sat on the back porch, soaking up the late-summer sunlight. Other days, she lay in bed, sometimes reading her Bible and sometimes watching the waves chase each other to shore, but mostly, she just slept. The hospice nurse, Lisa, stopped by every day to check on her, and her visits marked the time like the ticking of an old clock.

During these visits, Liam took advantage of the opportunity to run a quick errand or check on the boathouse. He and Levi had fallen into a routine—Levi looking out for Aidan and Liam taking care of Cadie. *Waiting for someone to die*—as Cadie had put it—was much more difficult than he'd imagined, and he'd even begun looking forward to food shopping because it offered a respite from the sadness that hung over the house like a dark cloud.

On the first night, when they'd all been gathered around

Cadie's bed, she had decided it was time to tell Aidan, and although frightened tears had trickled down his cheeks, they'd soon dried when she assured him that they'd see each other again—after *he* had lived a long, happy life, of course. "Will Tuck and Moby be there?" he asked, looking up at Liam, who was leaning against the door frame with his arms crossed, and Liam had brushed tears from his eyes and nodded.

One morning, toward the end of that first week, while Liam was running an errand and Levi was down on the beach with Aidan, Cadie had gone into the kitchen to make a cup of tea, and as she waited for the kettle to heat, she wandered over to the back door and gazed at the photo that was hanging there. She studied it, wondering who it was; then she caught her breath, realizing the little boy was Liam and the young couple were his parents—Levi's grandparents. Suddenly, Cadie realized that there was still so much she didn't know about him . . . and time was running out!

The tea kettle sputtered and began to whistle, demanding her attention, and as she turned to pick it up, Liam bumped open the door with his arms full of groceries. "Hey," he said with a smile. "You're up."

"Yes, I am! It's funny how I can feel absolutely miserable one day and kind of okay the next."

"Well, on one of your 'kind of okay' days, the boys and I have a surprise for you."

"You do?! What is it?"

"If I tell you," he said, setting down the groceries, "it won't be a surprise."

"I suppose not," she said, dunking her tea bag and wondering what it could be.

"Are you hungry?"

"A little."

"How about some toast and peanut butter?"

"That sounds good."

Liam pulled a fresh loaf of bread out of a bag, opened it, dropped two slices of bread in the toaster, and opened the cabinet for the peanut butter. "Crunchy or creamy?"

"Creamy," she said, sitting at the table with her tea. "I love that picture of you with your parents."

Liam looked up. "You recognized me?"

"Of course," Cadie said with a smile. "You look just like Levi did at that age, and your mom was beautiful. You look like your dad—who is very handsome by the way—but you definitely have your mom's eyes."

Liam chuckled as he smoothed peanut butter over the warm toast, cut it in half, and set it in front of her.

"What?" Cadie asked.

"Coop used to say that too," he said as he spread crunchy peanut butter on his toast.

"Well, it's true," she said, taking a bite. "Mmm, this is so good—you forget how good something as simple as toast and peanut butter is . . . especially when the peanut butter is all warm and melty."

"Melty?"

"Mm-hmm, see how it's all *melty* right here?" she said, pointing to the pool of warm, melted peanut butter.

Liam rolled his eyes. "Yes, I see," he teased.

Cadie took another bite and remembered she had another question. "Mm . . ." she said, her mouth full, "did you ever find your photo album?"

"Mm-hmm," he said with his mouth full too.

"Well?" Cadie asked, taking a sip of her tea. "Are you gonna show it to me?"

"Why do you want to see old photographs?"

"Because I want to know more about you . . . just like you wanted to know more about Levi."

"A bunch of old photos aren't going to tell you."

"Yes, they will—pictures *do* tell a story. . . ."

Just then, Aidan and Tuck burst into the kitchen with Levi behind them. "Guess what we saw?" Aidan said excitedly.

Cadie started to scold, "Hon, you're getting sand all over . . ."

But Liam gently put his hand on her arm. "What did you see?"

"Seals!"

"No way!" Liam said.

"Yes, way," Aidan said, nodding excitedly. "They swam right by us!"

"That's so cool," Liam said.

"I know!"

Cadie watched their exchange and couldn't help but smile. Suddenly, she felt a big, wet, sandy paw on her leg and looked down to see Tuck gazing longingly at her.

"Don't be a beggar, mister," Liam scolded.

"Does he like toast and peanut butter?" Cadie asked.

Liam laughed, shaking his head. "That would be the understatement of the century."

Cadie held out her last morsel, and Tuck took it ever so gently. "Good boy," she said softly as Tuck swallowed it whole and turned his attention to Liam.

"You see, it's not *us* he loves. It's our food!"

"He's too funny," Cadie said, laughing, and Liam, Levi, and Aidan all smiled—it was good to hear her laugh.

Suddenly, Tuck barked and hurried over to the screen door.

"Hello, there, Tuck," a familiar voice said.

Liam pushed open the screen door. "Hey, Mike, what've you got?"

"Hey, Liam, I have a registered envelope here with your address, but not your name," Mike said in a perplexed voice.

"What's the name?"

Mike looked at the envelope. "Acadia Knox."

"She's here. Does she have to sign for it?"

"No, you can sign," Mike said, holding out the card.

Liam looked at the name of the sender—it was from a lawyer's office. "Great," he muttered, shaking his head. "Does she *have* to accept it?"

"No," Mike said slowly, "but if she doesn't, whoever sent it can still proceed with whatever they're doing. That's why they sent it certified—so they can prove they tried to notify her—which is usually all that's required."

Liam looked at it again, trying to decide.

"Legal problems don't go away because you ignore them," Mike added, "and you're almost always better off knowing what they're up to."

Liam nodded. "Let me ask."

While he waited, Mike knelt down and scratched Tuck's ears. "You must've been for a swim," he said softly as the big dog wiggled around him.

Liam reappeared with the signed card and exchanged it for the envelope. "Sorry to be the one to deliver bad news . . . if that's the case," Mike said regretfully.

"What can you do?" Liam said. "Thanks, Mike."

Mike waved and Liam went back inside. He handed the envelope to Cadie. She tore it open, quickly scanned the contents, and looked up. "Well, he's definitely going through with it," she said in a resigned voice.

Chapter 33

The water cascading over Cadie's thin shoulders felt like a thousand needles pricking her sensitive skin. She tilted her head back, blocking the full force of the spray, and waited for the sensation to subside. Then she reached for the new bottle of shampoo Levi had bought after he noticed her hair was starting to come in. She took off the top, poured a small amount into the palm of her hand, lifted it to her nose, smelled its lovely, fresh scent, and smoothed it into the soft blond fuzz sprouting from her bald head. She couldn't remember the last time she'd shampooed her hair, and although she really didn't need to now, it felt luxurious, relaxing . . . *and* normal, and she wondered if people who were blessed with busy, cancer-free lives ever took the time to simply enjoy washing their hair with a fragrant shampoo. She smiled sadly . . . *probably not*—before cancer, she hadn't either.

She rinsed her head, reached for the washcloth, and washed with soap that was on the back corner of the tub—it was a masculine scent, but she didn't care; in fact, now she knew why

Liam always smelled so good. With one hand, she held on to the newly installed handicap bar and leaned over to wash her legs, but as she did, white-hot fire surged through her abdomen and she cried out, doubling over in pain and clinging to the bar. She sank to the floor of the tub, her tears masked by the water, and wrapped her arms tightly around her knees. Finally, when the pain eased, she lay back against the back of the tub and looked down at her skeletal body. Her breasts were so small they were practically nonexistent, and the sight of them brought back the stinging humiliation of her husband referring to them as mosquito bites.

She looked farther down at the protruding bones of her hips and watched the water pool in the sunken curve of her abdomen. The water splashed in it like rain drops in a puddle, and as she stared at the smooth skin of her abdomen—under which all hell had broken loose, she wondered—for the millionth time—why her body had betrayed her.

She lightly traced her finger through the stubble of pubic hair, which—like the fuzz on top of her head—was trying to make a comeback . . . and then lower still, curious to see if her body could still be aroused. It had been so long since she'd even thought about sex . . . never mind *had* it. Her encounters with Taylor had been pretty lackluster, and it made her sad to think that the only time she'd ever really enjoyed a truly amazing orgasm was when she was seventeen . . . and sadder still to know she'd probably never have another one, since there was no way Liam could be aroused by her thin, bony body . . . accentuated with a only disappointing pair of *mosquito bites.*

There was a knock on the door. "Cadie?" Liam called. "Are you okay?"

She sat up, grimacing as another surge of pain shot through her body. "I'm fine," she croaked, pulling herself up, and turning off the water. She dried off, wrapped the towel around her, and hobbled over to the counter where her medicine bottles were lined up. She hated taking painkillers because they made her feel drowsy . . . and she didn't want to sleep away the little time she had left, but after another surge of pain, she swore softly, opened one of the bottles, and popped a pill in her mouth. Then she closed her eyes and waited. Finally, she pulled on a pair of sweatpants and an old, soft, flannel shirt of Liam's, hung up her towel, and made her way weakly back to bed.

"How'd it go?" Liam asked, appearing in the doorway.

"Good," she said. "It felt really good to take a shower."

"Do you need anything?"

"No, thanks. I'm all set."

Liam nodded. "Well, would you be up to looking at some old photos . . . ?"

Cadie's face lit up. "Yes!" she said with a huge smile.

Liam pulled an album from behind his back and handed it to her.

"Sit down," she said, moving over to make room for him. Liam leaned back against the pillows as Cadie opened the leather book filled with photos that had been carefully tucked into white decorative, adhesive corners stuck to black paper pages. "Oh, my goodness!" she exclaimed, looking at the first few pages filled with old black and white photos of a gorgeous bride on the arm of a handsome groom. "These are beautiful!"

Liam put his hands behind his head and looked down at the photos. He hadn't looked at the book in years . . . and he'd never shared it with anyone.

"I love old black and whites," Cadie gushed. "Even though people rave about the pictures they can take with their phones and send to their computers, nothing compares to the rich elegance of an old black-and-white photograph on heavy, textured paper."

Liam smiled as Cadie "oohed" and "aahed" over the pictures of Lily and Daniel honeymooning in New Hampshire . . . and soon after, of Lily sporting a baby bump . . . and finally, of the proud parents holding their new son. Cadie turned the pages, commenting and pointing as the photos evolved from black and white to glossy, square, colored snapshots with white borders—all of a little boy in typical childhood settings: sitting in a pedal car under a Christmas tree; dressed as a pirate next to a jack-o'-lantern; wearing frog boots and proudly holding a frog; blowing out the candles on birthday cakes; leaning against a tree with his dad . . . or with his arms wrapped tightly around his mom's neck, giving her a kiss. But what Cadie noticed most about the little boy was that his ocean blue eyes were always full of a sweet serenity and innocence. "Look at you," Cadie murmured.

Then she turned another page and a handful of loose photos fell out. She picked them up and slowly looked through them—they were of the same boy—older now—sailing, hiking, eating clams . . . and there was one of him with another boy standing on the beach with their arms around each other's shoulders.

She looked through them again and noticed that something about him was different. She stared at the pictures, trying to figure out what it was, and then she realized that the innocent wonder was gone . . . and even though he was smiling, his eyes were solemn and sad.

"Who's that?" she asked, pointing to the second boy.

"That's Jack," Liam said. "He was my best friend—we were inseparable—we even enlisted together. He saved my life."

"Do you still keep in touch with him?"

"Sort of . . ." Liam said, "but I don't know if we will any longer."

"Why?"

"He's changed."

Cadie nodded, sensing his reluctance to talk about it. She looked back down at the pictures and smiled. "Here's the boy *I* knew!" she said, spreading out the last of the photos—they were of a slender teenager. There was one of him standing in the boathouse; another of him looking up from working on a boat; another with Cooper, and one of him standing proudly next to his restored runabout . . . and in the last photo he had his arm around a pretty girl. "Wow," Cadie murmured softly. "I remember when Coop took this picture."

Liam smiled. "Yeah, he told me I'd need it to remember you by because I'd probably never see you again . . . and he was right."

"He wasn't right—you're seeing me now!"

"True," Liam said, putting his arm around her, "but it's been a long time."

Cadie nodded and looked back at the pictures. "Thank you for sharing these with me."

"You're welcome," he said, kissing the top of her head. "Mmm, you smell good," he murmured with a smile.

"Thank you," she said flirtatiously. "It's my new shampoo."

"Surf Foam?"

She looked up in surprise. "How'd you know?"

"I saw it on the shelf."

"Thank you for doing this too."

"Doing what?"

"You know—all this—taking us in, taking the pressure off Levi, looking out for Aidan, and not letting me die in the hospital or in a stuffy apartment."

"Oh, it's nothing," Liam said with a grin; then he leaned over and gently kissed her lips . . . and Cadie realized, in surprise, that her body *could* still be aroused.

She leaned back against him and then Liam stretched out alongside her thin body and put his arm around her and they lay quietly together as a warm summer breeze drifted through the windows. She listened to his soft breathing and to his heart beating and thought, *His heart will continue beating long after mine stops. . . .*

Chapter 34

When Cadie woke up, Liam was gone, but curled up in the spot where he'd been was Moby. Cadie reached over and lightly touched the soft gray fur and Moby pushed his head up into her hand. Cadie scratched under his white chin and he purred. "What did I do to deserve *your* company?" she whispered softly, and he blinked, stretched out to his full length, and kept purring.

A moment later, the back door opened and Cadie heard the clicking of paws on the wooden floor. Then she heard Levi reminding Aidan to be quiet.

"It's okay," she called. "I'm awake."

Hearing her voice, Tuck bounded into the room and launched onto the bed, sending Moby scurrying. "You're such a big lug," Cadie said, laughing as he stood over her, licking her face.

"Hop down, Tuck," Levi scolded, following him into the room. "Sorry, Mom," he said, pulling him off the bed.

"It's okay, hon. He's fine. Really."

Levi shook his head. "No, it's not—his feet are wet and sandy, and now your sheets are wet and sandy too."

"They'll dry," she said, reaching for his hand, but he pulled away.

"Hey," she said with a frown. "What's the matter?"

"Nothing," he said, then stopped and looked back. "I'm sorry. I just have to fix a snack for Aidan."

"Come here," she said. "His snack can wait."

Levi reluctantly sat down and watched as the big dog cleaned himself next to the bed. "Tuck, stop," he scolded again, nudging him with his foot.

Cadie looked down at him and he thumped his tail happily. "He's just doing what dogs do," she said softly. "So . . . what's *really* the matter? Is taking care of Aidan twenty-four/seven getting to you?"

Levi shook his head. "No, it's fine."

"How come I don't believe you?" she said with a gentle smile.

"He just asks so many questions . . . and he needs to be entertained all the time. I never get a minute to myself . . . to just think or draw . . . or *anything*."

"That's how kids are—they're busy and curious. You were the same way."

Levi shook his head. "I could entertain myself—I used to spend hours drawing pictures."

"Why don't you give him a pad and some pencils? Maybe he has a knack for drawing too."

"Maybe," Levi said, sounding unconvinced.

"But that's not everything . . ."

Levi bit his lip and looked away.

"Hey," she said softly. "Look at me. . . ."

"I can't," Levi answered, shaking his head, tears stinging his eyes.

"Look at me," she said again, and as Levi turned, hot tears were spilling down his cheeks. "Oh, hon, it's going to be okay . . .

you're going to be okay . . . you're going to get through this. I'm so proud of who you are. You've grown up to be a wonderful man . . . and you're an amazing artist—who's already had a one-man show *on Nantucket,* of all places!"

Liam smiled and brushed his cheeks. "I know, but all I want is for you to be here. I'd give up everything if you'd just get better."

"I want to be here, too, hon, but things don't always work out the way we want. I'll be in here, though," she said, touching his chest. "At least I hope I'll be."

"You will be," he said, fresh tears filling his eyes.

"And you have a lot of other people who are going to fill your life with love—Liam, Aidan, Emma . . . and most importantly, kids of your own someday. By the way, when is Emma coming home?"

"Tomorrow."

"Are you picking her up?"

"I was going to, but it's too much with Aidan."

"You should go," Cadie said. "Aidan can stay here. I'm sure you could use a break from all this anyway."

"No, I . . ."

"Levi, I'm hungry," Aidan called from the kitchen, "and I just spilled the juice. . . ."

Levi groaned and shook his head, and Cadie smiled. "You're going and that's that."

Levi started to get up, but then turned and wrapped his arms around her. "Thanks, Mom," he said softly. And when he pulled back, he said, "You smell good."

"It's my new shampoo," she said with a grin.

"Hey!" Aidan said, peering around the door. "What's a man gotta do to get a little food around here?!" Levi rolled his eyes and headed for the door, but before he got there, he turned. "Emma wants to see you. Is that okay?"

Cadie smiled. "I'd love to see her . . ." She hesitated, searching Levi's eyes. "Don't let her go, Le—she's a lovely girl . . . and she's brave to want to come see me."

"I know," Levi said with a half smile. "I won't let her go."

Tuck pulled himself up and trotted after him and, moments later, she heard Aidan explain, "Don't worry about the spill, Le. Tuck got it."

Cadie looked out the window and watched the waves chasing each other to shore, one after another . . . continuously . . . endlessly—just as they would after she was gone. All of a sudden, the keenness of knowing that life *would* go on—that the world would keep turning—without her—was almost too much to bear. She pictured all the lovely things she would miss: Levi painting in his studio; showing his artwork in prestigious galleries; marrying his sweet Emma, cradling babies in his arms and bringing them to visit their silver haired grandfather. She could picture Liam sweeping their grandchildren up into his strong arms; taking them sailing and swimming, and teaching them how to make s'mores as they sat around a fire and looked at the stars.

And then she tried to picture Aidan. What would *his* life be like? How hard would it be for him when he was taken from Levi? Would her parents send him to some faraway prep school? Would he ever be able to have a dog? Would he lose his sweet innocence and curiosity? Would he ever again . . . *be happy?*

"Oh, God," she whispered. "Please take care of Aidan. . . ."

A moment later, a small voice startled her thoughts. "Here, Mommy, Levi made toast and peanut butter for you."

"Thanks, hon," she said, looking up. "Are you having some too?"

"I already had it," Aidan said as Tuck rested his chin on her bed and gazed at her.

* * *

Liam walked over to a small gray building behind the boat-house and pulled a set of keys out of his pocket. Although the structure wasn't nearly as old as the boathouse, a couple of sea-sons in the salty air had quickly weathered its cedar shake sid-ing and made it look like it had been there forever. Liam flipped through the key ring, came to a small silver key, slipped it into the lock, and turned it. The lock clicked open easily and he slid the heavy wooden doors to the sides, revealing a neatly swept bay. Originally, the barn had been built to store supplies: planking, frames, old masts, booms, and sails, but after Coop died, Liam had cleaned it out and used it to store only one thing. He stepped inside and lifted the corner of a heavy canvas cover, and the warm glow of mahogany and chrome sparkled in the sunlight.

Liam pulled the compressor over to fill the tires of the trailer with air, backed his truck up to the hitch, clamped it, and slowly pulled the old runabout out of the barn. Just as he did, a familiar black sedan pulled into the parking lot.

"Hey, John," he said, walking over. "I'm sorry I haven't got-ten back to you—things've been a little crazy."

John Alden nodded. "Don't apologize. I stopped by a cou-ple of times, but you weren't here, so I asked Sally if something happened and she said you had a family emergency, and I know you said it wouldn't be done this season, but I was stopping by to see if you'd come up with a figure . . . and if you needed any money up front."

"I appreciate that," Liam said.

John motioned to the Chris-Craft. "Whose is this?"

"Mine," Liam said.

John looked at Liam as if he were seeing him for the first time. "Yours?!"

Liam nodded, wishing John didn't look so surprised.

"She's a beauty! When'd you get her?"

"I've had her since high school," Liam said, wiping dust from the deck with a chamois. "Coop and I restored her."

"Wow!" John gushed. "How come I've never seen her before?"

"She's been in storage. I've had her out to refinish—but it's always been during the off-season."

John nodded. "Are you taking her out now?"

"No, not today . . . but soon, I hope."

"Well, I don't know how you could own such a gorgeous boat and not take her out once in a while—it's a sin . . . and it's not fair to *her* either."

Liam chuckled. "You're right. I never thought about it that way before."

"Well, anyway," John said, reaching into his shirt pocket. "We're heading back to Boston on Saturday and I wanted you to be able to reach me." He handed Liam a business card.

Liam glanced down at it and started to put it in his pocket, but then stopped. "You're an attorney?!"

John nodded. "Thirty years."

"What kind?"

"I'm a partner in a firm. We have lawyers that specialize in just about every field—divorce, bankruptcy, personal injury, immigration, estate planning, elder law. . . ."

Liam swallowed. "What's your specialty?"

"I've been at it so long I've become a bit of a jack of all trades, but lately, my focus has been on estate planning and, sometimes, depending on the client, custody."

Liam nodded slowly. "Do you have a minute?"

Chapter 35

The next morning Levi was up early, but when he shuffled into the kitchen, he found Liam already up, making scrambled eggs.

"Coffee?" Liam asked, nodding toward the pot.

"Mmm," he murmured, pouring coffee into a mug and looking out the window. "I can't believe it's still dark out at six o'clock," he muttered. "A month ago, the sun was up before five."

"I know," Liam said. "And it's getting dark earlier too. A month ago, it was still light out at nine, but now it's getting dark by seven."

"It's depressing. . . ." Levi mused gloomily.

"It sure is," Liam agreed. He scraped the eggs onto two plates and then spread butter on the toast that had just popped up. "Jam?" he asked.

"What kind?"

"Beach plum."

Levi frowned.

"Sally made it."

"Oh," he said with a smile. "Then, yes."

Liam chuckled as he spread the jam on both pieces of toast.

"It was really nice of her to bring over that big pot of soup last night," Levi said, sitting down. "I never thought I'd like kale."

Liam smiled. "I was skeptical too. It must've been the roasted vegetables that made it so good."

"Mmm," Levi agreed with his mouth full. "She's a sweet lady," he added. "I know Mom loved meeting her, and Tuck was so funny when he jumped in her car when she was leaving."

"He *is* funny," Liam said, shaking his head. "Whenever he stays with her, I have trouble getting him to leave. I think he might be happier if he just lived with her."

"Oh, I don't know," Levi said skeptically, looking down at the big dog asleep at his feet. "He follows you everywhere too."

Liam looked at the sleeping dog and smiled. "When do you think you'll be back?"

"Tonight, I hope. Are you sure you don't mind having Emma here too?"

"I don't mind," Liam assured him. "I'm looking forward to meeting her."

"All right, but I really feel like we've turned your world upside down."

"Maybe that's a good thing," Liam said with a smile. "And if you do get back tonight, and your mom feels up to it tomorrow, maybe we could take her for that boat ride."

Levi nodded. "That would be great."

Liam paused. "There's something else . . ."

Levi looked up in surprise. "What?"

He took a deep breath. "Well, I have a customer who is a lawyer, and yesterday, we had the chance to talk about your mom and Aidan . . . and I know this is crazy, but he said that even if your mom was financially able to fight your grandparents for custody, it's highly unlikely a court would give him to you."

"Why?" Levi said. "I'm capable of taking care of him. I have my own place, my own income, and I love him more than they ever will."

Liam shook his head. "I know, but he said a court won't see it that way. They'll look for his father first, and if he doesn't want him, they'll probably give him to his grandparents."

"That's not right!" Levi said in an angry whisper. "His father is long gone—he gave up all his parental rights in the divorce settlement, so he has no claim to Aidan . . . and his grandparents will probably ship him off to some boarding school."

Liam bit his lip and nodded. "I know. It's not right. I couldn't agree more. This attorney said there's another possible solution; it's kind of far-fetched and we might run out of time, but he said if I was willing to pursue it, he'd represent us."

Levi shook his head. "We can't afford a lawyer and you shouldn't pay for one either. You've done enough."

"I wouldn't be paying him—his sailboat is the one that's in for repair and we agreed to an exchange of services."

Levi frowned and shook his head. "I'm confused. How does this help? You just said a court wouldn't give me custody . . . so who would get Aidan?"

Liam took a deep breath. "I would."

Levi stared at him. "You'd be willing to do that?"

Liam nodded. "I would. I've been giving it a lot of thought and I've realized that I wouldn't *just* be doing it for Aidan . . . I'd also be doing it for me. It definitely would change my life, but I honestly think that it would be in a good way. Plus, I keep coming back to something your mom said: She said having you was like having a part of me with her . . . and if I adopted Aidan, I'd have a part of her with me." He paused. "How would you feel about that?"

"I think it would be great!" Levi said with a grin. "And, boy, would it ever piss off my grandfather!"

Liam chuckled. "I hadn't thought of that, but I bet it would."

After Levi left for the airport, Liam looked in on Cadie. She moaned softly and he left the door open so he could hear her if she called out; then he walked down the hall to check on Aidan. When he peered around the doorway, Tuck's tail thumped, but he didn't move—he was much too comfortable stretched out on the bed with Aidan's arm draped around his big neck. "It would definitely be wrong to separate you two," he said softly.

He walked back to the kitchen, refreshed his coffee cup, and stepped out into the cool morning air. The sun was just starting to come up, and as he sank into one of the chairs, he wondered if he *really* was prepared to take on the responsibility of another human being. Is anyone ever really ready? Had Cadie been ready to take care of Levi? Had Cooper been ready to take care of him? Just then, it dawned on him that he'd been Aidan's age when he'd come to live with Coop, and as he watched the sun peak over the horizon, he wondered if his uncle was playing a role in this turn of events. He could almost hear him whispering in God's ear, "Don't let that boy off easy—he needs a little excitement in his life."

He chuckled and looked up at the morning stars. "Thanks a lot, Coop," he said, and immediately, one of the stars blinked.

Chapter 36

Cadie woke up to the sound of voices outside her window. She looked out, her eyes adjusting to the bright sunlight; then she realized Aidan and Liam were working on something in the backyard. As her eyes adjusted she realized Aidan was looking at her window—as if he was making sure she wasn't watching. "I think she's awake," she heard him whisper.

Liam turned around. "There's no peeking," he scolded.

"I'm not peeking," she called back, and Tuck, hearing her voice, trotted over and pressed his wet nose against her screen. "Hey there, honey pot," she said softly. "Do you know what they're up to?" but the ever-faithful golden retriever—keeper of all secrets—just wagged his tail.

Cadie sat up higher, holding her abdomen. "Whatcha doin'?"

"Nothin'," Aidan called back, trying to stand so she couldn't see, but he wasn't tall enough to completely hide the wooden post they'd just put in the ground.

Cadie watched as Liam pointed to an empty gallon jug lying on the grass; then she saw Aidan pick it up and hurry toward the house.

While he waited for Aidan to come back, Liam turned to the window. "Do you need anything?"

"No, I'm just going to use the bathroom," she called back. "Then maybe I'll make some breakfast."

Liam looked at his watch. "You missed breakfast. It's time for lunch."

"Oh," Cadie said as she looked at the bedside clock and realized it was eleven-thirty! "Damn pain pills!" she muttered. "Is there any of Sally's soup left?"

"There's plenty. I'll be in to fix it in a minute."

"You don't have to come in. I can do it." She stood up, still holding her abdomen, and made her way slowly to the bathroom.

Ten minutes later, when she finally made it back to bed, Aidan was standing outside her window. "Look!" he said proudly.

Cadie looked across the yard and saw a post with a brand-new birdfeeder hanging from it, and on either side of the post, nestled between two new hydrangea plants, was a birdbath filled with fresh water. "Oh, my!" Cadie said. "That looks great!"

"Mm-hmm," Aidan nodded. "*And* we're going to hang a hummingbird feeder right here, outside your window," he added, pointing to the overhang above his head. "So you can watch the hummingbirds."

"That's wonderful, Aidan," Cadie said. "Thank you so much!"

"You're welcome," he said, beaming.

"Aid," Liam called from the porch. "Ready for lunch?"

"Yes," Aidan called back. "I'll be right there!" He looked back at Cadie. "Are you having lunch?"

Cadie nodded. "I'll meet you in the kitchen."

She wrapped her robe around her thin body, made her way

to the kitchen, and eased into the chair across from Aidan as Liam set a steaming bowl of kale soup in front of her. "Aidan, do you want some soup?" he asked.

"What kind?"

"Kale and roasted vegetable."

Aidan squinched his nose. "No, thanks. I'll just have grilled cheese."

Liam spread butter across a slice of bread and dropped it, butter-side down, into a frying pan. "How 'bout you, Cadie-did? Can I tempt you with one of my famous grilled cheese sandwiches?"

"*Cadie-did?*" Aidan giggled, looking at his mom.

"No, thank you . . . just soup."

"You should try Liam's grilled cheese, Mom. It's wicked good."

"Wicked, huh?" she said, raising her eyebrows.

"Mm-hmm," he nodded.

"May I change my order?" she asked, looking at Liam.

Liam smiled as he measured sugar. "You may," he replied.

"May I have half a grilled cheese with my soup?"

Liam nodded as he poured the sugar into a pot and proceeded to fill the measuring cup with water.

"You're quite the multitasker," she teased. "What are you making?"

"Hummingbird juice," he said, putting the pot on the stovetop and turning on the burner. "I never used to be a multitasker," he said, spreading more butter on bread and then flipping Aidan's sandwich. "But I'm learning."

Cadie smiled as she blew on her soup. "You'd be a good dad."

Liam looked up in surprise and searched her eyes. "Do you really think so?"

"Mm-hmm," she said, sipping the soup from her spoon.

"It's funny you should say that," he said as he cut Aidan's

sandwich in quarters and set it down in front of him. "Milk?" he asked.

"And pickles," Aidan said.

Liam looked back at Cadie. "There's something I want to talk to you about."

"What?" she asked, studying him curiously.

He flipped the second sandwich and glanced over at Aidan. "After lunch."

"Okay," Cadie said, frowning.

Liam cut the second sandwich in half, slid half onto the plate next to Cadie's bowl and half next to his, ladled soup into both, turned off the boiling sugar water, and sat down.

"Thanks for lunch," Cadie said, taking a bite of her sandwich. "Sally's soup is amazing."

"What about my grilled cheese?!" he asked, looking wounded.

"Oh," she said with a grin. "It's wicked good!"

Aidan smiled as he popped a pickle in his mouth.

"So, tell me more about Sally," Cadie said. "She owns a restaurant?"

"Yeah—Cuppa Jo to Go—it's a breakfast-lunch place. She's up pretty early every day."

"How long has she had the restaurant?"

"Oh, a long time . . . I can remember Coop bringing me there when I was Aidan's age. He and Sally spent a lot of time together."

"Do you think they were an item?"

Liam smiled and nodded. "I don't have proof, but as I got older, I noticed the way they looked at each other and I saw how mad Sally got when Coop drank too much . . . but then I found out she was married."

"How'd you find that out?"

Liam laughed, remembering. "Dimitri."

"Dimitri?"

"Yeah, he was Coop's drinking buddy and the father of one of my friends from high school—Tracey."

"Tracey?"

"Jack's wife."

"Hmm . . ." Cadie said with raised eyebrows. "Now we're getting somewhere."

"Can I take Tuck outside and see if the birds've found the feeder yet?" Aidan interrupted.

"Sure," Liam said, tousling his hair. "But don't get too close or you'll scare them off."

"Okay," Aidan said. "C'mon, Tuck," he called, heading for the door, but then he skidded to a halt and Tuck, who was right behind him, almost knocked him over. "What about the hummingbird feeder?"

"We'll hang it up after the sugar water cools."

"Okay."

Liam smiled. "Anyway, whenever Coop and Dimitri went out, Frannie—Dimitri's wife—would call and ask me to round them up. One night, I found them in their favorite haunt, but they were three sheets to the wind and I couldn't get them to leave, so I just ordered a beer and joined them. Dimitri started talking to Coop about a woman, and at first, I wasn't sure who it was. . . .

" 'Why the hell doesn't she divorce the son of a bitch?' Dimitri slurred. And Coop groaned, 'I've told ya before, Dimitri . . . because she's Catholic!' 'So?' Dimitri said, shaking his head. 'She doesn't need 'im—she's got the restaurant, and that place's worth a fortune.' 'Is not about the money,' Coop said. 'It's about 'er faith . . . *and* she says it's bad enough she's with me.' "

Liam grinned. "That's when I almost fell off my stool!"

Cadie smiled. "Good for him. I'm glad he had someone."

"Me too," Liam said, nodding, but then his face grew solemn. "Sally took it pretty hard when he died. . . ."

Liam looked down at Cadie's half-eaten lunch. "Not hungry?"

She looked down too. "I guess not. It was good, though."

Then she looked up at him. "So what did you want to talk about?"

Liam took a deep breath and let it out slowly. "Aidan."

Chapter 37

"I think you'd be a wonderful dad," Cadie said as Liam helped her back to bed. "But it's a huge responsibility. Are you absolutely sure?"

"Yes, I'm sure." Liam said, leaving out the word *absolutely.*

He sat on the bed next to her and Cadie searched his eyes. "I wish we'd had the chance to spend our lives together."

"I wish we had too," he said with a sad smile. "That's why we have to make the most of the time we have left." He hesitated, searching her eyes. "Cadie, I hope you know what an inspiration you are to me. I see the pain in your eyes and I know you're putting up a good front to make it easier for us . . ." He paused. "I don't think I could do it. I don't think I could keep smiling."

Cadie squeezed his hand. "I guess I've just come to realize there's no point in feeling sorry for myself. Everyone has to face death eventually, so I may as well go out with a smile on my face."

"That's just what I mean. . . ." Liam said, shaking his head.

Cadie saw tears glistening in his eyes. "Hey," she teased gently.

"There's no crying, remember? Even when I'm gone, I don't want you guys to be gloomy. I want you to celebrate."

Liam nodded.

"Promise?" she asked, raising her eyebrows.

"We'll try," he said, "but I can't promise."

They heard a sound outside the window and they looked up to see a hummingbird hovering near the new feeder. A moment later, another tiny bird buzzed by, squeaking and scolding, and then they chased each other, hovering and dancing in midair.

"I've never seen a hummingbird," Cadie whispered in awe.

"Never?!"

She shook her head. "I don't think Aidan has either."

"I'll go get him," Liam said, getting up. He hurried down the hall, and even though he was only gone a short time, by the time they got back, Cadie was sound asleep.

"Do you see them?" Liam asked softly, pointing out the window.

Aidan nodded. "That's so cool," he whispered. "They found it in no time."

"They did," Liam agreed.

As the afternoon went by, Aidan grew tired of watching the birds and Liam pulled down the squeaky attic stairs from the ceiling and climbed up into the dusty, hot attic to look for the box of books from his childhood, and when he came back down and set it on the porch, Aidan excitedly pulled it open and peered inside.

"Let's read this one," he exclaimed, pulling out a dog-eared copy of *Robinson Crusoe*.

"That's a good one," Liam said with a nod as Aidan climbed onto his lap.

An hour later, when Cadie came out onto the porch, Liam was still reading out loud, but Aidan was sound asleep. "Now I understand why you always wanted to live on an island by yourself," she teased. "Is Aidan going to be your man Friday?"

Liam looked up in surprise and smiled. "That may have been where the idea originated . . . and he might be. You never know!"

"You *do* realize he's asleep, don't you?"

"He is?!" Liam said, moving so he could see Aidan's face. "And here I thought he was just a good listener."

Cadie sat down next to him and watched a pair of cardinals fluttering from the scrub pines to the birdfeeder.

That evening, Levi and Emma caught the last ferry back to Nantucket, but by the time they got to the house, Liam was the only one still awake. "Your mom tried to stay up," he said, meeting them on the porch.

"That's okay," Levi replied, shaking his head. "We tried to catch an earlier ferry, but there wasn't room for the car."

Liam nodded and then turned to the pretty young woman standing next to him. "You must be Emma," he said with a smile.

Emma smiled back, revealing a dimple in one cheek. "I am . . . and you must be Mr. Tate," she said, extending her hand. "I'm so pleased to meet Levi's dad!"

Liam was immediately enchanted. "I'm pleased to meet you, too, but please call me Liam. I don't think anyone's ever called me Mr. Tate before!"

"Very well," she said with a grin. "*Liam* it is."

They chatted quietly for a few minutes and Liam confirmed that, if Cadie felt well enough the next day, the boat was ready.

Chapter 38

"I can't believe you still have her!" Cadie exclaimed when she saw the old Chris-Craft tied to the dock. She looked at Levi, on whose arm she was leaning. "This is the boat I told you about—the one your dad restored when he was in high school."

"I know, Mom," Levi said, smiling at his mom's enthusiasm. "She's beautiful."

Liam came up on her other side. "Soo . . . what do you think? Should we take her for a ride?"

"Really?!" Cadie asked.

"Really," Liam said with a nod.

"I . . . I don't know," she answered uncertainly. "I don't want to ruin everyone's fun."

"You won't ruin anyone's fun," Liam assured her. "C'mon," he said, taking her other arm.

"C'mon, Mom!" Aidan called from the dock. "C'mon, Emma!"

"We're coming, Aid," Emma called back as she carried one of the coolers and the beach bag down to the dock and set them in the back of the boat.

"Don't forget your life jacket," Liam called, pointing to a small vest lying on the dock.

Aidan slipped it on, then stood still so Emma could help him with the buckles while Liam and Levi helped Cadie—who was all bundled up in a hooded sweatshirt and sweatpants, and her pink hat—into the front seat. Then, Levi climbed in back with Emma and Aidan, and Liam untied the lines and climbed in next to Cadie. "You okay?" he asked.

"Fine," she said, feeling a nervous twinge in her stomach.

"Do you want a blanket?"

She nodded and Liam unfolded one of the blankets and gently wrapped it around her. "How's that?"

"Good," she said with a nod, and he smiled, hoping she was still strong enough to make the trip . . . and hoping he wasn't asking too much.

The day before yesterday, after John left, he'd set to work, getting the boat ready. He'd cleaned a mouse nest out of the engine, drained out the old fuel, filled the tank with fresh gas, checked the fluids, battery, and plugs, and then towed Coop's old, wooden skiff and an anchor out across the waves and been happily surprised to discover how smoothly she ran.

That morning, he'd packed sandwiches and Cadie's pain meds in one cooler and drinks in the other; set out folding chairs, filled the beach bag with extra clothes and blankets, and made sure there were enough life jackets on board for everyone; finally, he'd clicked on his marine radio, pressed in the button on the handheld mic, and made a radio check to his friend Nate who had an old Gar Wood called *Exodus* docked in a nearby marina—and even though he hadn't said his Coast Guard registration number in over twenty years, it spilled from his lips as if he'd used it just yesterday. "This is Tuckernuck II-Whiskey-Zulu-Victor-Five-Six-Niner-Five calling *Exodus*, over?"

"This is *Exodus*," Nate had responded immediately. "Holy shit, man! Have you got 'er in the water?!"

"I do!" Liam had responded with a grin.

Liam pushed the starter and the faithful, old runabout rumbled to life, her Yacht Ensign snapping in the wind, and as he pulled away from the island, he looked over at Cadie. She smiled, her face glowing in the sunlight . . . and in that one precious moment, with the cool wind rushing all around her, she forgot about having cancer . . . and simply enjoyed being alive!

Fifteen minutes later, as they neared Tuckernuck Island, Liam eased back on the throttle and waved to a little girl who was standing on the shore.

Cadie waved too. "It hasn't changed," she murmured softly, gazing at the sandy landscape and the long grass, swaying in the summer sun.

"Some things never change," Liam said as he guided the boat up alongside the skiff.

Transferring everyone and everything from the runabout to the skiff was a bit of a challenge, but they managed to pull it off without falling in, and then Liam rowed to shore. "Are you sure you don't want me to row?" Cadie teased.

Liam shook his head. "Not this time."

When they reached the beach, Levi hopped out, pulled the skiff up onto the shore, and helped Emma and Aidan out. Then he and Levi stood on either side of Cadie. "I can do it," Cadie said. "I'm not an invalid . . . *yet*." She steadied herself by holding on to the side of the boat, slipped off her sandals, pulled her sweatpants up above her knees, and started to walk slowly along the water's edge. Liam and Levi watched protectively and then looked at each other with raised eyebrows, each thinking the same thing—*she* must *be feeling okay!*

Five minutes later, after spreading blankets and setting up chairs, Liam looked over to where Cadie was standing near the water's edge. "I guess there's no time like the present," he murmured with an anxious smile.

Levi grinned, knowing what Liam had in mind. "Go for it!" he said.

As Liam walked toward her, Aidan called after him, "Can I come?" but Liam—whose heart was pounding—didn't seem to hear him.

"No, you stay here, Aid," Levi said, reaching into the beach bag for the Frisbee. "Here, catch," he said, waiting for him to look back.

"All right!" Aidan said, a huge smile spreading across his face as he held out his hands. "Emma, want to play?!"

"Sure, Aid, just let me put on my sunscreen."

Levi gently tossed the Frisbee to Aidan, and while his little brother hurried after it, he looked down the beach and watched his dad put his arm around his mom's shoulders.

"Do you feel up to taking a walk?" Liam asked.

"To the love shack?" Cadie teased.

Liam looked puzzled. "Love shack?"

"Don't you remember what a hit 'Love Shack' was that summer?"

"I remember the song, but I don't think I realized it was from that summer."

Cadie laughed. "I did . . . and whenever I heard it, I thought of your cottage."

"Is that why you have it on your phone?"

Cadie laughed. "It *is*—it always makes me smile."

They walked slowly along the beach. "Let me know if you think we should turn around," Liam said, pulling her closer. "I don't want to overdo it."

"I will," Cadie said, looking up at him. "Liam, I can't thank you enough for *doing* all this—every day, you do more . . . and I still can't believe you're willing to adopt Aidan."

"Why can't you believe it?"

"I don't know. I guess because you have your life and your work . . . and you're used to being on your own."

"I've only been on my own for a couple of years. Before that, Coop was still alive . . . *and* I can't really say that I've liked being alone. It's just the way it worked out. Besides," he said, "having Aidan will be like having part of *you* with me."

Cadie smiled sadly. "I'm praying it works out. Aidan will have a great time growing up here . . . with Tuck by his side too."

"Levi said Aidan's father gave up parental rights when you got divorced—is that true?"

Cadie nodded. "Yes, and we haven't seen him since—I heard he moved to an island in the Caribbean, so I wouldn't worry about him coming back into the picture."

"Well, that's good. John was concerned he might throw a wrench into the whole thing." Liam stopped walking. "I think the gate is along here somewhere," he said, pulling back some branches. "Here it is." They carefully stepped over limbs and bushes and stood in what once had been the front yard. Liam looked up and softly swore as Cadie whispered, "Oh, my goodness!" The wild rosebush they'd stepped under years earlier had grown so much that it now covered the entire house in a blanket of pink blossoms.

"I've never seen such a huge rosebush!"

"I know . . . and I can only wonder what it's doing to the siding and the roof!"

Cadie pulled her phone out of her pocket, tapped the camera icon, and aimed it at the house.

Liam frowned. "What are you doing?"

"Taking a picture."

"Your phone takes pictures?!"

Cadie nodded as she tried to fit the whole cottage into the photo.

"Here," Liam said, "why don't you stand in front of the cottage and *I'll* take the picture."

Cadie frowned. "I don't think I want to be in the picture."

"Why? You look cute."

Cadie rolled her eyes. "I don't know about that," she said, but then she showed him which button to tap and reluctantly walked over to stand in front of the tremendous rosebush.

"Ready?" Liam asked, and when Cadie mustered a smile, he tapped the button. "Is there a way to see how it came out?"

Cadie walked over and tapped the tiny image in the corner and the picture filled the screen. "Hey, that looks great," he said happily. "Look how your hat matches the roses!"

Cadie rolled her eyes again—she couldn't believe he thought she looked "cute" or that the picture had turned out "great." "I think you need your eyes checked," she said good-naturedly.

"What? Why?" he said, putting his arm around her. Then he looked up at the house. "Let's see if we can find a way in."

They picked their way gingerly through the overgrown yard, and although the back of the house had just as many roses creeping over it, the door was visible. "Whoever owns this place has a terrible caretaker," Cadie teased.

"I know—he should be fired!" Liam said, and as he jiggled the door, a pane of glass fell out and smashed on the granite steps. "Well, that's convenient," he said, reaching in and turning the knob. The door creaked open and as Cadie followed him inside, they heard scurrying paws.

"I think someone lives in here," Cadie whispered, and a moment later, a skinny orange tiger cat scooted out the door. "Oh!" she said, putting her hand on her chest. "How'd she get in here?!"

"Looks like she might've come through a window," Liam said, pointing to a second broken pane.

They looked around the room. "I guess it still needs work,"

Liam said with a smile. "But I bet it would make a great studio—what do you think?"

Cadie looked puzzled. "An artist's stu . . . do you mean for Levi?!"

Liam nodded.

"Wow! He'd love it—why didn't you ask him to come?"

Liam shrugged. "Because I wanted to come here with you . . . besides, I just thought of it. I'm probably never going to live here, but I don't want to let it go either . . . so maybe we can fix it up and turn it into a studio."

"That would be wonderful."

Liam shook his head. "It's the least I can do . . . for *my son*," he added with a grin.

Cadie smiled and looked around. "Why did you want to come here with just me?"

Liam bit his lip and felt his heart pound. Then he took a deep breath. "Because . . . I wanted to ask you something."

She gave him a puzzled look. "What?"

Liam reached into his pocket, pulled out a small velvet box, swallowed nervously, and slowly knelt down on one knee. "I already have Levi's permission—I figured he was the one to ask . . ."

Tears filled Cadie's eyes as she looked down at Liam's handsome, tan face and gorgeous ocean blue eyes.

"Cadie, will you marry me?"

She shook her head slowly. "You want to marry me *now?*" she whispered in disbelief.

Liam pressed his lips together and nodded.

"Oh, Liam, you're making the dream I've had in my heart my whole life come true. Yes, of course I'll marry you!"

Liam smiled, stood up, and slipped the ring on her finger. Then he wrapped his arms around her and, lifting her off the ground, gently kissed her lips. "I love you so much," he whispered.

"And I love *you*," she murmured.

As Liam set her down, he felt her flinch. "Are you okay?"

She nodded, mustering a smile, and then held her hand up to admire the ring. "It's beautiful!"

Liam looked at it too. "I guess we need to have it sized," he said, realizing how loose it was on her thin finger.

She nodded. "Maybe you should hang on to it until we do. I don't want to lose it."

Liam searched her eyes and shook his head. "No, I want you to wear it. We'll take care of it tomorrow."

He kissed her again and held her for a long time. Then they looked around one last time, closed up the little cottage, and walked slowly back to the beach. As they drew near, Levi saw them coming. "Well?!"

Liam grinned. "You're finally going to be legitimate!"

Chapter 39

As they pulled back up to the boathouse, the sky was on fire with gloriously pink and orange hues streaking across the sky. Cadie turned to Levi. "God has his paintbrush out," she said with a weak smile.

Levi nodded. "I know! He puts the rest of us artists to shame!"

Liam hopped out and quickly tied the lines. Then he reached out and took Aidan, who was half asleep, from Levi's outstretched arms and set him on the dock. "Don't fall in," he warned, steadying him. Levi handed Liam the coolers and bags, and helped Emma and Cadie out too. "I had a feeling this trip might be too much," Liam said as Cadie leaned on him. "We probably should've headed home a lot sooner."

"It wasn't too much," she insisted.

"Mmm," Liam murmured doubtfully.

"Besides, I loved every minute," she said, squeezing his hand, "and at this point, that's all that matters."

"Are you cold?" he asked, helping her to the truck.

"A little."

He turned the truck on and clicked the heat to low. "I can't believe I'm turning the heat on in August!"

"It might be August, but it feels like September."

"Will you be okay while I bring in the boat?"

Cadie nodded. "I'm fine . . . just tired."

"Okay, I'll be right back."

As Cadie watched Liam hurry back down the boat launch, she rubbed her abdomen, tears filling her eyes.

Levi and Emma loaded the coolers, beach bags, and chairs into his car, and Liam started to open the boathouse, but then he remembered the railcar was already occupied by John Alden's sailboat. He swore, not wanting to take the time to load the boat onto the trailer, so he just locked the doors again.

"How is she?" Levi asked as he walked by with the last of their gear.

"She *says* she's fine, but she always says that."

"Well, we're going to pick up the pizza. Do you want us to take Aidan?"

"No, he can go with us."

"Okay, we'll see you back at the house."

"All right," Liam said, hurrying down the ramp to make sure the boat was secure. "C'mon, Aid," he called, and Aidan threw the stones he had in his hand into the water and hurried after him.

As Liam approached the truck, he realized he couldn't see Cadie, and when he opened the door, he found her lying across the seat. "Cade, what's the matter?"

She moaned softly and Liam looked around the parking lot to see if Levi was still there, but his car was gone. "Can you sit up?" he asked, but she didn't answer.

"Is she dying?" Aidan asked, anxious tears welling up in his eyes.

"No, she just needs her pain medicine and it's in the"—he looked in the back of the truck—"cooler . . . which is in the damn car!"

"Okay, Cadie, you've got to move over," he said, lifting up her head and edging behind the wheel. "Aid, climb up here."

Aidan climbed up awkwardly and Liam closed the door, wondering what seatbelt law he was breaking as he spun the tires and pulled out of the parking lot. "Damn, it's hot in here!" he mumbled, rolling down the window, and then he remembered why it *was* hot and rolled it up again. For a brief second, he considered trying to find Levi and Emma, but then he thought better of it—there were at least five pizza places on Nantucket and they were all in opposite directions of the house . . . besides, there was probably another bottle of pain medicine at home.

"Is she going to be okay?" Aidan asked worriedly, as he watched his mom clutching her stomach.

"She'll be okay, pal. She just has a tummy ache," Liam consoled, trying to remember the last time he'd seen her take anything. He knew she hated taking the pain meds because they made her drowsy, but he also knew she needed to stay ahead of the pain, or it ran her over like a locomotive.

Ten minutes later, they pulled into the driveway, and after he'd lifted Aidan down, he gently gathered Cadie's featherlight body into his arms. She whimpered, but he whispered, "I'm sorry, Cade, but I have to carry you inside."

"It's okay, Mommy," Aidan said, trailing along behind them.

When Liam opened the door, Tuck bounded out happily. "Go get busy, Tuck," he commanded, letting the door slam behind them, but Tuck, hearing Cadie crying, just stared through the screen and watched as they disappeared down the hall. He barked, wanting to be let back in, but no one came.

Liam laid her on the bed and she pulled her knees up to her chest and lay still. He pulled the blanket up over her and hurried into the bathroom to scan the pill bottles—there were two empty oxycodone bottles and a full bottle of something called Roxanol. He studied the label uncertainly, trying to figure what it was . . . and then he saw the word morphine. Had she taken morphine before? He didn't want to give her something she'd never taken because he didn't know how she'd react, but he had to give her *something* . . . and what the hell was taking Levi so long?!

In the next room, he heard her cry out and then he heard Aidan softly telling her it was okay. His heart pounded. What had he been thinking, taking her out all day?! He obviously knew nothing about caring for someone who was dying! Nothing! You certainly don't take a dying person on an all-day joy ride, and you definitely need to be better educated about their medicine. What had the hospice nurse said about morphine? Was it slow release or would it help right away? He couldn't remember. Cadie cried out again and Liam swore again. "I'm just giving it to her," he said, filling a cup with water.

He sat on the bed and coaxed her to sit up. She turned her head and he slipped a pill in her mouth; then he got her to take a sip of water. "Did it go down?" he asked. She nodded and lay back on the pillow.

"Is she dying?" Aidan asked again in a trembling voice, his eyes full of tears.

Liam looked up, searched the little boy's eyes, and pulled him onto his lap. "Oh, pal," he said softly. "Everybody dies sometime . . . but your mom isn't dying tonight. She's too much of a fighter."

Aidan nodded. "I don't want her to die . . . *ever.*"

"I don't want her to die ever either," Liam whispered into

his wispy hair. They sat there for a long time, holding on to the hope that she wouldn't die . . . *ever,* and then Tuck, who was still waiting outside, barked, and Aidan looked up. "I think he wants to come in."

"I think he does too," Liam said with a half smile.

Chapter 40

Lisa was there first thing the next morning, and while she helped Cadie bathe and put on fresh pajamas, Liam changed her sheets. Then they both helped her back to bed. Although the pain was finally under control, and the bath, fresh linens, and pajamas felt wonderful, Cadie was still exhausted and drifted off as soon as her head hit the pillow.

Lisa looked up at Liam and smiled. "She showed me her ring—it's beautiful!"

"Yes, well, we did too much yesterday," he said, regretfully. "This is all my fault."

Lisa put her hand on his arm. "No, don't blame yourself—you're doing the best you can in very difficult circumstances. I know you want to make every day count . . . *and* every moment last, but you have to allow some downtime . . . for *both* of you."

"I know. I just wanted to do it before . . . before it was too late."

"I completely understand—trust me! And you're right—she's going to start to lose the little strength she has left, and you and Levi are going to have to be very diligent about making sure she's not in pain. If you don't think you can manage it, you need to let me know."

Liam shook his head. "We can do it."

"Do you have any more questions about her meds?"

"No, I think I've got it now."

Lisa nodded as she jotted something on a slip of paper and handed it to him. "This is my cell phone number. You can call me anytime—day or night."

Liam nodded. "There are some other things Cadie and I need to take care of . . ."

Lisa smiled. "Give her a couple days and get her to eat. She's not giving up yet."

"Thanks, Lisa."

"You're a good guy, Liam—she's lucky to have you, but you need to get some rest. Promise me you'll let Levi take a shift, so you can take a nap."

"I promise," Liam said with a weary smile.

After she'd left, Liam looked in on Cadie and realized Tuck was lying beside her. "I just changed those sheets, mister," he scolded softly, but Tuck just gave him a sad look. Liam shook his head and wondered if dogs could tell when someone was dying. He went back into the kitchen, poured a cup of coffee, and sank into a chair. He knew their situation wasn't unique— there were people all around the world who were, at that very moment, keeping watch at the bedsides of loved ones who were dying. Somehow, though, that realization was little consolation— he still felt as if they were in a broken-down boat alone . . . on stormy seas without a paddle! He looked down and realized Cadie's Bible was on the table. He pulled it toward him and looked at it—it was open to Psalm 42—and as he slowly read the words, he was filled with an overwhelming sense of peace. *This is what Cadie has been talking about,* he thought. *This is what I've been missing.* He turned the page and continued to read.

A half an hour later, he closed the Bible and gazed out the window. Then he reached into his wallet, pulled out John Alden's card, and dialed. It rang once before going straight to voice mail. Liam cleared his throat. "Hey, John. It's Liam. I was wondering if you might have time to meet with me this afternoon . . ." He paused. "It's kind of urgent."

As he hung up the phone, he heard car doors slamming. He went out on the porch and saw Levi and Emma, with their arms full of grocery bags, making their way toward him. Aidan's arms were full, too, but his were wrapped around a pot with a tremendous white lily in it. "This is Mona," he said matter-of-factly. "She's for my mom."

Levi chuckled and shook his head. "He means it's a Mona Lisa lily. He and Emma picked it out."

"Is there more?" Liam asked, coming down the steps.

"No, this is it," Emma said, handing him a bag.

They set everything on the counter and Liam surveyed the pile. "I don't think you bought enough food!"

"Emma's going to help out with the cooking. She claims it's easier to plan a week-long menu than to try to figure out one day at a time." He grinned. "Who knew?!"

Emma shook her head. "No offense, but men just don't know how to plan ahead—at least when it comes to meals. My mum always says, 'Men get hungry and go to the store to buy something to satisfy their immediate hunger, but it never occurs to them that maybe, while they're there, they should buy something for the next day too. It simply doesn't occur to them that they're going to get hungry again!' *And* my mum's right— my brothers and dad are the same way."

Liam and Levi looked at each other and smiled—it was definitely going to be nice to have a home-cooked meal!

"How's Mom?" Levi asked as he emptied the bags.

"Lisa was here and she helped her in the bathroom and I changed the sheets. Then we went over the meds again." He looked at the clock. "She took a pain pill at ten, so she can have another after two, but she said the morphine might make her even drowsier—everyone reacts differently, so we'll have to see . . . maybe she'll be *less* drowsy. Anyway, will you guys be okay if I go run a few errands?"

"We'll be fine," Levi said, unplugging Cadie's phone from its charger. "Take this with you, though, so I can reach you."

Liam took the phone and slipped it in his pocket. "Oh! I'm expecting a call from the attorney—his name is John Alden. If he calls, can you give him this number?"

Levi nodded. "Do you think you might have time to swing by the elementary school?"

Liam frowned. "Why?"

"Because it's almost Labor Day and everybody's already out buying school supplies . . . and if Aidan's going to go to school out here, he needs to be registered."

Liam opened the fridge and pulled out the leftover pizza from the night before. "I'm also going to the town hall to find out what we need to get a marriage certificate." He pried a piece of cold pizza off the top of the pile. "You guys should have this for lunch," he said, motioning to the plate, and as he pushed open the screen door, he took a big bite. "See you in a bit."

A moment later, he came back in. "What grade?" he asked with his mouth full of pizza.

"Second!" Aidan chimed.

Chapter 41

Liam was standing in the quiet Nantucket Elementary School office, filling out the registration paperwork, when the B-52's broke into song. He looked up, startled, remembered the phone, and reached into his pocket. "I'm never going to get used to carrying this phone," he muttered; then he noticed that the two secretaries were looking at each other and smiling.

He stepped out into the hall to take the call and returned a moment later. "I think I'm going to have to take this stuff home," he said. "There are some things I'm not sure about."

"That's fine," one of the secretaries replied, getting up and walking over to the counter. "Here's a school handbook and a schedule of upcoming events. Will your son be taking the bus?"

"I'm not sure," Liam said, startled by the weighty responsibility inferred by the words *your son.*

"Okay, well, you can let us know. School starts Tuesday— the day after Labor Day, but there's an open house on Friday."

"This Friday?!" Liam asked, looking perplexed. "Labor Day is *next* weekend?"

The secretary nodded, wondering how a grown man could not know this.

Liam saw the look on her face and quickly recovered. "I mean, I can't believe summer is over, can you?"

"No, I can't," she said glumly. "Anyway, when you bring in your son, he'll be able to see his classroom and meet his teacher, Mrs. Polley—she's a real sweetheart."

Flustered by the entire conversation, Liam gathered up the papers. "Thank you," he said, smiling. "Oh," he said, holding up the phone, "this is my wife's."

The secretary smiled. "If you say so . . ."

Ten minutes later, Liam was standing in the town clerk's office. "Hey, Liam," the town clerk's secretary said, looking up from her desk. "What can I do for you?"

"Hey, Luce," Liam said, looking hopefully past his old high-school classmate into the dark office behind her. "Is Tom here?"

"No, he's on vacation. Can I help you?"

Liam inwardly groaned—Lucy Reynolds was the biggest gossip on the face of the earth, and if he asked her about a marriage license, everyone on the island would know about it before he even got home. He looked around to see if there might be a pamphlet lying on the counter.

"Are you looking for something specific?" Lucy asked. "Voter registration? Dog license—did you get Tucket his new license? Because if you didn't, I'm afraid there's a late fee . . ."

"No," he said, shaking his head. "I hate politics and Tuck is up to date. What I need is . . ." He paused and took a deep breath. ". . . information about getting a marriage license."

"Ahh . . ." Lucy said, smiling knowingly as she stood up. "Are we ready to take the plunge?"

Liam groaned inwardly again. *How can she smile like that when she's never even been married?* "I'd just like to know how one goes about it," Liam said, attempting nonchalance.

"Well," Lucy began, sensing his desire for discretion, "the couple—whoever they may be—must appear in person and apply for the license, and they must bring in picture IDs. Then, there's a three-day waiting period, and after that, they're free to wed."

"That's it?!" Liam said in surprise.

"That's it," Lucy confirmed.

"Do you have an application?"

"Right here," Lucy said, reaching under the counter.

Liam quickly looked it over. "Do you happen to know if there's a justice of the peace on the island?"

Lucy brought her hand to her chin. "Hmm . . . well, Tom is—but as I said, he's on vacation . . . but I think Sally Adams is . . ."

"Sally is a justice of the peace?!"

"Well, she used to be . . . whether she stayed current, I'm not sure, but I can probably look it up. . . ." she said, opening a drawer.

"No, that's okay," Liam said as he headed for the door. "Thanks."

Lucy looked up in surprise as the door closed. "You're welcome," she called back; then she hurried back to her desk, sat her wide bottom back in her chair, and picked up her phone. "Guess who was just in here asking questions about a marriage license!"

After a quick stop at the jeweler's to drop off Cadie's ring, Liam pulled in to the boathouse parking lot and realized John was already there. He got out, looked around, and saw him standing on the dock. "Hey," he said, walking down the ramp. "Sorry I'm late."

"You're not late," John said, looking at his watch. "I'm early, for a change."

Liam unlocked the boathouse and turned on the lights. "C'mon in," he said.

John followed him back to the tidy desk that had once been Cooper's and then glanced over into the workshop and saw *Pride & Joy* cradled on the rail car. "Hey, you *did* start working on it! I didn't think you had." He walked over to survey the broken planks lined up on the floor.

"I did," Liam said, standing next to him, "but I didn't get very far."

"That's okay," John said. "I know how it is when life throws you a curve."

Liam chuckled and shook his head. "I think life's actually throwing a no-hitter at the moment."

John nodded, sitting down across from him. "So what have you decided?"

Liam reached into his shirt. "I brought the letter from Cadie's father's attorney."

John looked it over. "I know Frank Collins—he has a high-powered office in New York, but since Cadie lives in Massachusetts, the case will be decided here. Anyway, are you willing to try for custody and does Cadie agree?"

"Yes, I'm willing, and Cadie loves the idea."

"Okay, then the first step—which we should take right away—is to draw up a will. Do you know if she has one?"

"I don't," Liam said regretfully.

"It doesn't matter," John assured him. "A new one will override any previous documents, and the one I draw up will be simple and straightforward—it will not only take care of any possessions, but it will also, more importantly, state her wishes regarding legal guardianship for her son. It's not complicated. She just designates the person or persons she hopes will be willing to raise him. She can name you first and Levi second. Under normal circumstances—when there aren't any challengers—a document like that would be sufficient, but since we already know her father is going to challenge it, we have to be ready . . . and then there's the boy's father."

"From what I gather, he's given up all rights and has no interest in Aidan."

"That may be, but Cadie's father might reach out to him and offer to pay him to *show* interest and then later take the boy off his hands—you never know to what lengths people will go. We have to be ready for anything."

"You're right about that—I'm sure there's nothing that's below him," Liam said.

John nodded. "Unfortunately, the world is full of people like that." He paused. "Did you happen to bring that paper?"

Liam nodded and handed him the form Cadie had filled out with all of her pertinent information. "Great, I'll get right to work on the will, and when it's ready, I'll stop by so she can sign it." He tapped his pen on the paper. "Let's see," he murmured, "is there anything else?" He paused. "You should also know you don't have to wait to start the adoption process. Do you have a computer?"

Liam shook his head and John chuckled. "*Why* am I not surprised? Well, it doesn't matter. I'll brink the appropriate paperwork when I stop by," he said, jotting a note on Cadie's form. "I guess that's it," he added, scanning the paper. Then he looked up and smiled. "If you're going to raise a child in this day and age, you should probably get a computer. Everything from signing up for swimming lessons to applying to colleges is online these days." Liam nodded, but John could see he wasn't convinced. "I probably have an old one you could have."

"Thanks," Liam said, "but I think I'll wait to see if I really will be raising a child." He paused. "By the way, I asked Cadie to marry me."

"You did?! What'd she say?"

"Yes," he said with a grin, "and now, Levi wants to change his name. Maybe later, you could help us with that too."

"That's easy," John said, smiling. "People change their names all the time." Then he frowned. "But hasn't he been working on establishing himself as an artist? Won't it set him back to not keep the name people are just beginning to recognize?"

"I asked him the same question, but he said he doesn't care."

John nodded. "So when's the wedding?"

"After we apply for the license, there's a three-day waiting period . . . so if we go tomorrow, we'll have it by Friday."

"That just might help your case too," John said thoughtfully. "If you're married to Cadie and adopting Aidan, it will show the court you're truly committed. By the way, is Aidan starting school here?"

"Yes, I was just there filling out the paperwork."

"Perfect. That'll help too," John said. "The court won't want to uproot him if he's settled in and doing well." He stood up. "I guess that's it for now, Liam. If we run into any obstacles I have an old classmate who's a judge . . . *and* she has a place on the Vineyard," he added with a smile. "By the way, how's Cadie doing?"

"She's hanging in there. I wore her out yesterday so she's recovering today. But she's so amazing—no matter how bad it gets, she just keeps smiling."

"My mom died of cancer," John said with a nod, "and she always kept up a good front. It takes a special person to face the end of life with a smile on their face. Not everyone can do it. If it were me, I'd be miserable and no one would want to be around me."

Liam followed him to the door. "I can't thank you enough, John," he said, extending his hand.

John nodded. "Please tell Cadie I'm looking forward to meeting the woman who stole the heart of Nantucket's most eligible bachelor. And tell her not to worry."

"I will," Liam said, and as he watched John pull away, he regretted that he'd never taken the time to get to know him. He'd always thought of him as just another customer with too much money, but he was wrong—John was kind and willing to help . . . *and* he'd had a mom who'd smiled in the face of death. A person who'd been raised by a woman like that couldn't be half-bad. Maybe *he* was the one with the attitude . . . and maybe *he* shouldn't assume so much!

Liam's last stop was Cuppa Jo to Go. "Hey, Liam!" Sally said when he walked in. "I heard the big news," she said as she wiped down the counters.

"Are you kidding?!" Liam said, shaking his head.

"Word travels fast."

"Who told you?"

"Chase . . . or maybe it was Devon—I can never keep their names straight . . . but they're taking all the credit."

He shook his head again. "It's that damn Lucy Reynolds—she shouldn't be allowed to work in the town hall—she's got her nose in everybody's business."

"People were bound to find out," Sally consoled as she emptied coffeepots and cleaned around them.

"Hold on," Liam said, reaching for the last pot. "I'll have some of that, even though what I could really use is a good, stiff drink."

"I have some beer in back," Sally offered.

"You do?!"

She nodded.

"You want one?" he asked, walking behind the counter to help himself.

"Sure," she said, looking up at the clock as she locked the front door.

He opened two bottles and she sat down across from him at one of the tables.

"Congratulations!" she said, tapping her bottle against his.

"Thanks," he said, taking a sip.

"She must mean a lot to you."

"She does. We never had the chance to be together."

Sally nodded. "I remember Coop talking about you two. His heart broke when he saw how crushed you were."

"It did?"

She nodded. "He never let on, but he was a pretty romantic fella."

"Noo," Liam said with a teasing smile.

"Mm-hmm," Sally said, taking a sip of her beer.

"Well, sometime you're going to have to tell me how you know that."

"Mm . . . maybe," Sally teased.

"Anyway, before Lucy got on her speed dial, she said you were a justice of the peace . . . are you still?"

"I *am*," Sally said.

He smiled. "What are you doin' Friday night?"

"Having wedding cake at your house," she said with a laugh.

Chapter 42

The following morning, Lisa stopped by with a wheelchair and a dozen cider doughnuts. Cadie reached into the box, pulled one out, and took a bite. "Oh, my, I think I've died and gone to heaven," she said with a sugary grin.

"I thought I might get you to eat one of those," Lisa said with a smile. "I worked at Downyflake when I was in high school, and I definitely ate more than my share of their famous doughnuts," she added, rubbing her stomach. "I was one of the few freshmen who *lost* fifteen pounds when I went away to college."

Liam surveyed the offerings in the box, and then, smiling at Aidan, recited, "As you ramble on through life, brother, whatever be your goal; keep your eye upon the donut . . . and not upon the hole!"

Aidan laughed. "I'm keeping my eye on this one," he said, taking a huge bite. "Mmm . . . I think I've died and gone to heaven, too, Mommy!"

"They are yummy," Cadie said, discreetly breaking off half and putting it back. "Thanks, Lis!"

"You're welcome. I'm glad you're feeling better. I also thought you could use a wheelchair—in case your fiancé decides to take you on any more adventures."

"Our next adventure is to the jeweler's and then to the town hall," Liam said.

"Well, have fun and don't do too much."

"Don't worry," Liam said. "I learned my lesson."

As Lisa gathered up her things, Emma and Levi came in from taking Tuck for a walk. "Hello," she said as Tuck bounded across the room to say hello, but halfway there, he skidded to a halt, lifted his nose into the air, followed the lovely new scent over to the doughnut in Cadie's hand, sank to his haunches, and gazed at her.

"Oh, my goodness," Lisa said with a laugh. "What a beggar!"

"You've got that right," Liam said. "He definitely knows how to use those sad brown eyes."

Lisa shook her head. "I've got one just like him," she said, pushing open the door.

After she'd gone, and Cadie had given her last morsel to Tuck, Levi and Emma split a doughnut . . . and then they split another. "Wow!" Levi said. "I'm going to have to move here just so I can have these doughnuts every day."

Liam chuckled. "Don't let Sally hear you say that!" Then he turned to Cadie. "Are you ready to head out?"

"Yes, I just need to use the loo and take a pain pill. We won't be gone longer than four hours, will we?"

"No, but bring the bottle just in case," Liam said as he went outside to put the wheelchair in the back of the truck. "And your driver's license!" he called over his shoulder.

After stopping at the jeweler's—where Cadie slipped on her newly sized, sparkling, pear-shaped diamond—they headed to the town hall. "The secretary is a real busybody," Liam warned as he helped Cadie into the chair.

"That's okay," she said with a smile "I hope she tells the whole world we're getting married!"

Liam chuckled—how come he hadn't thought about it that way? How come his biggest concern was keeping his business private and not letting the world in? "I wish you'd stick around a little longer," he said with a smile. "I still have a lot to learn!"

"You're learning already," Cadie teased. "Look at the limb you're walking on!"

"You're not kidding," he said.

When he wheeled Cadie into the office, Lucy was on the phone, but when she saw Liam standing at the counter, she quickly got off. "Hi, Liam, what can I do for you?"

"I'd like to apply for a marriage license."

Lucy frowned. "I must've forgotten to tell you that you *both* have to appear. . . ."

"We *are* both here."

"You are?" Lucy said in surprise, standing up and walking to the counter. "Oh!" she said, seeing the frail, petite woman wearing a pink Red Sox cap sitting in the wheelchair. "I'm sorry—I didn't see you."

Liam handed the application and their driver's licenses to her, and Lucy made copies and told Liam he could pick up the license on Friday. "Does Cadie need to come?" he asked.

Lucy shook her head as her mind raced with questions.

"Okay, thanks," Liam said, turning the wheelchair around while a stunned Lucy watched them go.

"Did you see the look on her face?" Cadie said, grinning. "Do I really look *that* bad?"

"I *did* see the look on her face—it was priceless . . . and no, you don't," Liam assured. "You look beautiful. I especially like your new hat."

"Thanks," she said, "my sons got it for me."

"I know," he replied as he helped her into the truck. "You have some fine sons."

"I do," she said.

Liam walked around to the driver's side of the truck. "Do you feel like getting a bite to eat?" he asked.

Cadie looked out the window, wishing she had the strength to celebrate. "I better not," she said, mustering a smile.

"That's fine," Liam said. "It was just a thought."

"You must be hungry, though . . ." she said. "Why don't you pick something up?" She paused. "You know what would be good?"

"What?" Liam asked curiously.

"A milkshake," Cadie said, her eyes sparkling. "I love chocolate milkshakes . . . and I'd like to have one last—"

"You've got it," Liam interrupted, not wanting to hear the rest of her sentence. "The best place for shakes is the pharmacy . . . and we have to go there anyway to pick up a prescription."

"Perfect," Cadie said, leaning back in her seat.

While Liam went into the pharmacy, Cadie gazed out the window at all the vacationers who were making the most of the last full week of summer. Other than her boat trip two days earlier, she hadn't been out in the world in almost two weeks. During that time, people had gone to the movies and to dinner; they'd gone to the beach and shopped for T-shirts; they'd wandered through galleries and bookstores; *and* they'd continue to do all those things *after* she was gone. The thought was so hard to take.

"Do you ever try to wrap your mind around the concept of *eternity?*" Cadie asked as they sat in a quiet beach parking lot, sipping their shakes.

"Hmm?" Liam asked uncertainly as he swallowed.

"You know—*infinity and beyond . . .*" Cadie said, gesturing heavenward. "Eternity . . . the endless time that happens after you leave this earth."

Liam shook his head. "I try not to think about it."

"It's really hard to imagine the sun shining and the stars sparkling, the moon glowing, the birds singing, the crickets and cicadas chirping and buzzing, and all the other precious things that make up this wonderful life . . . still happening after you're gone. It seems like they should stop too."

Liam looked over. "This conversation is pretty depressing. . . ."

Cadie smiled sadly. "I'm sorry. It's just . . . it's all I think about lately."

"I thought you had an unwavering faith," he said softly.

Cadie shrugged. "I don't know about unwavering. I do have a strong faith, but I still have doubts about God's plans—especially when they don't align with mine."

"I know what you mean," he said. "When my parents died, I couldn't understand what plan God could possibly have for my life—I couldn't understand why they had to die. But then you said I'd brought light to Coop's life, and that it wouldn't have happened if my parents had lived. I'd never thought about it that way before. I guess we *do* have to trust that there's a greater plan we don't always see." He paused and looked over. "And as far as eternity goes, I've heard it's much better in heaven. Jesus even has a room all set up for us when we get there," he said with a smile.

Cadie gave him a suspicious look. "Have you been reading my Bible?"

Liam grinned and took a sip of his milkshake.

Chapter 43

On Wednesday night, a fierce thunderstorm rumbled across Nantucket, leaving in its wake air so cool it prompted even the hardiest islanders to reach for their flannel.

"Sheesh!" Liam exclaimed as he stood on the porch in his boxers. "Let me know when you're done," he called, leaving Tuck squatting in the woods as he went back in to pull on jeans and a shirt. When he came back, Tuck was sitting on the porch, swishing his tail. "C'mon," he said, holding the door open. "You're certainly a lot happier than you were last night," he said as he poured kibble into Tuck's bowl. "You're so silly to let thunder bother you, you know that?" he said, and Tuck wagged his tail in agreement.

Liam set Tuck's bowl down next to Moby's untouched food, reminded Tuck not to touch it, and turned to the next order of business—coffee. "Where *is* Moby?" he wondered out loud, trying to remember the last time he'd seen him.

Just then, Aidan wandered into the kitchen. "Are there any doughnuts left?" he asked hopefully.

"There's *one* left," Liam said, holding up a ziplock bag.

"Do you think anyone wants it?"

Liam shook his head. "Nope, it has your name on it."

"It does?! Where?"

Liam laughed. "I don't mean that literally . . . I mean it figuratively."

Aidan frowned.

"That means it's for you." Liam said, putting it on a plate.

"Oh," Aidan said uncertainly.

"I'll explain it better after I have my coffee."

Aidan nodded and took a big bite as Tuck plopped down next to him.

"Tuck, leave Aidan alone," Liam scolded, nudging him with his foot. Then he noticed that both bowls were empty. "I told you not to eat Moby's food," he said sternly, and Tuck swished the tip of his tail guiltily, his eyes full of sad remorse.

Liam shook his head. "Aid, have you seen Moby?"

Aidan nodded. "Yesterday—he had something in his mouth."

"He did?"

"Mm-hmm . . . it was gray and furry. Levi buried it."

"Was it a mole?"

Aidan shrugged. "What's a mole look like?"

"It's a little bigger than a mouse and it has a funny nose."

"Does it have big feet?"

"Yes."

"It was a mole," Aidan said matter-of-factly.

Just then, the phone rang. "Hello?" Liam said, wondering who was calling so early. "Hey, John," he said. "Yes, ten should be fine . . . Thanks . . . See you then."

As he hung up, Emma shuffled in, pushing back her hair. "Mornin', loves," she murmured, reaching for a mug.

"Mornin'," Aidan replied.

"Coffee's not quite ready," Liam said, and she nodded as she sat down across from Aidan—still holding the mug in her hands. "You're awfully cheerful, mister . . ." she said, eyeing his sugary cheeks. "Wait a minute! Did you eat the *last* doughnut?!"

Aidan giggled as he swung his feet. "Mm-hmm. Liam said it had my name on it."

"Oh, no," Emma said, shaking her head. "It most definitely had *my* name on it."

"Mm-mm," Aidan said, shaking his head.

"Well, I'll need to see it then," she said.

"You can't see it," he giggled. "It's all chewed up in my stomach, and besides, there wasn't *really* a name on it—Liam meant it figure-tively."

"Did he now?" Emma said with a chuckle.

"Mm-hmm."

Liam listened to their exchange and smiled to himself. Cadie was right—Emma was so good with the boys, and she'd definitely be a comfort to them when they needed it most.

At around ten-thirty, Liam heard Tuck barking and looked out the window to see John Alden getting the official Tuck Tate greeting. "C'mon, Tuck," he called, and the big dog bounded up the porch steps.

"Hey, John," Liam said, shaking his hand. "Thanks for coming."

"No problem," John said. "You have a great place."

Liam nodded. "Coop bought it in the early seventies. It was pretty overgrown and run-down, but he worked on it tirelessly, clearing the property and creating the gardens, and then he spent years restoring and adding on to the cottage—it was a labor of love."

John looked around admiringly. "I'd love to find an old fixer-upper and retire to work on it . . . and leave the crazy legal world behind. Cooper did it right," he said enviously.

"He did," Liam agreed, surprised that a man of John's caste could be envious of the life of a lowly boatwright.

"Anyway," John said, holding up an official-looking folder. "I have Cadie's will and the adoption paperwork for Aidan. I took the liberty of filling out the basic information on the computer, just to make it easier. I hope that's okay."

"That's fine," Liam said, holding the door. "It's a little too chilly to sit outside."

"I know," John said as he stepped inside. "It feels like autumn."

Cadie was sitting at the table and John immediately walked over to shake her hand. "It's nice to meet you," he said, and even though Liam had explained their situation, her gaunt appearance reminded him of his mom and it caught him off guard.

"It's nice to meet you too. I can't thank you enough for helping us."

"I'm happy *to* help," John said with a genuine smile.

He sat down across from her and went through the will, explaining each part, including where it named Liam as Aidan's legal guardian.

"It's perfect," Cadie said.

"Good," John replied; then he looked up at Liam. "You said there'd be a couple of friends here who could serve as witnesses."

"Yes," Liam said, standing. "Emma and Devon are down on the beach. I'll get them."

Cadie watched him go and then turned to John. "I appreciate what Liam is trying to do," she said quietly, "but my father won't give up easily. Do you really think it'll work?"

"I think so," John assured her. "Liam has many things working in his favor, and it will definitely help that Aidan will be in school out here. The court will be reluctant to take him out of a situation in which he is thriving, especially so soon after losing his mother," he added gently.

Cadie nodded, finding it odd that her death could somehow be an advantage for her son. Just then, Emma and Devon came in and witnessed her signing the documents, and then signed them too.

That afternoon, Liam took Aidan shopping for school supplies—a venture that resulted in several moms looking up with surprise as the local boat builder shopped for sneakers and backpacks with a cute little blond-haired boy in tow. Liam noticed them looking and smiled as he ran his long brown fingers through his thick, sun-streaked hair, causing them to almost trip over their own children.

When they finally got home, it was nearly five o'clock and the savory stew Emma was making was already simmering. "Sorry," Liam said, putting the onion she'd asked for on the counter.

"No problem," Emma assured him. "I saved a little fat and I'll just brown it up and throw it in."

Liam lifted the top off Coop's old Crock-Pot and the rich aroma of simmering beef and vegetables drifted through the kitchen. "Mmm, it has been a long time since the kitchen smelled this good, hasn't it, Tuck?!" Liam said with a grin, and the big dog looked up at him and thumped his tail.

"Has he been underfoot all afternoon?"

"Noo," Emma said with a smile as she skillfully chopped the onion, "but he has been keeping an eye on my every move." She threw a hunk of fat into the hot skillet, slid it around with the knife, and added the onion. Immediately, the aroma of frying onion filled the room too.

"It smells so good in here," Cadie said, leaning weakly against the doorframe. "I wish I had more of an appetite."

"You're up!" Liam said. "How do you feel?"

"Okay," she said, sitting down in the nearest chair.

Liam frowned. "Would you like something to drink?"

"A cup of tea would be good." She looked at the bags near the door. "How was school shopping?"

"It was great!" Aidan said, showing off his new sneakers.

"Wow! Those are sporty," she said, admiring his new white canvas high-tops.

"You know who else is going to like those?" Emma said.

"Who?" Aidan asked.

"Levi. He loves retro sneakers."

"That's the artist in him," Cadie said with a smile. "Is he here?"

Emma shook her head. "No, Devon asked him to stop by the gallery. The show wraps up this weekend, so we have to pick up the paintings that haven't sold."

"Do you know how many *did* sell?" Cadie asked as Liam set the tea in front of her.

"Eleven!" Emma said with a huge smile. "Devon said it was the best show they've had."

"That's wonderful," Cadie said, wrapping her hands around the warm mug. Then she looked back at Aidan. "What else did you get, hon?"

"A new backpack," Aidan said proudly as he slipped it over his shoulders.

"Nice," Cadie said with a nod. "I love the color."

Aidan nodded. "There's an open house at my school tomorrow. Do you want to come?"

Cadie searched his face—so full of hope. "Of course I'll come," she said. "I can't wait to meet your new teacher and see your school."

"Great!" Aidan said with a grin.

"Hey, Aid," Liam said. "Would you take Tuck out and throw the ball for him?"

"Sure," Aidan said. "C'mon, Tuck!"

After he'd gone outside, Liam sat across from Cadie. "Are you sure you're going to be up for that?"

"I'm sure," Cadie said determinedly. "And even if I'm not, I'm going. I'm not missing something so important."

"Okay," Liam said, reaching for her hand.

"Levi and I would like to go too," Emma chimed in. "We don't want you to feel like Aidan's going to be completely your responsibility, Liam—we want to help out in any way we—"

Just then the phone rang and Liam reached to answer it. "Hello?" He paused. "Oh, hey, John . . . He's just noticing now? Yes, no problem, I'll see you in a few minutes." Liam hung up the phone. "John's son's wallet has been missing since he ran the boat up on the rocks. He thinks it might be in the boat, so John was wondering if I could meet him there to take a look." He paused and looked at Emma. "Is there time before supper?"

"Of course, go ahead."

Ten minutes later, Liam found Jordy's wallet under the seat, and when John got there, he didn't even have to get out of his car. "Thanks, Liam—sorry to drag you out."

"No problem—you're doing plenty for us."

John laughed. "I actually think I'm getting the better end of the deal."

"I don't know about that," Liam said.

"Well, remember, if you hear anything more from Cadie's father or his attorney, have them contact me. Don't get into a discussion . . . and please keep me posted on Cadie."

"I will," Liam said with a half smile, waving as John pulled away.

He walked back into the boathouse to turn off the lights, and as he did, he heard tires pulling into the parking lot. "What'd you forget, John?" he murmured, but when he looked out, he saw a dark SUV with Vermont plates parking next to his truck. He frowned uncertainly and then realized it was Jack.

"Hey, man," Jack said, seeing him.

"Hey," Liam said. "What're you doing here?"

"Is that any way to greet your best bud?" Jack asked, sounding wounded.

"I just mean you're never out here . . . and now, you've been here twice in a month. . . ."

Jack shook his head slowly. "She left me, Li. She took the kids and . . ."

"What?" Liam asked in surprise.

"Tracey left me . . ."

"Is she out here?"

"I dunno . . . she's been gone three freakin' days and she doesn't answer her freakin' phone, so I came out here, ya know, thinkin' she might be at her parents' house, but it's all closed up . . . so I went to The Brotherhood and had a couple . . ."

"A couple?" Liam said with a chuckle. "Man, you look toasted!"

Jack waved him off. "I'm fine . . . 'cept I can't find my family. Even the freakin' dog's gone . . ."

"What happened?"

"I dunno. I came home from a business trip and she wasn't home, so I waited, thinking they're just out somewhere, but then it got dark and they still weren't home . . . and then she doesn't answer her damn phone. Finally, I was so beat I just went to bed, and in the morning, they *still* weren't home."

"Did you call the police?"

"No, what the hell are they gonna do? Turn it into a federal case with a lot of publicity that I don't need."

"Do you have any idea why she left?"

"She's probably tired of me screwin' around. . . ."

"You think?" Liam said, rubbing his temple.

"You got any beer?" Jack asked.

Liam eyed him. "Don't you think you've had enough?"

"I told you I only had a couple. But if this is the warmest reception I'm gonna get, I can leave."

"No, I'm sorry—I just have . . ." Liam paused and shook his head. *This is the last thing I need right now. . . .* "C'mon in . . ." he said, not wanting to explain.

Jack followed him inside and Liam opened the fridge and took out a couple of beers. "Want to sit outside?"

"Sure," Jack said, looking around. "I meant to ask you last time, do you still have your boat?" Liam nodded as he opened the bottles and handed one to Jack. Then he walked outside to the picnic table next to the boathouse.

"Where is it?" Jack asked, and Liam motioned to the barn, suddenly thankful he'd come by to put her away the day before.

"Do you ever take her out?"

"Sometimes."

Jack frowned. "Are you pissed at me or something?"

Liam clenched his jaw. "Yeah, actually. I am."

"Why?"

"Because you're so damn lucky, Jack, to have Tracey and two great kids, and yet, you treat her like crap. I just can't believe how much you've changed."

"I haven't changed, Liam. I've always been a shit and you, of all people, should know that."

"No, you haven't," Liam said. "When we were in high school . . . *and* in the marines, you . . ."

"I cheated on Tracey."

Liam's eyes narrowed. "I just can't believe the man I've always thought of as my best friend—who saved my life—is such an ass."

"Saved your life? *What* are you talking about?"

"When we were under attack and you threw yourself on top of me," Liam said, shaking his head. "How can I ever turn my back on you after that?"

Jack stared at him. "I didn't throw myself on top of you, Liam. *You* saved me."

Liam frowned. "What?"

"Yeah, man . . . you saved me."

Liam shook his head. "I don't remember it that way. . . ."

"Probably because you got hit in the head . . ." Jack paused. "Li, you've always been the good guy . . . and I, well, I've always been a little less than perfect," he said with a smile. "Do you remember that comic strip, *Goofus and Gallant*?"

Liam shook his head.

"It's a comic strip that used to be in a kids' magazine about two boys—Gallant was always the gentleman and Goofus did everything wrong . . . and when we were growing up, I always thought of you as Gallant and me as Goofus. My mom even used to ask me why I wasn't more like you." He shook his head. "And if Tracey was smart, she would've ended up with you."

Liam swallowed. "What are you gonna do?"

"I don't know," he said. "I've tried to change, but I absolutely suck at it." He shook his head. "She's better off without me." He downed his beer. "Want another?"

"No," Liam said, getting up.

"Want to go to The Brotherhood?"

Liam shook his head. "No." He hesitated, trying to decide how much he wanted to share. "I've got some stuff goin' on."

"That's fine," Jack said with a smile. "Mind if I grab another for the ferry?"

"No, help yourself."

Jack went into the boathouse and came back out with two beers. "Thanks, man. I owe you."

"No, you don't," Liam said. "But let me know how Tracey is."

"I will," Jack said. "*If* I find her," he added with a smile. He turned and headed to his vehicle, but then stopped and turned around. "Hey," he called, "did you ever find out if that artist was related to what's her name?"

Liam shook his head. "No, I never found out."

Jack nodded.

Chapter 44

The next morning, Aidan was up and dressed before anyone else had even opened their eyes. "I'm ready for the open house," he whispered, nudging Liam.

"Hmm?" Liam murmured, opening one eye.

"Open house . . . you know . . . at my school," he whispered.

Liam squinted at the clock. "That doesn't start 'til ten, pal."

"How long is that?"

"Four hours."

"Oh," Aidan said gloomily.

Liam looked him over and realized he already had on his sneakers. "You look very nice, though."

Aidan nodded, and seeing the disappointment on his face, Liam suggested, "Since we have time, how'd you like to help me make French toast?"

Aidan smiled brightly. "Sure!"

"Okay," Liam said, sitting up, "give me a minute."

As Aidan shuffled to the kitchen, Cadie whispered, "Good morning."

"Good morning," Liam said, looking over. "Sorry we woke you."

"You didn't wake me . . . I've been awake." She paused. "You're so good with him."

"Am I?"

"Mm-hmm."

Liam smiled skeptically. "Do you need anything?"

"No, I'm fine . . . but I think I might venture to the bathroom in a bit and take a shower."

"Okay, well, don't hesitate to call me if you need help."

"Ha!" Cadie said. "Even though you're going to be my husband," she said, admiring his broad chest, "you're *not* going to see me naked."

Liam frowned. "I've seen you before . . ."

"That was a long time ago, and I definitely don't look like the same."

Liam sat on the edge of the bed. "I don't care what cancer has done to your body, Cade. I'll always think you're beautiful."

Cadie smiled sadly and looked away. Through the blur of tears, she saw a flash of red. "Look," she whispered, wiping her eyes, "Mr. Cardinal is having his breakfast. He comes for a bedtime snack at dusk too, and he and the little missus chirp back and forth that all is well."

"Is that what you think?" Liam asked with a smile.

Cadie nodded. "It *is* what they're saying. It's peaceful . . . but at the same time, it's melancholy—like "Taps"—it's as if they're saying the day is over, but God is near."

Liam smiled and watched as the female landed on the feeder too.

"Hi, Mom," Aidan said, appearing in the doorway.

"Hi, hon," Cadie said.

"I'm helping Liam make French toast."

"You are? Well, you two better get going," Cadie said, nudging Liam.

"Yup, I'm coming," Liam said, getting up.

After Liam had pulled on his jeans and T-shirt and disappeared down the hall, Cadie made her way slowly to the bathroom, turned on the shower, brushed her teeth, and took a pain pill. Then she pulled back the curtain and braced herself for the sensation of a thousand needle pricks. She held on to the handrail and let the water rush over her body—and even though it stung, it felt good. She ran her hand over her sunken abdomen, keenly aware that, every day, her body was growing weaker— *Is this the last time I'll be able to shower on my own? It's so strange to experience death in slow motion.* She pushed the thought from her mind, washed the fuzz on top of her head, quickly ran the washcloth over the rest of her thin body, rinsed, turned off the water, reached for her towel, lost her balance and fell.

Tears filled her eyes, and almost immediately, she heard Liam's voice on the other side of the door. "Cadie?!" Are you all right?!"

She could hear his concern, but all she could do was groan.

"Cadie, I know you don't want me to see you, but I have to come in. . . ."

"No," she moaned.

A moment later, he was kneeling beside her. "Are you okay?"

She nodded.

"What hurts?"

"My head . . . and my elbow," she said rubbing the side of her head.

"Can you stand up?"

Cadie held on to the side of the tub as Liam helped her up. Then he wrapped the towel around her and pulled her against him. "I'm so sorry," he whispered. "I'm so sorry you fell . . . I'm so sorry this is happening . . . I'm sorry for *everything*. And I *do* still think you're beautiful." Hot tears streamed down Cadie's cheeks as she felt his strong arms holding her tightly, her heart aching for all that could've been.

Chapter 45

"I thought you said you didn't know how to cook?" Levi said. "So far, we've had burgers, pancakes, *and now,* French toast . . . and even the lady with no appetite has managed to eat a whole piece," he added, smiling at Cadie.

"Best French toast *ever,*" she said with her mouth full.

"Well, as I've said before," Liam said, "every man needs to know how to make pancakes and burgers, but today, the French toast was *all* Aidan—he beat the eggs, added the milk, vanilla, and cinnamon, and dipped every slice of bread for exactly the right length of time—so they soaked up the perfect amount of egg mixture. And then, the most important part, of course, is the snow . . . and he's a pro at sugar sifting."

Aidan beamed proudly. "Every man needs to know how to make French toast."

"They also need to know how to help clean up," Liam said, pushing back from the table. "When I was growing up, Coop used to wash the dishes while I dried . . . so here you go," he said, tossing a dishtowel in his direction. It landed on Aidan's head, and he pulled it off, grinning, and stood ready to dry.

* * *

"What time is Sally coming over?" Cadie asked as they pulled into the elementary-school parking lot.

"Around four . . . *and* she's bringing dinner."

"She *is?*"

"Mm-hmm."

"What's she bringing?" Aidan asked from the seat between them.

"Lobster," he said as he pulled into a spot.

"Cool!"

"Mmm, I love lobster," Cadie murmured. "I haven't had it in years."

"That's what I heard," Liam said, climbing out and lifting the wheelchair from the back of the truck.

Levi and Emma, who'd parked nearby, walked over. "How's your head?"

Cadie ran her finger over the tender spot above her temple. "I've got an egg," she said, adjusting her pink Red Sox cap. "Good thing I'm wearing a hat."

Liam wheeled the chair through the doors and they were immediately greeted by the staff who looked up Aidan's name and directed them down the hall. "You're so lucky," one lady said, smiling at Aidan. "Mrs. Polley is one of my all-time favorite teachers."

Aidan nodded, and as they walked down the hall, he turned to Cadie. "Did you hear that?"

"No, what?" Cadie asked.

"She said Mrs. Polley is one of her all-time favorite teachers!"

"That's wonderful, Aid," Cadie said, her heart swelling with happiness for him.

"Is this it?" Aidan asked, peering into room 24.

"C'mon in," a cheerful voice called, and Aidan stepped tentatively into the classroom. "You must be Aidan!"

"How'd you know?!" Aidan asked in surprise as Mrs. Polley reached out to shake his hand.

"Because I heard I was getting a very smart new student, and I could tell—just by looking at you—that *you* are very smart."

Aidan beamed as he looked up at her kind face.

"Would you like to see your desk?"

He nodded and Mrs. Polley led him over to a desk near the window.

"It even has my name on it," he exclaimed.

"There's a surprise inside too."

Aidan reached into the desk and pulled out three new pencils—red, blue, and green—all with *Aidan* printed on them. "Cool!"

Mrs. Polley turned to greet everyone and then looked straight in Cadie's eyes. "I'm looking forward to having Aidan in my class."

"Thank you," Cadie said. And suddenly realizing the important role this lady would play in Aidan's life during a very difficult time, whispered, "Thank you very much."

"You're welcome," Mrs. Polley said softly.

Then she told them about the curriculum she had planned for the year—including a whale watch and a project about shipwrecks. "That'll be right up your alley," she said, smiling at Liam.

They toured the rest of the school and then looked through the doors to the playground. "Can we go out?" Aidan said hopefully.

Liam looked down at Cadie. "I think we better get going, pal."

"We'll go out with him," Levi offered. "You and Mom can head home."

"Are you sure?"

"Positive. Oh, and we might stop somewhere for lunch or ice cream."

"Or *both*," Emma said with a grin.

"All right, well, we have to stop at the town hall, but we're heading straight home after that."

"Okay, see you later!" Aidan said, pushing open the door and running across the grass to join the other kids.

Chapter 46

"Got lobstah?" Sally said with a smile as she maneuvered a big cooler through the screen door and set it on the floor. As soon as she stood up, Tuck jumped up and put his big paws on her shoulders and slobbered her with kisses. "I'm happy to see you too!" she said, laughing. "You look so handsome with your Valentine bandana!" Then she noticed Aidan standing shyly in the doorway. "And you look handsome too," she said, admiring his blue oxford shirt and paisley bow tie.

"Thanks," he said as he lifted the top of the cooler and peered inside. "I thought lobsters were red."

"They are . . . after you cook 'em," she explained, motioning to the heavy metal pot already heating on the stove.

"How many are here?" he asked, trying to count the crawling brown crustaceans.

"Six."

"Everyone gets their own?!" he asked in surprise. "I don't know if I can eat a whole one."

"Well, you don't eat the *whole* thing. The best part is right here," Sally said, holding up a lobster and pointing to its tail. "There's a lot of meat in here . . . and in the claws, but that's about it. You crack the shell, pull out the meat, and dip it in melted butter with lemon . . . and mm-mm, it's so good, you'll think you died and went to heaven!"

Aidan smiled at Sally's enthusiasm . . . and also because heaven was starting to sound like a pretty good place!

"Hey, Sal," Liam said, coming into the kitchen, tying his tie.

"Look at you!" Sally said admiringly.

"Look at you, too," he teased, admiring her white slacks and cobalt blue linen blouse.

"Thank you," Sally said, looking down and realizing there was dog hair on her slacks. "I knew I shouldn't wear white over here," she said, laughing, "but I have to make the most of these pants—no white after this weekend, you know, and they probably won't fit after the long winter."

"You're so old school," Liam teased. "Lots of people wear white after Labor Day."

"Not me."

Aidan, who'd been listening to the conversation, looked up in dismay. "Does that mean I can't wear my new sneakers to school?"

"Yes, you can," Liam said, shaking his head. "That silly rule doesn't apply to sneakers."

"That's good," Aidan said, sounding relieved.

"Do you have more food to bring in?" Liam asked.

"I *do*—I have a potato salad, a Caesar salad, corn on the cob, and carrot cake."

"Wow! I had no idea you were making so much."

"Hey," she said, holding Liam's smooth face in her hands, "such an important event doesn't happen every day . . . and if Coop were here, we'd be having fireworks too."

Liam smiled and pulled her into a hug. "Thanks, Sally."

"Can we have fireworks tonight?!" Aidan asked hopefully.

"I'll have to see if there're any left from Coop's stash," Liam said. "But right now, we need to bring in the rest of the food."

"Okay!" Aidan said, hopping down to help.

Sally started to follow him, but Liam held out his hand. "The boys and I will get it—it's the least we can do."

"Okay," she chuckled. "Maybe I'll go check on the bride . . ."

"Good idea," Liam said. "She and Emma are getting ready."

Sally disappeared down the hall and found Cadie and Emma in the throes of trying to pin Cadie's white linen dress—in which she was absolutely swimming.

"Need some help?" Sally asked.

"Yes, please," Cadie said, shaking her head. "This dress used to fit like a glove, but now I think I could fit two of me in it."

Sally reached for the pin cushion and skillfully tucked and pinned the dress so that the pins weren't even visible. "Just don't move too much or you'll get pricked," Sally said, stepping back. "You look lovely!"

"Thank you," Cadie said, easing into her wheelchair and pulling a blanket over her lap. "Of course, I'll be wearing this blanket, too, so no one will even see my dress."

"You'd look beautiful wearing a sack," Emma said, clasping a string of pearls around her neck.

"Mmm," Cadie murmured doubtfully.

"Anyone up for a little celebratory nectar?" Sally asked, producing a small silver flask.

Cadie raised her eyebrows and smiled as Sally unscrewed the top and handed it to her. She took it from her and noticed there was fancy engraving on the side: *To my sweet Sally . . . Yours Forever, W.E.C.* "Hmm . . ." she said, eyeing Sally. "Is this from Cooper?"

"Maybe," Sally said with a grin.

Cadie took a sip and handed it to Emma. "Cheers!" Emma said with a grin as she tossed it back, licked her lips, and handed it back to Sally.

"Cheers *and* blessings!" Sally said, winking at Cadie and taking a swallow. Then she slipped the flask back into her bag. "Shall we?"

"Yes," Cadie said, feeling a little light-headed.

Emma maneuvered the wheelchair into the kitchen and Levi, who was holding the door, grinned and announced, "Here comes the bride!"

"Oh, my!" Cadie said as she looked around at the festively decorated porch. Christmas lights glittered brightly along the wainscoted ceiling and bouquets of white balloons swayed along the railing.

"See the table, Mom?" Aidan asked.

"It looks beautiful!" Cadie said, admiring the white linen tablecloth set with silver, and decorated with flickering candles and white hydrangea blossoms. "You guys . . ." she said, her eyes glistening with tears. "You've made it so special."

"I helped," Aidan said happily as Cadie pulled him into a hug.

"Well, it looks lovely."

Just then, Liam came up the steps carrying a bouquet of blue hydrangea blossoms. He'd put on his jacket and he looked very dapper as he stood in front of her. "That's because it's *for* someone special," he said with a smile, handing her the freshly cut blooms and kissing her cheek. "*And* there's no crying," he added, gently brushing away her tears.

"They're not sad tears," she said, smiling. "They're happy."

Liam nodded. "Are you ready?" he asked.

"I am—I want to walk, though," she said, handing him the blanket.

"Okay," he said, helping her stand and offering her his arm. Together, they walked slowly to where Sally was waiting. Cadie stood as straight as she could, stubbornly ignoring the pain, and gazing into Liam's eyes. Then Sally spoke briefly of their star-crossed past, asked them to repeat the vows they'd prepared, waited as they slid on the gold bands Aidan was holding tightly in his hands, and delivered a lovely benediction. "You may kiss your bride," she said with a smile.

Liam leaned down, and for the very first time, gently kissed his wife's lips. "I will love you forever," he whispered, pulling her in his arms

"And I will love *you* for all eternity," Cadie whispered back.

"Hooray!" Aidan, Levi, and Emma all cheered as Tuck barked and wiggled around them.

Chapter 47

"Dinner was delicious, Sally," Liam said as he nested the last of the empty bowls into the back of her Outback. "And that carrot cake was amazing. I can't thank you enough—you made it so special."

"You're very welcome, my dear," Sally said affectionately. "I'm so glad you were able to find some of Coop's old fireworks—I love those rockets, and I think Aidan did too."

Liam nodded. "*He* did . . . but Tuck definitely didn't. After I lit the first one, I remembered why we stopped shooting them off."

"It's too bad he gets so upset."

"It's the same with thunder."

"Oh, well," she said with a sigh. "We all have our idiosyncrasies."

"We do," Liam agreed with a chuckle.

"Well, you better get back to your girl," Sally said, nodding toward Cadie, who was still sitting near the fire. "It's been a long day."

"It has been, but she never complains; she just soldiers on, no matter how she's feeling."

"That's a rare trait. If it were me, I'd be a cranky, old bitch."

"No, you wouldn't," he said with a smile.

"You're a good guy, Li," Sally said, hugging him. "Your uncle, in spite of his shortcomings, did a good job raising you . . . and I'm sure you'll do a good a job, too—if not better—raising Aidan."

"We'll see," he said.

"Have a good night."

"You too. Talk to you soon."

"You better!" Sally said, waving.

Liam watched her go and then walked over and sat beside Cadie. "Should I throw more wood on?"

"No . . . not for me anyway," she said, looking up at the stars. "I hate for this night to end, but I'm afraid I'm fading fast."

Liam nodded and reached for her hand. "That's fine."

"Did you thank Sally?"

"I did."

"I'm sorry I couldn't help clean up."

"The bride doesn't get kitchen duty."

"I know, but the kids ended up doing it all."

"They didn't mind, and besides, they're already done. I think they've even gone to bed . . . I know Aidan's sound asleep with Tuck curled up next to him."

Cadie nodded. "It was all so nice. . . ."

"Mmm," Liam agreed, squeezing her hand.

"Everything was delicious—I wish I could've eaten more." She watched the bright orange sparks of light from the fire shoot up into the night sky; then her eyes were drawn to several white blossoms on the stone wall. "Are those moonflowers?!"

Liam followed her gaze. "Yes, Coop planted them a long time ago, and now, the vine has completely taken over."

Cadie smiled. "When I was a little girl, my grandfather had a moonflower vine and he and I would sit out on summer nights and wait for the blossoms to open. He used to say that those little flowers, blooming at night, were a reminder that God never stopped working . . . or caring for us—even in the darkest of times. Isn't it funny that I should be reminded of that now?"

Liam smiled. "I don't know. It seems to me someone recently told me that God's timing is perfect."

"Me?" Cadie said with a laugh.

Liam nodded. "So, is this the same grandfather who had the runabout named *Stardust*?"

"It is," Cadie said in surprise. "How did you remember that?!"

"I remember everything," Liam said with a smile.

"But that was a long time ago."

"I still remember."

"You would've liked him . . . and he you—he wasn't anything like my parents."

"He was your mom's dad, right?"

"Yes, and my uncles were all great men, too, but my mother—who was the youngest and only girl—was always a challenge . . . at least, according to my grandfather."

"I guess it doesn't matter how good you are at parenting," Liam said, shaking his head. "Some kids are just born difficult. Look at John Alden—he's a great guy, but his son Jordy isn't anything like him." He paused. "And look at you! Look at the amazing person you are . . . in spite of your parents."

Cadie laughed. "That's true. Although my biggest fault was not being strong enough to break free and follow my heart . . . and look where it got me."

"It got you here . . ." Liam said, "married to me."

"Which took a while . . . *but* which, I also think is absolutely *the* most amazing thing!"

"Me too," Liam said, standing up and gently lifting her into his arms. He kissed her, carried her inside, and helped her change into her pajamas.

"Lay with me," she whispered.

Liam unbuttoned his dress shirt and lay down next to her.

"I'm sure you can do better than that," she teased.

"What do you mean?" he asked softly, leaning on one arm.

Cadie hesitated uncertainly. *Is there any way on earth that this sweet, gorgeous man could ever be aroused by my frail, cancer-ravaged body? Or will he be embarrassed when he isn't? Will I ruin everything by asking him?* She closed her eyes and willed herself to speak. "I won't break."

Liam touched her cheek and searched her eyes. "Are you sure?"

She nodded, and in the soft glow of the moon's light, Liam slowly undressed and slipped under the covers beside her. "Mmm, you're so warm," she murmured, feeling his long, muscular body pressing against hers.

"I don't want to hurt you," he murmured, gently kissing her lips.

"You won't . . ." she said, feeling him hard against her.

"I want you so much," he whispered, lightly tracing his fingers over the curves of her body.

"I want you too," she murmured, touching him.

They lay side by side, exploring each other's body, until finally, he eased above her and slowly pushed himself deep inside . . . and then they both caught their breath, forgetting everything . . . the past . . . the pain . . . the longing . . . the loss, and loving with an intimacy and abandon that knew no bounds.

Chapter 48

The calendar promised two more weeks of summer, but by Tuesday morning, the warm weather definitely seemed to be in the rearview mirror. Liam glanced at the thermometer when he let Tuck and Moby out into the darkness and shivered. It was barely forty degrees. "What the heck happened to summer?"

He went back inside and peered into Aidan's room. "Hey, pal," he called softly. "It's time to get up."

"I don't want to go," Aidan said tearfully.

"How come?" Liam asked, sitting on the edge of his bed. "You've been looking forward to it all weekend."

"I just don't."

Liam lightly brushed back his wispy blond hair. "Mrs. Polley has your desk all ready and she's going to be waiting for you."

"I *just* don't want to go," Aidan said, turning away.

Liam took a deep breath and shook his head. *Now what? I can't just let him lie here and not go—kids don't skip school just because they don't feel like going. Do I sternly demand he get up, get dressed, and have breakfast? Or do I just leave him be-*

cause there's a lot going on in his world right now? Liam looked out into the darkness and tried to remember how he'd felt on his first day of school. It had been just after Christmas break and he vaguely remembered feeling nervous and homesick, missing his parents. . . . *And what had Cooper done?*

"How'd you like to go to Sally's for breakfast?" he asked.

"Today?" Aidan said, his voice muffled by his pillow.

"Yes. On the way to school."

"Can Mom come?"

Liam hesitated, recalling the pain Cadie had had over the weekend. "You can ask her, but I think she'll probably want to stay home."

Just then, Tuck let out a plaintive bark.

"Can Tuck come?"

"Sure," Liam said.

"Okay," Aidan said, sitting up and pushing off his covers. "Is Mom making my lunch?"

"No, I am, remember? We talked about this—all the things you like."

"PB and J."

"And tropical punch."

"And yogurt and cookies."

Liam nodded. "I think I can handle it."

"Don't forget the special ingredient," Aidan reminded.

"What's that?"

"Love—Mom always says love is what makes everything taste so good."

"Oh," Liam said, pulling him into a hug and feeling how small he was. "If we're going to go to Sally's, you need to get up and get dressed."

"Aye, aye, Captain," Aidan said, saluting him with a grin.

Liam chuckled and headed back to the kitchen to let Tuck and Moby in.

Five minutes later, Aidan appeared, dressed in a T-shirt and shorts, and Liam looked up from making coffee and shook his head. "You're gonna need more on than—"

"I tried to wake Mom to see if she wanted to go," Aidan interrupted in a worried voice, "but she won't wake up."

"What?!" Liam said, a shadow falling over his face. He tousled Aidan's hair as he hurried past him. "Cadie?" he said, trying to control his voice. "Cadie," he repeated, stroking her cheek. It felt cold and he reached for her hand. "Hey, Cade . . ." He pressed his fingers against her wrist and felt a faint pulse.

"Is everything okay?" Levi asked, coming into the room with Emma behind him, pulling on her robe.

Liam nodded as Cadie stirred and opened her eyes. "Hey, Cade," he said softly.

"Hey," she said groggily, looking around. "How come you're all here? What's the matter?"

"Nothing's the matter," Liam assured her.

But then Aidan leaned against her bed and innocently explained, "I tried to wake you to see if you wanted to go to Sally's for breakfast, but you wouldn't wake up."

"Oh," Cadie said, looking confused.

Liam looked at Levi and they each knew what the other was thinking—*it's just a matter of time* . . .

Finally, Emma broke the silence. "So, you two are going to Sally's?" she asked, putting her hand on Aidan's shoulders.

"Mm-hmm," Aidan said with a nod.

"Well, you're going to have to put on long pants and a sweatshirt," Emma said with a shiver. "It's chilly." She guided Aidan back to his room and left Liam and Levi alone with Cadie.

"How're you feeling?" Liam asked, squeezing her hand.

"Tired," she said. "And I need to use the bathroom."

"Do you want me to carry you?"

"Sure," she said with a weak smile, knowing there was no way she'd make it on her own.

Liam looked at Levi. "Want to finish packing Aidan's lunch?"

Levi nodded, his eyes glistening.

Ten minutes later, after helping Cadie back to bed and assuring her everything was okay, Liam reappeared in the kitchen. "I know you need to pick up your paintings today," he said, "but do you mind staying here until I get back from taking Aidan to school?"

"I don't mind," Levi said.

"When he woke up, he didn't want to go to school, so I bribed him with breakfast at Sally's."

"Bribery's good," Levi said with a smile as he slipped a juice box into the canvas lunch bag. "In fact, breakfast is a good idea—he adores Sally. How come he didn't want to go to school?" he asked, looking puzzled. "I thought he was looking forward to it."

"I thought so too. I don't know if he's nervous or if he's afraid to leave her."

Levi nodded. "I know how he feels. Emma and I were planning to take the paintings back to Boston after we picked them up, but now I'm afraid to go that far—I'm afraid I won't be able to get back . . ."

"Nothing's going to happen today," Liam said. "You *should* go."

"How do you know that? How will *we* know . . . ?"

Liam shook his head. "I don't know."

"Are you ready, Cap?" Aidan asked, coming into the kitchen wearing jeans, his new sneakers, a sweatshirt, and his backpack.

Levi frowned. "*Cap?*"

"It's short for captain," Aidan said with a grin.

Levi realized he'd never heard Aidan address Liam by any

name—he'd never called him Liam or Mr. Tate *or* Dad—and it suddenly dawned on him that he probably hadn't known *what* to call him.

"Don't forget your lunch," Emma said, turning him around, unzipping the top of his backpack, and slipping his lunch inside.

"So much for a shower," Liam said, running his hand through his hair, pulling a flannel shirt on over his T-shirt, and reaching for his keys. "There're eggs," he said, nodding to the fridge.

"That's all right," Levi said, holding up his coffee mug. "We're all set. We'll grab something on the way too."

"Okay," Liam said. "I'll be back in a bit."

"Have a good day, pal," Levi said, giving Aidan a high five before pulling him into a hug.

"Bye, love," Emma said, hugging him too.

"Do you want to say good-bye to Mom?" Levi suggested, and then wished he hadn't.

"Sure," Aidan said, hurrying down the hall. They all stood silently, waiting, and when he reappeared, he said, "She was asleep, so I just gave her a kiss."

"Okay, let's go," Liam said, holding the door.

"C'mon, Tuck," Aidan called, and the big dog almost knocked him over as he hurried out the door.

After the truck pulled away, Emma poured a cup of coffee and headed down the hall to take a shower, and Levi wandered back to his mom's room and sat on the edge of her bed. "Oh, Mom," he whispered. "Please don't go yet." Then he just sat there, watching her breathe, time slipping by.

"Hey," Emma said, peering into the room. "Your turn."

Levi nodded, stood up, and followed her back to Coop's old room.

"Are you okay?" she asked.

"Not really," he said, sinking onto their unmade bed and holding his head in his hands.

Emma put her arm around him. "I'm so sorry, Levi," she said softly. "Waiting is pure hell."

Levi nodded, tears filling his eyes.

"My granddad had cancer," Em continued, "and the end was miserable for everyone—it's a terrible way to go. Terrible for everyone." She paused. "Did you know it's legal in Oregon for doctors to assist a person who is terminally ill in death?"

"No," Levi said, shaking his head. "They should make it legal everywhere. I hate seeing her in so much pain. It's inhumane to make people suffer . . . and it's inhumane to make their families suffer."

"I couldn't agree more," Emma said.

"I don't want her to die," Levi said, his voice choked with emotion, "but at the same time, I just want it to be over . . . and the only way for it to *be* over is for her to die. It's crazy, Em. I feel so selfish."

"You're not selfish, Le. You're a wonderful son and you've been there for your mum every step of the way. Your love is why you're suffering so much. It's perfectly normal to want the pain and misery to end . . . the human spirit can only take so much."

Levi groaned in anguish. "Where is God in all this?"

"He's closer than your own breathing," Emma whispered, searching his eyes.

Levi shook his head. "I know one thing—if I ever get sick, we're moving to Oregon."

Emma smiled. "Same for me."

He reached for his towel. "Thanks for being here, Em," he said, gently kissing her cheek.

Liam parked in front of Cuppa Joe and Aidan hopped down as Tuck trotted up the worn steps. "Wait for us," Aidan called. They went inside and Tuck immediately wiggled his way behind the counter.

"Well, hello there!" Sally said, laughing.

Aidan gave her a hug. "We're here for breakfast."

"You are?"

"Mm-hmm . . . we're on our way to school."

"Well, what can I get you?"

"A blueberry muffin!"

"Make that two," Liam said wearily as he reached for a coffeepot.

Sally took two huge blueberry muffins out of the glass case and looked over at the tall, dark haired boy with horn-rimmed glasses working behind the counter. "Jase, you okay for a minute?"

Jase flashed a smile as he made change for a customer. "Yup."

Then Sally turned back to Liam. "How is she?" she asked as the muffins heated.

"Not good," Liam said, shaking his head. "She's in a lot of pain and she's needed so much morphine, she's hardly ever awake."

"That's what happens," Sally said, putting the warm muffins down on the table and joining them. As soon as she sat down, Tuck moseyed over to rest his head on her lap. "I hate to say this, Liam, but it probably won't be much longer. . . ."

Liam nodded and looked over at Aidan to see if he knew what they were talking about, but he was busy peeling the paper off his muffin. "Sally, can you open this for me?" he asked, sliding his milk carton toward her.

"Sure, hon," she said, prying open the cardboard top. "Are you ready for your first day?"

"I guess so," he said, swinging his feet.

"Mrs. Polley is a wonderful teacher."

"I know," he said, taking a sip from his straw.

"She comes in here on her way to school sometimes."

"She does?!" Aidan said in surprise, looking around.

"Mm-hmm, but probably not today—she's probably already *at* school today, getting ready."

Aidan nodded, his body swaying slightly to the rhythm of his swinging legs.

"Is Lisa coming today?" Sally asked, turning back to Liam.

"Yes," he said, glancing at his watch as he sipped his coffee.

"Well, I think you should talk to her about having someone there round the clock."

"I will," Liam said.

"Do you want me to wrap your muffin?"

Liam looked down and realized he hadn't even taken a bite. He smiled sadly. "I guess so . . . sorry."

"Don't be sorry, hon. You can have it later when you're hungry." She disappeared behind the counter and came back with a waxed paper bag.

"Thanks, Sally," Liam said, standing. "Thank you for everything."

Sally gave him a hug. "You're more than welcome, my dear. Please keep me posted."

"I will."

Sally turned to Aidan and scooped him up. "Have a great first day, hon . . . and tell Mrs. Polley I said hello—she and I go way back."

"I will," Aidan said, wrapping his arms tightly around Sally's neck.

She set him down and held Tuck's head in her hands. "You be good, too, mister," she said, and Tuck licked her cheek and wagged his tail as if to say, "I will."

Chapter 49

Levi and Emma carried the last of the paintings up the stairs to the spacious studio on the top floor of an old warehouse that looked out over Boston Harbor. "I love your space here," Emma said, setting down the painting in her arms. "I can't believe the rent is such a bargain."

"I know. I think I'm going to keep it even after the cottage is ready. They're so different."

"And the art that comes from them will be too."

"You're right—it's funny how the setting influences the outcome; here I'm always working from photographs, but when the cottage is ready, I'll be able to do a lot more plein air painting, which will be nice—I haven't had the chance to do that since college."

"Something to look forward to," Emma said with a smile.

"I need something to look forward to . . . although I'm going to miss being able to show my mom what I'm working on," he said sadly.

"I think you're going to find she's closer than ever—it'll be as if she's looking over your shoulder."

"I hope so," Levi said, pulling her into his arms. "One thing she's already told me is not to let go of *you*."

"She's a smart lady," Emma teased.

"Well, I told her I already knew that."

"Smart boy," she added, laughing.

"And I never will," he added, kissing her full lips.

"Even if we have to move to Oregon someday?"

"Even then," he said, kissing her neck and pushing her blouse down over her shoulder.

"Mmm," she murmured, pulling him toward the unmade bed that was pushed up against the windows, but as she lay back across the sun-warmed sheets and watched him pull his sweater over his head, she realized his eyes were glistening.

He dropped his sweater on the bed and sat down next to her. "I'm sorry, Em, I shouldn't have started anything. I thought I could . . ." he said, "but I just can't. All I can think about is how much pain she's in . . . *and* how time is running out."

"Shh . . . it's okay," Emma whispered.

Levi lay back against the pillows next to her with tears streaming down his cheeks. "My heart feels like it weighs a hundred pounds . . . and it's all I can do to drag it around behind me."

Emma stroked his soft hair. "A month from now . . . or six months from now, when the time is right, Le, we'll make love again. There's no hurry."

Levi turned to search her eyes. "I need to head back, but you don't have to go. I know you have things to take care of . . . I know you have stuff to do."

Emma frowned. "I'm going back with you."

He smiled sadly and wrapped his arms around her.

Chapter 50

On Tuesday afternoon, a light rain began to fall across Nantucket and the dark clouds and fog hung stubbornly over the island right through Thursday. By Wednesday, Cadie had stopped eating, and although Lisa tried to limit her meds so she'd be awake, her pain without them was crushing. At Liam's request, she and another nurse started taking turns staying at the house, and although they said they wouldn't be sleeping while they were there, Liam gave up his bed and slept in Coop's old recliner so they'd be close to Cadie if she needed them. On Thursday night, Moby hopped up on the bed and nestled on the quilt next to her . . . and Liam—who'd never seen his cat show compassion—found it oddly comforting that the old fellow seemed to understand. Even happy-go-lucky Tuck was subdued and often wandered into the room to rest his chin on the bed or gently nudge her hand.

On Friday morning, the sun finally broke through the gloomy clouds, bringing with it blue skies and a balmy breeze. Liam pushed open the kitchen windows to let in the fresh air and went to see if Lisa needed anything. As soon as he walked in the room, he realized Cadie's breathing had changed—it was shallow and more labored. "Is everything okay?" he asked with a frown.

Lisa turned to look at him and shook her head. "You need to decide if you want Aidan to be here."

"Do you think it's today?"

"I do," she said gently.

Liam shook his head. "I-I don't know . . ." he stammered.

"It should be whatever feels right to you." She paused, seeing his dismay. "I'll get Levi."

Liam sat on the edge of the bed and held Cadie's hand. "What would *you* want, Cade?" he whispered softly. "Aiden is *so* young . . . but he knows what's happening. Would you want him to be here?" He searched her unresponsive face and then looked up and realized Levi had come into the room. "What do you think?"

"I don't know either," Levi said, brushing back tears.

Just then, a hummingbird landed on the feeder and they both watched as it hovered outside the window, looking at them. "It's a part of life," Levi said, "but I don't want him to be scarred for life."

Emma stood in the doorway with Aidan and then put her hands on his shoulders and guided him over to the bed. "Hi, Mommy," he whispered softly, touching Cadie's hand. To their surprise, she stirred and opened her eyes.

"Hi, hon," she murmured, and then she turned to look out the window. "Did you see how blue the sky is today?" Aidan nodded solemnly and she squeezed his hand. Then she looked at each of them and smiled wistfully. "I've known such love," she whispered.

Moments later, she was gone.

PART III

For the trumpet will sound, the dead will be raised
imperishable, and we will be changed.

—I Corinthians 15:52

Chapter 51

Liam stood silently, watching the last rays of the September day dance across the waves. *It's over,* he thought. *The seemingly interminable wait for death is over. Cadie is gone . . . and now we are left to pick up the pieces of our lives and move on— with work and school and whatever else will occupy our time. Our lives* without *her.* He closed his eyes and recalled how, when Cadie's breathing had become almost imperceptible, Lisa had opened a window. "For her spirit to pass on," she'd said, and a warm breeze had whispered through the window, rustling the curtain.

He ran his fingers through his hair, rubbed his eyes, and watched a flock of piping plovers chase the waves. He felt something wet nudge his hand and then heard a light thump on the sand. He looked down and saw a soggy tennis ball at his feet. "Life goes on, doesn't it, old pal?" he said with a sad smile. He picked up the ball and tossed it, but Tuck only took a few half-hearted steps before he just sat down and gazed at it. "I know how you feel," Liam said, kneeling next to him. Tuck licked Liam's cheek and then lay down and put his big, golden head between his paws.

"Oh, pal," Liam said, sitting next to him. "You and I—we should know better. This is what happens when you put your heart on the line."

"Hey, Dad," Levi said, coming up behind them.

Liam looked up. "I don't think I'm ever going to get used to being called *Dad.*"

"Yes, you will, and someday, you'll be called Grandpa too." He knelt down next to him and stroked Tuck's soft fur. "Anyway, the undertaker just called, and he's on his way."

Liam nodded. "I'll be right up."

"Okay," Levi said, turning to walk back to the house.

Liam watched him go and then looked back at the waves. He'd always thought it was crazy that grieving people were expected to deal with the business-like details of their loved ones' arrangements within hours of losing them: Writing an obituary so it will appear in the paper in a timely fashion; choosing a coffin or cremation; deciding where to bury—or scatter—the remains; choosing hymns and readings, not to mention planning a party-like reception for an unpredictable number of people—all while you're feeling your absolute worst. And even though he'd balked when Cadie had brought up the subject, he was glad, now, she told him what she wanted.

"You don't have to tell my parents," she'd instructed matter-of-factly. "They probably won't come anyway—especially since I want my ashes to be scattered, not buried."

"Maybe you should write this down," Liam had suggested, blinking back tears as he listened to her casually talk about it.

"There's *only* one other thing . . ."

"What's that?"

"I want it to be a celebration—no tears—and maybe Emma could sing a hymn."

Liam had nodded, trying to muster a smile. "I can't promise

anything—I mean, we'll try to make it celebratory, but there might be some tears." He paused. "What hymn?"

"Something upbeat," she'd mused thoughtfully, humming a few notes of one of her favorite hymns, and Emma, who was sitting in the next room, recognized it and smiled.

At least it will be simple, he thought . . . and *we don't have to plan a party.*

Cadie's service *was* simple and beautiful—just the way she wanted. On Tuesday morning, after Levi stoically read from John 14 and Aidan helped Liam take the top off the box of ashes and then held Sally's hand, Emma slipped her guitar strap over her head, strummed a few notes, adjusted the strings, and sang the hymn Cadie had hummed that day—"Lord of the Dance"—her sweet voice carrying over the sand. Finally, with the wind whispering through the grass, Liam tearfully walked to the water's edge and released the ashes across the gentle waves of Tuckernuck Island.

They stood and watched in silence until Aidan whispered, "Play it again, Em."

She looked down and smiled. "Only if you'll sing it with me this time. . . ."

He nodded and Emma started to softly strum her guitar again.

On the ride back, the runabout skipped lightly across the waves, but the hearts of her passengers were as heavy as anchors, each of them feeling as if they were leaving someone very important behind.

"The purpose of life is to sow seeds of love, encouragement, wisdom, and forgiveness," Levi read as they sat around the kitchen table the next morning. He looked up from the worn, leather journal Cadie had filled with quotes, verses, prayers and sketches. "Look at this drawing," he added, sliding the book across the table. Liam and Emma both leaned forward to look at the sketch of a little boy.

Emma smiled. "If that isn't Aidan, I don't know who it is!"

Liam nodded. "Now we know where you get your talent, Le."

Levi shook his head. "I had no idea she could draw *or* that she kept a journal."

"It's a real treasure," Liam agreed.

Levi paused and looked up at Emma. "I think now would be a good time."

She smiled and nodded.

"A good time for what?" Liam asked.

"Mom wanted us to give you something," Levi said, "when the time was right."

Liam watched curiously as Levi disappeared down the hall and came back with a large, flat package wrapped in brown paper. "This was in my show—so you may remember it, but before the show even opened, Mom bought it, and she made Devon and Chase promise not to tell me. When I arrived, I realized it had sold and I couldn't believe it. Of course, they wouldn't tell me who bought it, so I didn't find out until the show ended . . . when Em and I went to pick up the paintings that hadn't sold." He paused. "By then, Mom was pretty out of it most of the time, but one morning when she happened to be awake, I told her I would've given her the painting if she'd told me she wanted it, but she said no, she wanted to *buy* it—and she wanted to give it to you. I tried to explain that she could've saved a lot of money, but she didn't care—she wanted to support me." He paused and searched Liam's eyes. "When she bought it, she didn't even know if she was going to see you again."

Liam nodded, and as Levi pulled away the paper, his heart stopped—it was the painting of the island. He stared at it in disbelief, remembering how he'd admired it and how disappointed he'd been when Tracey explained what the red dot meant. "I love it," Liam said, misty-eyed. "When I first saw it, I wondered how you had captured it so perfectly."

Levi smiled. "I worked from the old photos Mom had taken—she said they were from the last day she saw you. The photos are beautiful. The sun is setting behind the trees and the island is bathed in a warm, rosy glow."

"Well, you captured it perfectly. I've often recalled how beautiful the sky was that evening," he said, nodding approvingly. "I love it," he said again, and then looked at Levi and Emma. "Where do you think I should hang it?"

"Over your bed," Emma said. "The lighting in there is perf—"

Just then, there was a knock at the door and Tuck scrambled to get up. "Hey there, Tuck," a familiar voice said as Tuck nudged the door open with his nose and went out to greet the mailman.

"Hey, Mike," Liam said.

"Hey, Liam," Mike replied, kneeling to give Tuck a treat.

"What've you got for me?"

"Another certified letter that needs a signature," Mike said, holding out the card.

"Great," Liam muttered as he looked at the name of the sender.

"Sorry," Mike said.

Liam nodded. "I'll forgive you this time, but don't bring any more."

Mike smiled as he stood up. "I'll try not to."

Liam took the envelope inside, sat down at the table, and scanned the letter from Carlton Knox's attorney.

"What's it say?" Levi asked.

Liam shook his head in disbelief. "It says your grandparents—due to their extensive financial support of Aidan and his mother—

have been granted temporary custody until the court makes its final decision. It's effective Wednesday, September sixteenth." He glanced at the calendar. "That's today!"

He reached into his pocket, pulled out John's business card, walked over to the phone, and dialed. A moment later, he was leaving a message and looking worriedly at his watch. "He's not there . . . and I have to pick up Aidan."

"I'm going with you," Levi said.

"Someone has to stay here in case he calls back."

"He has Mom's cell phone number."

"But I left the home number in my message. . . ."

"I'll stay," Emma said. "You two go."

Chapter 52

As soon as Liam pulled into the elementary-school parking lot, he saw Carlton Knox standing in front of the building with a police officer while a woman they didn't recognize held Aidan's hand.

"Holy shit," Levi growled in disbelief.

Liam parked the car and they made their way through the crowd of parents picking up their children. "Excuse me, Officer," Liam said as they approached. "What's going on? You can't just come to school and take my child without notifying me."

The officer immediately stood straighter, as if he'd been warned about a possible confrontation. "Sir, please step over here," he said.

Liam's heart pounded as he stared at Carlton. "*I'm* Aidan's guardian," he said, trying to control his anger. "You have no right to take him."

"*I'm* his grandfather," Carlton snarled, "and I have *every* right. I have a court order that says I've been granted custody until the court's confirmation."

"I don't care what you have," Liam said, his voice rising.

"His mother's dying wish was for me to be his guardian—it says so in her will."

"Do you have the will?" the policeman interrupted.

"I don't have it on me. My attorney has it."

The woman shook her head and, without an ounce of sympathy, stated, "I'm afraid Aidan will be staying with his grandparents until further notice."

Liam eyed her. "I'm sorry . . . I didn't catch your name."

"Michelle Logan with DCF," she said, extending her hand.

Liam ignored her outstretched hand and looked back at Carlton. "Cadie doesn't want you raising Aidan."

"Ms. Logan," Levi interrupted, trying to gain control over the unraveling situation. "Aidan is settled here—he's started school; he loves his teacher; and he's happy. It's wrong to take away him from his home right after he lost his mother."

"I'm sorry, but we have the court order right here," she said, holding up an official-looking document.

Liam looked down at Aidan and saw tears in his eyes. "How can you take him?" he asked angrily. "He obviously doesn't want to go."

The DCF agent looked down at Aidan. "It's okay, hon," she soothed, squeezing his hand, but Aidan pulled free.

"I won't go," he cried. "I want to stay with Cap."

A crowd began to gather around them curiously, but the policeman motioned for them to move along. Then he turned back to Liam. "Sir, please come with me," he said, trying to motion to Michelle Logan to take Aidan to her car, but when she picked him up, he started to howl.

Liam glared at Carlton. "You can't even grant your daughter her dying wish, you son of a bitch," he seethed.

"Stay away from my grandson, you pathetic piece of shit," Carlton growled.

Suddenly, all the years of pent-up anger were summoned to Liam's fist, and in the next moment, he lunged at Carlton, and although Levi made a valiant effort to step between them, he couldn't stop Liam's fist from connecting with Carlton's chin, knocking him to the ground.

"Arrest him," Carlton demanded, rubbing his chin. And before Liam knew it, his throbbing fist was in a handcuff, and Levi was shouting, "Dad, give me your keys and don't resist!"

With his free hand, Liam tossed his truck keys to Levi. "Call John Alden," he shouted. "Tell him what happened."

Carlton struggled to his feet and watched as Liam was led away. "Good luck getting him now," he sneered.

Liam swore repeatedly as the officer ducked his head into the back of the cruiser. "I can't believe this is happening," Liam growled. He looked out the window and watched as Aidan, still howling, reached out for Levi. "Oh, Cadie, I screwed up," he whispered, feeling anguished tears streaming down his cheeks. He wiped them on his shoulders. "Your father's right—I'm never going to get custody *now*."

Two hours later, a different police officer peered into Liam's cell. "Well, well, well, if it isn't Liam Tate. What the hell'd you do, Li?"

Liam looked up. "Hey, Frank," he said, "something stupid, obviously."

"I've never known you to do *anything* stupid," his old classmate said, reaching for his keys.

"I did this time," Liam said, shaking his head.

Frank unlocked the door. "Not to worry. Sally bailed you out—you're free to go."

Liam walked to the main desk, collected his wallet and watch, and gave Sally a long hug. "I really messed things up, Sal."

"So I heard."

"I think I've lost him."

"You never know," she murmured.

"How come *you* bailed me out? Where's Levi?"

"He and Emma are on their way to Boston to pick up the will. Your attorney said he'd send it overnight, but Levi said he didn't want to take any chances."

Liam sank heavily into the passenger's seat of Sally's wagon and shook his head. "I can't believe this is happening."

"It'll work out, Li. Once you have the will—which appoints you as guardian—her father won't have a leg to stand on."

"Even after I assaulted him in front of DCF and a police officer?!"

Sally looked out the window and didn't say anything, and Liam glanced over. "Your silence speaks volumes."

"I'm sorry," she said. "I'm trying to think of a way to justify that."

"There isn't a way."

"Have you eaten?" she asked, changing the subject.

"I'm not hungry. If you could just drop me off, I'll just wallow in my misery."

"Suit yourself," Sally said with a sigh.

"It's *shoot* yourself," Liam corrected.

"I won't be able to leave you alone if you talk like that," she said, pulling into his driveway.

"You know I'm only kidding, Sal."

"I know," she said, giving him another long hug, "but try not to worry too much—you and Aidan are meant to be together."

"We'll see," he said skeptically as he got out of the car. "Thanks for bailing me out," he added.

"Anytime," she said with a half smile.

"Hopefully not *anytime* soon," he said, closing the door and tapping the roof of her car. He watched her pull away, waved, and then walked toward the house.

As soon as he opened the back door, Tuck landed his big paws on his shoulders and slobbered him with wet kisses.

"Hey, pal," Liam said, holding him up. "I know, I know—I just got out of your favorite car. Unfortunately, Sally's already on her way home." He held the door open so Tuck could go out. "Need to get busy?"

Tuck trotted down the stairs and looked up the driveway to make sure Sally was really gone; then he headed across the yard. Liam turned on the outside light, scratched Moby behind his ears, and read the note Levi had left. Then he opened the fridge, grabbed a beer, opened it, took a sip, and realized Emma had left a plate with a note taped to it instructing him to *Just Nuke!* ☺ He shook his head, feeling lucky to have them both in his life. He heard Tuck lumbering up the porch steps and went over to push open the door. The big golden trotted in, wagging his tail expectantly, and Liam chuckled. "And I *know* you've already eaten," he said. "Levi left a note, so you can't fool me." Tuck gazed at him innocently as if he didn't remember eating and Liam shook his head. "Nice try, though."

He stood in the middle of the quiet kitchen and looked around at the spotless counters. He'd always thought he'd kept things pretty shipshape—for a bachelor—but Emma went beyond tidy—when it came to a neat house, she was what Coop would call "OCD."

As Liam pulled off his shirt and turned on the bedroom light, he noticed the hospital bed was gone, and his bed, which Emma had made up with fresh sheets, was back in its original spot with Teddy propped up on the pillow. *Everything's back to normal,* he thought, *whatever that means.* He pulled the soft flannel shirt Cadie had liked to wear on over his T-shirt and realized Levi had hung the painting too. Emma was right—over his bed was the perfect spot—the painting's earthy colors went well with the color of the walls.

Liam reached for his beer, and with Tuck moseying beside him, went outside. As soon as he'd settled into a chair, Tuck rested his chin on his lap and Liam stroked his noble head and looked into his solemn eyes. "It's just you and me again, pal—like old times." Adjusting to a house full of people had been a challenge at times, and it had made him realize how set in his ways he'd become, but now that everyone was gone, it was even harder. He looked up at the dusky sky, sparkling with diamonds, and listened to the waves tumbling to shore, and then over the sound of the ocean, he heard a faint chirp. He looked around and, in the waning light, saw a female cardinal flutter to the stone wall. She cocked her head from side to side, studying him and chirping. Moments later, she flew away.

As quickly as she'd come, she was gone, and Liam whispered, "Was that you, Cade?"

Chapter 53

On Thursday morning, Levi and Emma returned to Nantucket, bringing Cadie's will with them. They were only able to spend the night, though, and after breakfast, they headed back to Boston.

As soon as they'd gone, Liam called John Alden but only got his voice mail, and when John finally called back later that day, he told Liam he'd submitted a copy of Cadie's will to the court and requested an expedited decision. Then he asked Liam about the encounter he'd had with Carlton Knox. "Don't worry," he assured him. "It sounds like he was trying to provoke you, and although that's no excuse for hitting him, what's done is done." His words weren't much solace, though, and after Liam hung up, he paced the floor, reliving the whole episode.

The next day, John called back and reported that—in light of Cadie's will—Aidan was going to be moved to foster care.

"Aidan's going to be so confused," Liam lamented. "How can they keep moving him when he just lost his mom?"

"It definitely seems screwed up," John consoled, "but I promise you, it's a positive sign. Another good thing is they accepted our request for an expedited court date. You need to be in Boston on Monday, October fifth, at nine a.m., clean-shaven and nicely dressed. And if you see Carlton Knox, stay away from him."

"Got it," Liam said, sounding a bit relieved.

After rattling around the house all day Saturday, Liam tightened the laces of his running shoes. Although there'd been a time when autumn on the island had broken his heart, he'd come to love the lonely desolation and silent beauty. As he ran, he lightly touched the gold band on his finger, and prayed, with all his heart, that Aidan would be allowed to come back and live with him.

The next two weeks dragged by as if they were pulling a tremendous, barnacle-covered anchor along the ocean floor. Liam couldn't believe how quiet the house was without the constant comings and goings of life . . . as they'd prepared for death. *It was ironic,* he thought, *that death could bring so much life to a house,* and so, to avoid the lonely silence, he began spending long hours at the boathouse.

The days were getting colder and he spent one entire afternoon, splitting firewood and stacking it in the woodshed behind the boathouse; then he carried several armloads inside. When the last log was stacked along the wall, he opened the creaky, iron door of the ancient Vermont Castings woodstove, crumpled up some newspaper, and started to throw it in, but he stopped when he noticed the date—Saturday, August 2—the day before Levi's opening. He smiled sadly, thinking of everything that had happened since then. *Who would've guessed life could change so much in six weeks' time?* He stuffed the newspaper in the stove, piled kindling and wood on top of it, struck a wooden match, and gently fanned the flame with the dustpan. When it started to catch, he added more wood, closed the door, turned the ceramic handle to open the damper, and listened to it crackle and hum. "Ah, Coop," he murmured, recalling how much his uncle had loved a fire in the woodstove. "This one's for you," he said, and Tuck moseyed over, licked his cheek, and curled up on a nearby rug.

"Now for the boat," Liam said, turning to survey the pile of broken planks still stacked on the floor. He walked over to the sailboat and ran his hand lightly across the wooden deck. "Don't you worry," he whispered softly, "there are some things I can't fix, but there are also some I can."

He pulled out his measuring tape, measured some of the longer pieces, walked over to a pile of oak planking, neatly stacked in the back of the shop, pulled out a few lengths, laid them on the floor, measured again, and began the slow, meticulous process of using the broken planks to make new forms.

The hours drifted by and Liam became so caught up in measuring, cutting, steaming, and fitting wood, he didn't even notice it was getting dark . . . until there was a knock on the door, followed by a questioning voice. "Hello?" Tuck scrambled to his feet and hurried over to the door.

Liam looked up. "Hey, Sally," he said, lifting off his safety glasses.

"Hi, you two," Sally said as Tuck almost knocked her over. "I haven't seen you in a few days and I've been worried, so I stopped by the house with some supper, but it was dark." She surveyed the wood scattered everywhere. "How *are* you doing?"

"We're doing," Liam said with a sad smile. "Just trying to stay busy . . ."

She nodded. "You haven't been by for a cup of coffee . . . or any other form of sustenance all week, so I thought you might like some supper . . . lasagna, garlic bread, and salad."

"Mmm . . . sounds good, Sal. To be honest, I haven't even thought about food."

"Well, you need to think about it once in a while—especially after that little boy comes to live with you."

"*If* he comes to live with me," Liam corrected, taking the

food from her. "Can you stay a minute?" he asked, pulling two chairs up to the stove.

"A minute . . ." she said, sitting down. "Have you had any news?"

"Just that he's in a foster home and our court date is October fifth."

"Wow, that's soon!"

"Not soon enough," Liam said, putting the food on the workbench.

"How come he's in foster care?"

"Because that's what the court decided after we presented the will. John says it's a good sign, but I'll only believe it when it happens."

"Do you want me to go with you?"

"No . . . thanks, but I'm planning to stay over with Levi and Em, so I was wondering if you could look after Tuck and Moby again?"

"Of course," Sally said, holding Tuck's head in her hands and looking into his soulful, brown eyes. "Do you want to come visit me again?" she asked, and Tuck wagged his tail as he happily licked her cheek.

"I also put you down as a reference, so if they call, try to say something nice."

Sally smiled. "I will . . . even if it involves lying."

"Thanks," Liam said with a smile. "They're coming to see the house Friday . . . and interview me."

"Well, they'll be impressed, I'm sure."

"I think they're visiting his teacher too."

Sally nodded. "I'm sure Barb will only say nice things."

"I hope so. It all seems pretty involved."

"Well, you know what they say . . . *No good deed goes unpunished.*"

"That's for sure," Liam said, shaking his head.

"Are you going to eat?"

He glanced at his watch. "I think I'll take it home."

"Well, you might want to warm it up when you get there."

"I will," Liam promised.

She stood and pulled her jacket around her. "It's downright frigid out there . . . but it's nice and toasty in here. Coop taught you well." She rested her hand on his cheek. "Good night, my dear. Keep me posted . . . and bring that little fellow over for a muffin or cinnamon bun when you get him back."

"I will, Sal. Thanks."

Sally turned to Tuck. "And I'll see *you* soon!"

Chapter 54

Liam looked out the window of Levi's apartment and watched the leaves chase each other across the cobblestone streets. "It looks like it's going to snow any minute."

"It feels like it too," Emma said, pulling her sweater around her.

"Are you sure you don't want something to eat?" Levi asked, handing Liam a cup of coffee. "Em made pumpkin muffins."

Liam shook his head. "I wish I could, but my stomach is tied in knots."

"Everything's going to be fine," Emma assured him. "And afterward, we'll go to The Gallows for lunch and celebrate, and you and Aidan can take the muffins home."

Liam ventured a smile, "The Gallows, eh? That's kind of prognostic." He took a sip of his coffee, glanced at his watch, and wished it was already *afterward*. "We should go."

A half hour later, they walked up the courthouse steps and saw John waiting near the entrance with his briefcase. He was on his phone, but when he saw them, he smiled, and a minute later, he slipped his phone in his pocket and joined them. "No worries," he said, shaking hands. "We got this!"

Emma squeezed Levi's hand and Liam smiled, daring to hope. "Is Aidan here?"

"He is—he's with a rep from DCF . . . and if all goes well, he'll be leaving with you." John glanced at his watch. "Let's go in."

They followed John into a small room with several rows of chairs, two tables, and a podium—it was nothing like the elegant courtroom Liam had expected; it was more like a classroom, and it was much less intimidating. He sat down at one of the tables next to John, and Levi and Emma sat behind them.

"Your confrontation with Carlton may not even come up," John said as he looked through his papers. "To the best of my knowledge, he hasn't filed charges."

Liam nodded, feeling his heart—and head—pounding. He rubbed his temple, inadvertently touching his scar, and looked around the room again—it reminded him of the room he'd waited in with Jack when they joined the marines. Suddenly, his mind flashed back to the look of dismay he'd seen on Coop's face when he told him he'd enlisted . . . and then he remembered the pained look he saw when he said he didn't care if he died. As soon as the words had spilled from his mouth, he'd wished he could take them back. "I'm sorry, Coop," he murmured. "I didn't mean it . . . I *did* care."

"What?" John said, glancing over and giving him a puzzled look.

Liam looked up and remembered where he was. He shook his head as if to clear it. "N-nothing," he stammered. "I was thinking about something else." He rubbed his temple, thinking, *Where the hell did that come from?* It had been years since he'd thought of that day—it was almost as if he'd blocked it out . . . and now, it had come back to him as clearly—and as keenly—as if it happened yesterday.

Just then, Carlton and Libby Knox came in with their attorney and sat at the table across from them. John stood to shake hands with their attorney, but the Knoxes looked straight ahead. The next moment, a guard came through a door behind the bench, asked them to rise, and announced the judge, and as they stood, an older woman in a sweeping black robe came through the door. "You may be seated," she said, peering over her glasses.

Forty-five minutes later, it was over. The Knoxes' attorney presented their case—which was based on their years of financial support, as well as their familial rights, but the judge—who'd already reviewed Cadie's will and Liam's background, including his military service—had no patience for their claims. "The boy's mother has clearly stated in her will that she would like Mr. Tate to be her son's guardian, and since he has already begun adoption proceedings, has a sound reputation, is a respectable businessman, and is financially secure, it is the court's decision that her wishes be followed. If the grandparents are interested in visitation rights, they can request them, but custody is hereby granted to Mr. Tate." And with the bang of her gavel, Liam was granted custody of Aidan.

John turned to him and smiled. "Congratulations! I told you there was nothing to worry about."

"I couldn't've done it without you," Liam said, barely able to believe it. "Thank goodness you had the foresight to draw up that will."

"That's my job," John said.

"Now I have to *do* my job," Liam said with a smile, "and finish the work on your boat."

"There's no hurry. Besides, Jordy hasn't learned a thing. Last week, he wrecked my Beemer!"

Liam shook his head in disbelief. "Is he okay?"

"Yeah, he's fine," John said, looking over Liam's shoulder.

Liam turned.

"You did it!" Emma said, her eyes gleaming as she hugged him.

Levi hugged him too. "I know Mom's smiling," he said, his voice choked with emotion. "I can't thank you enough."

Liam stepped back and looked in his eyes. "It's for me too."

Just then, the door opened and Aidan ran down the aisle into Liam's arms. "Oh, man, I missed you!"

Aidan grinned and squeezed him back. "I missed you, too, Cap."

Just then, Liam looked up and saw Carlton and Libby Knox stalking silently out of the room.

Chapter 55

"It's snowing!" Aidan shouted as they came out of The Gallows.

"It is indeed," Emma said, pulling her hood up.

"Snow on October fifth!" Levi said, shaking his head.

"That's New England for you," Liam said, pulling up his collar.

"Do you want to stay over tonight?" Levi asked. "The weather's supposed to be better tomorrow."

"No, we'll be fine," Liam replied. "Besides, *someone* has already missed too many days of school," he added, tousling Aidan's hair.

"Well, you better get going, then," Levi said, pushing his hands into his pockets, "before the roads get bad." Then he felt something in his pocket and pulled it out. "I keep forgetting to give this to you," he said, holding out Cadie's cell phone.

Liam frowned. "I don't need that."

"She wanted you to have it," Levi said. "It's for emergencies, and now that you have Aidan, it'll come in handy if he—or the school—needs to reach you."

Reluctantly, Liam took the phone.

"Here's the charger," Levi said, pulling a thin white cord out of his other pocket. "You have to charge it once in a while or it won't work—the battery icon is on the upper right corner," he added. "It tells you how much battery you have left."

"We'll see," Liam said skeptically.

"I'll show him," Aidan volunteered.

"There you go," Levi said with a laugh. "Do you want me to change the ringtone?"

"Change 'Love Shack'?!" Liam asked, looking horrified. "Are you kidding?"

Levi laughed. "I thought you might like a regular ringtone . . . or at least something less intrusive."

Liam thought about his old stuffed bear, Teddy, and Coop's old mailbox and realized he felt the same way about Cadie's ringtone—the one that had made her smile: He didn't want to ever let them go. "No . . . leave it," he said.

"Suit yourself," Levi said with a shrug.

"It's actually shoo . . ." Liam started, but then stopped.

"Have you got your muffins?" Emma asked. Liam held up the bag and she smiled. "Good—in case you get stranded!"

"I hope we *don't* get stranded, but if we do," he said, looking down at Aidan, "it'll be the first of many adventures, right, pal?"

Aidan nodded.

They gave hugs all around, and as Levi and Emma walked away, Liam called after them, "Don't be strangers!"

"We won't," Em promised.

"We're going to visit so often you're going to get tired of us," Levi called back.

"That'll never happen!"

"Maybe we'll come out for Columbus Day," Levi said.

"Sounds good!" Liam said, waving.

* * *

Heavy, wet snowflakes splattered against the windshield of the old pickup as they drove back to Hyannis, but the snow never amounted to much on the roads. Conditions took a turn for the worse, however, when they bumped onto the ferry—it was almost as if they were driving into a different world. Blinding snow and whipping winds buffeted the nearly empty vessel, and Liam and Aidan abandoned the truck and hurried up the stairs to the cabin. Liam bought two cups of cocoa topped with whipped cream, and they sat at a table and ate their muffins.

Aidan looked out at the swirling snow and whitecaps. "Do you think we *will* get stranded?"

"No, we'll be fine," Liam answered. "The captain's made this trip countless times—I bet he could do it blindfolded."

Immediately, Aidan pictured an old sea captain with a blindfold on, swaying in the bridge with his hands on the big wooden steering wheel. "Blindfolded?!"

"Mm-hmm," Liam said with a nod. "When I was your age, Coop and I came across in a storm much worse than this."

"You did?!"

Liam nodded. "It was right before Christmas and it was the last ferry, so it was stormy *and* dark."

"Why were you with your uncle?"

Liam hesitated, realizing Aidan didn't know much about his past. "Because my parents had died."

"Oh," Aidan said quietly. Then ventured, "How'd they die?"

"In a car accident."

Aidan nodded thoughtfully. "So, you're kind of *like* me."

Liam searched his face and smiled. "Kind of . . ."

Aidan took a sip of his cocoa. "I can't wait to see Tuck—he's going to be beside himself when he finds out I'm going to be living with him."

"He sure is," Liam said with a laugh. "He's missed you."

"I've missed him too . . . *and* Moby, although he's still *aloof.*"

"He *is,* but he has a friendly side too."

"I know—like when he curled up on Mom's bed," Aidan said, eating the last bite of his muffin. "I love these muffins," he added with his mouth full.

"They are good—you'll have to tell Sally about them."

"Mmm," Aidan agreed, looking out the window again. "We're almost there!"

Liam looked out the window and saw the outline of the island. "There she is."

Aidan crumpled up his muffin paper. "Islands are girls too?!"

"Yes, they're *feminine*," Liam said, impressed that Aidan remembered their conversation about objects having gender. "In fact, some people call Nantucket *The Gray Lady*."

Aidan watched the churning waves and wondered if the sea life liked being tossed around. "What about whales?"

"Feminine," Liam confirmed. "That's why Ishmael, Captain Ahab's mate, when he spots Moby Dick calls out, 'Thar *she* blows!' "

"Who's Captain Ahab and Ishmael?"

"You don't know who Captain Ahab and Ishmael are?!" Liam asked, looking shocked. "That's almost as bad as not knowing what a s'more is."

Aidan giggled and shook his head.

"Captain Ahab is Nantucket's most famous literary character."

"He is?"

Liam nodded. "He's the one-legged sea captain who hunted Moby Dick."

"Was Moby Dick a whale?"

"Moby Dick was the biggest, meanest whale that ever lived in the waters off Nantucket."

Aidan frowned. "Why'd they say, 'Thar *she* blows!' if Moby Dick was a boy?"

"That's a good question," Liam said, and as he stood up to throw away their trash, he wondered how many more questions Aidan would ask that he wouldn't be able to answer. "Maybe you should ask Sally," he suggested as they made their way down the stairs to the truck.

When they pulled up in front of Sally's house, she was sweeping the snow off her front walk, and Tuck, who was busily pulling dry lily stalks out of the ground, stopped his landscaping and bounded over to greet them. "You did it!" Sally cried, dropping her broom and scooping Aidan into her arms.

"We did it," Liam said, smiling as she hugged him too.

"Sally," Aidan said, giving her a quick squeeze, "if Moby Dick was a boy, how come Ishmael shouts, 'Thar *she* blows'?"

Liam eyed Sally with raised eyebrows as he waited for her to answer, but Sally didn't miss a beat. "Oh, that's just what sailors say when they see a whale—it doesn't matter if it's a boy or a girl."

Aidan slid to the ground, seemingly satisfied, and wrapped his arms around Tuck's neck. "Guess what, boy?" he whispered into his thick golden fur. "I'm going to live with you!" Tuck's tail thumped happily and he licked Aidan's cheek.

Chapter 56

"Are you sure you want this tired, old bear?" Liam asked as he tucked the stuffed bear from his childhood next to Aidan. Aidan pulled the bear close and nodded, and Liam tousled his hair and stood up to turn off the light.

"Aren't you going to listen to my prayers?" Aidan asked.

"I wasn't sure if you wanted me to," Liam said, sitting back down and pretending he hadn't forgotten. Just then, Tuck moseyed in, put his chin on the bed, and then launched his whole body onto the bed. He stretched out next to Aidan and rested his big head on his chest. Aidan smiled, clasped his hands together on top of Tuck's head, and solemnly closed his eyes. "Now I lay me down to sleep. I pray the Lord my soul to keep. Thy love go with me through the night and wake me up in the morning light. God bless Mom, Levi, Em, Sally, Tuck, Moby, Cap . . . and me. Amen." He opened his eyes and searched Liam's face. "Do you think Mom can hear me?"

Liam pressed his lips together. "I'm sure she can. She's watching over you every minute."

"I thought so," Aidan said, stroking Tuck's head. "Good night, Cap."

"Good night," Liam said, gently brushing the wisps of blond hair from Aidan's forehead and thinking how much he looked like Cadie. "Sleep tight."

"Don't let the bed bugs bite," he murmured sleepily. "Love you."

Liam smiled. "Love you too," he said softly, kissing both of them and turning off the light. Even though it was only eight o'clock, he was exhausted and his head was pounding. He filled the sink with hot, sudsy water, and while he washed the plates from their celebratory supper—pancakes—he wondered if Sally had an old cookbook she'd lend him with some foolproof Crock-Pot recipes. He rinsed out the sink, dried his hands, and realized "Love Shack" was playing in his pocket. He slipped the phone out, saw Levi's name, and slid his finger across the screen. "Hey," he said. "Yep, we made it back, although it was snowing pretty hard when we were coming across . . . yes, he's all tucked in . . . and Tuck's right beside him . . . and I'm right behind them. How're you two doing? Mm-hmm . . . Yes, I'll remember to plug it in . . . Mm-hmm, in the bottom . . . I saw it. Yes, Aidan showed me the little switch on the side, but I'm afraid if I turn off the ringer, I won't hear it . . . No, I doubt I'll feel it . . . Okay, we'll see . . . Thanks . . . I will . . . You too . . . Talk to you soon . . . Say hi to Em . . . Love you too . . . G'night."

Liam sat at the kitchen table and studied all the icons on the screen, wondering what each one did. He lightly tapped the red musical note on the bottom right and was surprised to see his name appear. He tapped it, and immediately two song titles appeared. He tapped the top one, and "The End of the Innocence" began to play. Smiling, he tapped the second one, and the slow, haunting whistle from Guns N' Roses's 1989 hit "Patience" began to play; he paused, his mind drifting back to that fateful summer day. Then, as the song played, he tapped the screen again and touched the Photos icon; then he tapped Camera Roll and the screen filled with tiny squares. He touched the last square, and a photo of Cadie filled the screen. He stared at it—it was the one he'd taken of Cadie standing in front of the cottage, the one where her pink hat had perfectly matched the blossoms that had cascaded over the roof. "Hey," he said softly, gazing at the sweet smile that had stolen his heart so long ago.

As he listened to the songs that had reminded Cadie of him, his eyes filled with tears, and long after they'd ended, he continued to gaze at the dark screen.

In the back of his mind, he heard a faint meow, wiped his eyes, and got up to open the door. As he did, a gust of cold wind rushed in, bringing leaves with it, and then Moby trotted proudly in behind them.

"Hold on, there, mister," Liam said, eyeing him. "What've you got?"

Moby looked up at him, sauntered over, and dropped a dead, furry body at his feet.

"You caught a mole?!"

The gray cat sat on his haunches and licked his paws casually as if it was no big deal.

"I'm impressed!" Liam said, scratching his ears. The old cat pushed his silky head into Liam's palm and purred, and a moment later, he got up and sauntered down the hall. Liam picked up the lifeless rodent and put it on the porch for an early burial. Then he turned off the kitchen lights and headed down the hall. As he walked past Aidan's room, he looked in and realized Moby had curled up on Aidan's other side. He shook his head and then continued down the hall. He turned on the bathroom light, and while he waited for the water coming out of the faucet to warm up, he looked around. It had been almost three weeks since Cadie died, and he still hadn't had the chance—or the initiative—to take down the handicap bars, and although

Emma had thrown away all the medicine bottles that had been on the counter, when he opened the cabinet to get some aspirin for his head, he found more.

He gazed at Cadie's name on the labels and new tears filled his eyes. He leaned against the bathroom door and wondered how long it would be before little things—like a name on a medicine bottle or an old song—didn't overwhelm him with waves of grief.

Chapter 57

Aidan shuffled sleepily into the kitchen. "Are we going to Sally's for breakfast?"

Liam looked up from making lunch. "I wasn't planning on it. We still have leftover pancakes."

Aidan yawned, stroking Tuck's head. "I'd rather go to Sally's—like we did on the first first day."

Liam glanced at the clock. "Well, I guess it depends on how quickly you can get ready."

Aidan's face brightened. "I can be quick," he said. "C'mon, Tuck, let's go! We're goin' to Sally's, and you know what that means—bacon *and* muffins!" He raced down the hall with Tuck trotting happily after him.

Liam shook his head. "Life goes on, doesn't it, Mobe?" he murmured, and the gray cat, who was dozing on a kitchen chair, opened one eye. "That reminds me—I need to take care of your late-night conquest." He finished making Aidan's sandwich, pulled the wax paper out of the drawer, tore off a piece, and wrapped it with the same neat folds he'd been making since he was Aidan's age. Then he tucked the sandwich into Aidan's lunch bag, added a juice box and some cookies, and glanced at the clock again. "Almost ready?" he called.

"Almost," Aidan called back.

"I'm going outside," he called, slipping on his jacket.

"Okay, I'll be right out."

"Don't forget to brush your teeth."

"But I haven't had breakfast."

"Well, you won't have the chance afterward."

"Okay."

Liam opened the door, realized how mild it was, and took his jacket off again. "Who would've thought we had snow yesterday?" Hearing his words, Moby looked up. "Want to go out?" he asked, and the old cat hopped off the chair, arched his back, and tiptoed slowly toward the door. "Take your time," Liam said. "We're not in a hurry." Ignoring his sarcastic comment, Moby brushed slowly through Liam's legs, swishing his tail.

Once outside, he sniffed the body of the deceased and waited while Liam went to get a shovel. "Where should his final resting place be?" Liam asked, walking around the yard and pressing down the soft maze of tunnels. He followed several trails that all seemed to lead to the birdfeeder. "I wonder what the attraction is here," he murmured to the cat. "Maybe we should put him *here* so all his moley friends can see what happens when they tunnel through *this* yard . . . what do you think, Mobe?" But Moby, who was licking his paws and wiping them over his ears, seemed indifferent to the site of the mole's final resting place. Liam kicked away a small pile of leaves that had accumulated around the hydrangeas and pushed his shovel into the earth. Then he snugly wrapped the mole in the paper towel, set it gently in the hole, and covered it with dirt.

"Whatcha doin'?" Aidan asked, appearing at his side.

"Burying a mole."

"Moby caught another mole?!"

"Yep," Liam said as Tuck nosed around the fresh dirt.

"Do moles go to heaven?"

Liam frowned, realizing that here, already, was another question to which he didn't know the answer.

"They do," he replied.

"I bet God doesn't like it when they dig tunnels in heaven," Aidan said with a grin.

"I bet He doesn't mind as much as I do," Liam replied with a chuckle. He looked up. "Ready?"

"Yup."

"You guys go hop in the truck. I'll be right there."

"Okay. C'mon, Tuck," Aidan said, skipping toward the truck with Tuck at his heels. They climbed in and waited while Liam put the shovel in the shed.

"Got your lunch?" Liam asked, climbing in.

Aidan nodded. "It sure is warm today," he said, leaning over to roll down Tuck's window. "And it was snowing yesterday!"

"I know," Liam agreed, watching Tuck lean out the window. "I think we're going to have a thunderstorm later though—which won't make Tuck happy."

"How come?" Aidan asked, putting his hand on Tuck's back.

"I don't know—he's just always been afraid of thunder."

"You shouldn't be afraid," Aidan whispered softly in Tuck's ear as he stroked his long copper-colored fur. "It's just the angels bowling. Hey, maybe Mom will be bowling too!"

Ten minutes later they were sitting by the widow in Cuppa Jo when Aidan saw Sally coming over with a tremendous muffin topped with cinnamon streusel. With a smile, she set it in front of him. "Wow!" he exclaimed. "I didn't know you had pumpkin muffins!"

"We have *everything*," Sally said jovially, kissing the top of his head, "especially for my favorite customer."

"Me?!" Aidan asked as he peeled off the muffin paper and took a big bite. "Mmm, this is really good," he mumbled with his mouth full of muffin. Sally laughed and hurried back to help wait on the growing line of customers.

Liam unwrapped his breakfast sandwich, broke off a piece of bacon, and gave it to Tuck, whose big head was resting on his lap. Then he took a sip of coffee and watched the customers coming through the door. In the off-season, almost everyone who came into Sally's was a native Nantucketer, and he waved to several of them. He glanced at his watch. "Need to hurry up, pal, or we'll be late." As he said this, he saw a woman with dark wavy hair come in with two blond-haired kids in tow. He frowned and waited for her to turn around, but the boy turned first, and when his eyes met Liam's, a flicker of recognition crossed his face. He pulled his mother's sleeve and then motioned to their table, and she turned to look. Immediately, a huge smile spread across her face, and then, as her children watched in dismay, she left their coveted spot near the front of the line. The kids hung back, hoping she'd return, but instead, she motioned for them to follow. The boy groaned, looking longingly at the glass case full of pastries and muffins, and then followed his sister, muttering, "We're gonna be late."

"Hey," Tracey said with a smile.

"Hey yourself," Liam said, standing to give her a hug. As he did, Tuck emerged from under the table and wiggled around them.

"Mom," T. J. said, finding his smile, "he looks just like Boomer!"

"He does," Tracey agreed, petting the big golden retriever. "What's his name?"

"Tucket," Liam said. "What are *you* guys doing here?"

"*We,*" Tracey said, putting her arms around her kids, "are headed to school . . . *and* we're probably going to be late . . . *again.*"

Liam eyed her with surprise. "School?!

She nodded, and then realized Aidan and Olivia were eyeing each other shyly. "Liv, can you say 'hi'?"

"I'm sorry," Liam said apologetically. "This is Aidan, and we're headed to school too." He put his hand on Aidan's head. "So, does that mean you're living out here?"

Tracey nodded. "I left Jack, Li. It's a long story. I've been meaning to call you, but it's been so hectic getting the kids settled." She nodded to Aidan and eyed Liam with raised eyebrows. "The last time I saw you, you were flying solo. How is it that you have such a cute, little breakfast partner?"

Liam laughed. "It's a long story too. Maybe we should drop the kids off and then talk."

"Okay," Tracey said, "but I have to feed mine first." She turned to survey the line and was happy to discover there wasn't one.

"Do you want a coffee?" Liam asked over his shoulder as he refilled his cup.

"Sure," Tracey said, riffling through her wallet, looking for the twenty she'd stuffed in it that morning.

"How do you take it?"

"Light and sweet."

Liam shook his head as he polluted her coffee with sugar and cream.

"So, what's good here, Aidan?" Tracey asked as the little boy crumpled up his muffin paper and walked past her to throw it away.

"The pumpkin muffins," he said with a sugary grin.

Tracey laughed at his enthusiasm and looked at T. J. and Olivia. "How does that sound?"

They both nodded. "I'm also getting a coffee," she said, handing the young man behind the counter the twenty she'd finally found.

"So, who's your teacher, Aidan?"

"Mrs. Polley."

"That's Olivia's teacher too!" Tracey said. "Did you hear that, Liv? Aidan's in your class."

Olivia frowned uncertainly and Aidan explained, "I've been away. Today's my first day back."

Tracey eyed Liam again as he handed the coffee to her and he grinned. "I told you—it's a long story."

"I can't wait to hear it," she said.

Just then, Sally came out from the kitchen, wiping her hands on her apron. "Ah! I see your paths have finally crossed," she said with a twinkle in her eye. "I've been wondering when that would happen."

"Hi, Sal," Tracey said, giving her old employer a hug.

"It's about time you stopped in," Sally teased. Then she noticed Jase waiting to give Tracey her change. "This one's on the house, Jase—Tracey used to work here."

Jase shrugged, dumped the change back into the drawer, and gave Tracey back her twenty.

"Thanks, Sal. You didn't have to do that."

"I know I didn't have to. I *wanted* to," she said, pulling a big piece of bacon from behind her back and holding it out to Tucket. He took it politely and she kissed the top of his head.

"If you're ever looking for help, Sal, let me know. I'm on my own now."

"I *am* looking for help," Sally said, looking up in surprise. "Jase is moving back to Boston. When can you start?"

"Whenever you'd like," Tracey said.

Sally turned to the boy behind the counter. "When are you moving, Jase?"

"Next Saturday," he said as he made change for a customer, "but I'd like to start packing sooner than that."

"Can you start Monday?" Sally asked, turning back to Tracey.

"You bet," Tracey said.

"Perfect," Sally said, putting her arm around her. "It'll be like old times."

Chapter 58

"Do you remember when we were here at the end of the summer," Tracey asked as they sat at the picnic table next to the boathouse, sipping their coffee, "and I said I had to drop Jack off at the airport, but I joked that I didn't really know where he was going?"

Liam nodded, trying to remember through the fog of the last two months, the conversation they'd had back in August.

"Well, even though I was joking at the time, I found out he really *didn't* have a business trip. He was going to California to spend time with the mother of his youngest child—at least *I think* he's the youngest."

"How'd you find that out?"

"She called and left a message!"

"No!"

"Yes, she said something about not being able to meet him at the airport. She must've known we had caller ID. Everyone does these days."

"I don't," Liam said.

"*Why* am I not surprised?" Tracey teased, rolling her eyes.

"Anyway, I think she wanted me to find out, so after I heard her message, I looked on Jack's Facebook page—to see if she was one of his friends—and there she was . . . and when I clicked on her page—which, of course, didn't have any security settings—I saw pictures of her with Jack and a little boy who looks just like T. J. That's when I lost it! Even though I've always wanted the kids to have a full-time dad, this was too much.

"I threw some stuff in a suitcase, loaded the kids and the dog in the car, and started driving. At first, I didn't know where we were going. I just needed to *go* . . . I needed to figure things out. We ended up driving all the way to my parents' house in Florida!

"I knew, right away, I couldn't stay there, though, so I asked them if I could use the house up here. My dad jumped at the idea—he doesn't like it just sitting here empty. So we drove back to Vermont, and when I knew Jack wouldn't be there, we picked up a few more things, and came out here."

"Jack was here, you know. . . ." Liam said.

"He was?!"

"He was looking for you. In fact, we sat right here and talked."

"I didn't know that," Tracey said, shaking her head. "When was that? I mean, when in the midst of all that *you* were going through?"

"It was the night before Cadie and I got married."

"Oh, I'm so sorry, Li," she said apologetically.

"It's not your fault."

"It is, in a way—if I hadn't left him . . . or if I'd at least answered my phone, he wouldn't've been looking for me." She paused. "How was he?"

"Drunk . . . and self-absorbed."

"What else is new?" Tracey said, her voice edged with sarcasm.

"Although he did ask, when he was leaving, if I'd ever found out if Cadie was related to Levi."

"What'd you tell him?"

"I told him I hadn't."

Tracey nodded, sipping her coffee. "It's so nice out today," she said, taking off her fleece jacket. "I can't believe we had snow yesterday and it's in the seventies today. I also can't believe you clocked Cadie's father!"

"I know—it was really stupid . . . but it sure felt good," he added with a grin.

"How's Aidan doing?"

"He seems okay. He misses her and gets teary at times—especially at bedtime."

"Well, there's no one on earth who can better understand how he feels."

"Having Tuck helps too," Liam said, nodding to the big dog lying in the warm sunshine. "They're inseparable."

Tracey smiled. "Dogs have a way of making the hard times more bearable. There was no way Jack was getting Boomer—I love him too much—he's such a big mush. In fact, we will have to get Tuck and Boom together—they'd have a great time!"

Liam smiled. "That would be fun."

Tracey looked out at the landscape dotted with boats that had been pulled out of the water and winterized with heavy-duty plastic white covers. "Do you still have that runabout you had in high school?"

"I do," Liam said with a smile.

"You do?! Where do you keep her?"

"In the barn," he said, nodding over his shoulder.

"Do you know you've never given me a ride?"

"I haven't?!" Liam teased with an impish grin.

"No," Tracey said, sounding wounded.

"Well, we'll just have to fix that."

They were both quiet, each lost in their own thoughts, and then the comfortable silence between them was broken by the sound of "Love Shack" coming from Liam's pocket. Tracey watched in quiet amusement as Liam slipped the iPhone out of his pocket, glanced at the screen, and answered it. "Yes, this is he . . . Okay, thanks, Mrs. Polley, I'll be right there."

He slid the phone back in his pocket. "I guess Aid's feeling a little out of sorts. Mrs. Polley said not to be alarmed—she just thinks he's feeling a little blue and maybe I should pick him up."

"That's certainly understandable after all he's been through," Tracey said. Then she smiled. "Nice ringtone!"

"Thanks," Liam said, grinning as he stood up.

Tracey handed her empty cup to Liam. "I can't believe you're a dad!"

"I can't believe it either!"

"Married, widowed, cell-phone–carrying father of two! A lot has happened in the last six weeks!"

He nodded. "*And* we're getting a computer."

"No!" she teased.

"Yup, Levi is bringing one out the next time he comes."

"Well, I guess you're not an island anymore!"

"No," he said slowly, surprised by her observation. "I guess I'm not."

Chapter 59

As soon as Liam walked into the school office, he saw Aidan sitting in a chair with his backpack at his feet, and the look on his face said it all. He scooped him into his arms. "Having a tough day, pal?"

Aidan nodded, gazing tearfully over Liam's shoulder. "I just miss her," he said, "and I can't think about anything else."

"I know how that is," Liam said as they walked across the parking lot. "You should look over there, though," he said, pointing to the truck. "Your pal's waitin' for you."

Aidan looked—his cheeks still wet—and saw Tuck watching from the truck. Liam set Aidan down and he ran over and climbed up on the seat next to him, and Tuck immediately started licking his wet cheeks. "Hey," Aidan said, giggling.

"He likes your salty tears."

Aidan smiled and buried his face in Tuck's long, soft fur, drying his tears.

Ten minutes later, they pulled into the driveway, and Liam noticed the sky was slate gray and the air was eerily still. He rolled up the truck windows, and as they walked toward the house, thunder rumbled in the distance. Immediately, Tuck's ears flattened against his head and his flag of a tail sank between his legs.

"It's okay, Tuck," Liam consoled, but when a cold gust of wind swept across the yard, swirling golden leaves into the dark sky, and a streak of white lightning split the heavens, Tuck raced toward the house.

"He really *doesn't* like storms," Aidan said, watching the leaves chase him across the driveway.

"No, he doesn't," Liam agreed, opening the door.

"It's okay, Tuck," Aidan said, dropping his backpack next to the door and laying down next to him under the table. He draped his arm around Tuck's neck. "You don't need to be afraid. It's just a thunderstorm and it'll be over before you know it."

Tuck looked up at Aidan and the tip of his tail wagged; then he put his big head on Aidan's lap and closed his eyes. A moment later, they were both sound asleep.

Liam turned on the stove light and filled the kettle with water, and while he waited for it to get hot, he listened to the rain hitting the windows—it was coming down sideways, and lightning was splitting the sky every few minutes, followed by long, low rolls of thunder. He looked under the table and couldn't believe his eyes. From the time Tuck was a pup, he had cowered under the table during storms, and no amount of coaxing would bring him out. But now—with Aidan next to him—he didn't even notice the storm rumbling outside.

The kettle started to sing and Liam poured hot water over his tea bag and let it steep. He rarely drank tea—coffee had always been his get-up-and-go drink; tea was more of a comfort thing, and at the moment—like Tuck—he needed a little comfort. He dunked the teabag a few more times and gave it a squeeze. Then he splashed a little milk into it, cupped his hands around the mug, and walked over to look out the window.

As he watched the rain coming down, he thought about Tracey's comment and realized it was true—after a lifetime of losing loved ones, he'd pulled away from the world and become a recluse—an island that no one could touch . . . or hurt . . . or love. And he'd been perfectly content living that way . . . until Cadie had swept into his life like a summer storm—full of love and life and faith . . . and the way she lived . . . and the way she died . . . had changed him. He *wasn't* an island anymore.

"Did it stop raining?" Aidan murmured sleepily.

"Yes," Liam said.

He sat up, rubbing his eyes. "I've got your ball, Tuck," he said softly. "Storm's over. . . ." He bounced it and Tuck opened one eye. "Want to play?"

Tuck thumped his tail and scrambled to his feet.

The late-day sun illuminated the tops of the trees, making the rusty golden colors shimmer like flames against the dark gray clouds and bathing the yard in a rosy hue. Raindrops sparkled from every surface, and as Liam watched, a female cardinal landed on the wall. Tuck was dancing on the wet grass, waiting for Aidan to throw the ball, and as soon as he did, he charged after it, scooped it up, raced back, and dropped it at Aidan's feet again. Smiling, Aidan picked up the soggy ball, hugged Tuck's noble head, and playfully whispered, "Are ya ready?"

Tuck began to dance again, waiting, and Liam smiled.

This is what heaven must be like. . . .

Epilogue

Nine months later

Liam wiped down the mahogany surface with his favorite soft chamois and then pushed the 1955 Chris-Craft Sportsman—which had spent the last two weeks nestled on the marine railcar—out of the boathouse. The classic, old runabout edged toward the water, sunlight glinting off her newly varnished surface, and then Liam stopped the winch so Aidan could slip her Yacht Ensign into the socket on her transom. Liam walked back to the stern and stood next to him. "What do you think?" he asked.

"It's perfect!" Aidan said, admiring the new name that had been painted across her transom in elegant gold script: *Cadie-did!*

They heard another vehicle pulling into the parking lot and looked up.

"Sally sent along blueberry muffins!" Tracey called as she opened the door for Boomer to hop out. Seeing him, Tuck raced over and the two dogs greeted each other, nose-to-nose, tails wagging. "I think they *must* be brothers," T. J. said, laughing, as he lifted a beach bag and cooler out of the car.

Liam walked over to help and Tracey smiled. "She also sent a bottle of champagne so we can have a proper christening."

"That's very thoughtful," Liam said, shaking his head, "but she should know better—there's no way we're smashing a bottle on new varnish."

"Well, we'll just have to drink it, then!" Tracey said with a grin.

"Hi, Aid," Olivia and T. J. called as they trotted down the ramp.

"Your boat's beautiful," T. J. said with an approving nod. "I'm gonna have a boat like this someday."

"It's a *runabout*," Aidan corrected, "and Cap's gonna help me restore one too."

Tracey laughed. "Raisin' him right, I see."

"Of course," Liam said as he lifted their things into the back and walked up to the boathouse to start the winch. "We've already picked one out—a 1955 Barrel Back."

"I always knew you'd make a good dad," she said.

Liam smiled but didn't say anything as he waited for the runabout to float free. "Aid, grab the forward line and tie it to the dock cleat."

T. J. and Olivia watched enviously as Aidan tied the knot.

"Jack called," Tracey said softly.

"Yeah?" Liam said, closing the boathouse doors. "What'd *he* have to say?"

"He's moving to California. He said this part-time dad thing wasn't working out."

"And just like that, he's leaving?"

"Just like that."

Liam locked the doors and shook his head, and then, seeing the sad look in Tracey's eyes, wrapped his arms around her.

"I'm sorry, Trace. I know you gave it your all—more than he deserved." He kissed the top of her head. "If it's any consolation, I'm glad you're here," he added with a smile.

Tracey smiled. "I'm glad I'm here too."

"C'mon, Mom," T. J. called.

"We're coming!"

The dogs moseyed down to the dock, and Liam lifted them into the back of the boat. "Hope you guys have your sea legs on," he teased as he helped Tracey into the front and untied the line. "Are you all set?" he asked, checking their life jackets.

"We are, Captain," they said, grinning.

Liam pushed the starter and the motor rumbled to life, water spitting from its tailpipe. He engaged the clutch and slowly pushed the throttle up with his thumb. Then he looked back and realized the dogs were leaning against the sides, their noses quivering.

As they made their way out of the cove, Liam saw a gorgeous eighteen-foot sloop cutting through the waves with her proud sail billowing. He pointed, and as they drew near, they waved and John Alden waved back.

Liam pushed the throttle higher, and as they sped across the water, he turned to check on the kids and then looked over at Tracey. Her white blouse made her early-summer tan look even darker—*it's all that olive oil she has running through her veins,* he thought, smiling to himself. She looked up, caught him looking at her, and smiled, her jade green eyes seeming to see right through him.

Ten minutes later, the outline of Tuckernuck Island came into view and Liam slowed down. He motioned for T. J. to come forward, lifted him over the back of the seat, and set him down behind the steering wheel. Tracey smiled as she watched Liam showing him how to use the throttle and, when the boat accelerated, letting him steer. Before they reached the island,

Olivia and Aidan both had turns, too, but when they drew closer to the island, Liam took over again and asked Aidan to show T. J. and Olivia how to throw the fenders over the sides.

They slowly circled the island, waving to two boys who were fishing, and then they swung around to a secluded stretch of beach. Liam skillfully maneuvered the runabout up to a brand-new wooden dock and cut the engine. The dogs wiggled excitedly, anxious to jump out but Liam told them to sit, and they gazed forlornly at him as they sank down.

Liam looked at Aidan again and motioned for the two boys to hop out. They scrambled eagerly onto the dock and waited for Olivia to toss them the lines.

"Aid, do you remember how to tie a dock line?" he called.

Aidan nodded, catching Olivia's line.

"Can you show T. J.?"

He nodded again and the two boys huddled over the dock cleats.

When both lines were secure, Liam set the beach bags and coolers on the dock and lifted out the dogs. "Good job," he said, inspecting their knots.

"Hi!" a voice called and they all turned. A huge smile spread across Aidan's face as he dropped his beach bag and sprinted toward Levi, just about knocking him over as he jumped into his arms. "Hey, Sport," Levi said, giving him a hug. "It's good to see you too! Sheesh, you're getting heavy—what the heck have you been eating?!"

Aidan laughed and slid to the ground as everyone else greeted Levi too. "Em's got lunch all ready," he said, taking a cooler from Tracey. "C'mon, she can't wait to see you."

"How's the dock holding up?" Liam asked, surveying their handiwork.

"Pretty well," Levi said as they walked toward the beach. "It's definitely easier than transferring everything to a skiff and rowing ashore. Can you imagine trying to lift these two dogs from the runabout to the skiff?"

Liam laughed. "Yeah, they'd probably have to swim ashore or we'd all end up in the drink!"

"What's *the drink?*" Olivia asked.

"It's the water, silly," Aidan answered.

Levi smiled. "I also don't know how we would've gotten all the building supplies and furniture out here—it would've been impossible."

Liam nodded. "It was a good idea."

As soon as they stepped onto the sand, the dogs made a bee-line for the water, charging headlong into the surf. "I'm surprised they didn't jump right off the dock," T. J. said with a laugh.

They walked along the water and then followed the new, wide path that led to the cottage. "Oh, my!" Tracey said, admiring the tremendous blue hydrangea blossoms and wild pink roses.

"Most of the plantings were already here," Levi explained. "We just pruned them back . . . *and* weeded. We also made charts so we'd be able to restore them to their original glory and we quickly discovered they were just traditional, old-fashioned gardens with black-eyed Susans, echinacea, bee balm, and Emma's favorite, lilies . . . and we planted Mom's Mona Lisa lily out here too—it's huge!"

Tracey nodded. "It sounds like you've been busy!"

"If you keep it up," Liam teased, "you're going to want to live here year-round."

Levi laughed. "I doubt if Em would agree to that!"

They stopped to admire the cottage—which was also in the midst of restoration. "It looks great!" Liam said, admiring the newly installed twelve-over-twelve window sash and cedar shakes on the roof. "Very nice! And I see the rosebush is finally under control."

Levi nodded. "That wild rose was breathtaking—the way it wrapped over the house, but it definitely wasn't good for the structure, so we had to cut it back. It's already filling in, though," he added, gently touching a blossom. They heard a sound, then the front door opened and an orange tiger cat scooted out. Emma peeked out. "I thought I heard voices," she said, giving them all hugs and squeezing Aidan the longest. "Come on in!" she said, opening the door wide.

"I think I'll bring the dogs around back," Levi said, "since they decided to go for a swim."

They all stepped over the new oak door sill into the bright, airy room.

"It's gorgeous," Tracey said, looking around.

"We wanted to keep as much of the original structure as possible," Levi explained when he came in. "We didn't know if we'd have to replace the old, wide-board floor, but after we sanded it down, we realized there was still plenty of wood left, and as you can see, it turned out great."

Liam nodded approvingly. "You did a nice job." He looked around at the new sheetrock.

"No primer or paint yet," Levi said with a smile, "but we're getting there. It's small, and we only plan to be here in the summer months—at least for now." He looked at Emma. "I don't know if Em could do year-round . . . besides, we . . ." he started, but Em raised her eyebrows and he stopped. "Anyway, this side is the living area," he said, gesturing to the open great room, "and the other side doubles as bedroom and studio. My easel is set up in there now, but eventually, I'd like to add on another room."

They all walked over to peer into the studio. "Very nice," Liam said with a nod, and then realized there was a canvas sitting on the easel. He walked over for a closer look. "Wow! This is great!"

Levi smiled. "Thanks. I'm working from several photographs, but the one in the center is my favorite."

Liam studied the photos as tears filled his eyes. He bit his lip and looked at the canvas again. "You've really captured her," he said softly.

"Thanks," Levi said, putting his hand on Liam's shoulder.

"So, are you guys hungry?" Emma asked.

Aidan, T. J., and Olivia all nodded enthusiastically.

"Well, I hope you like chicken salad."

"Sounds good!" Tracey said. "And Sally sent blueberry muffins."

"Oh, I forgot about those!" Aidan said with a grin.

They trouped through the sunny kitchen, admiring the new cabinets and counters, and out to the patio, on which an old-fashioned iron table was set for lunch.

"This is lovely, Em," Tracey said as the kids all squeezed together on the matching bench, elbowing each other and giggling.

"Look at you three!" Em laughed. "I bet you're nothing but mischief when you're together!"

"You're right about that," Liam said with a laugh. "They're as thick as thieves."

They sat down around the table, the ever-hopeful dogs strategically positioning themselves *under* the table, and then Levi gave thanks. As they passed around the croissants and snowflake rolls to make sandwiches, they chatted about everything from the remaining updates to the cottage to the price of propane . . . and from the new show Levi was having in the fall to the catboat Liam was building.

Finally, stuffed with chicken salad and Sally's blueberry muffins, they sat back, and Tuck rested his head on Liam's lap. "That was really good!" Levi said, rubbing his belly. "You outdid yourself, Em."

She nodded and winked at him.

"Ah," Levi said with a grin, "I just got the proverbial wink and a nod—which means I can finally tell you—before I burst, that Em and I have some news . . ."

They all looked up, waiting.

He smiled, his eyes sparkling. "I don't know if you noticed that Em is looking a little rounder," he said, reaching for her hand, "but that's because we . . . are . . . expecting!"

"Oh, that's wonderful!" Tracey exclaimed.

Aidan frowned. "Expecting what?" he asked.

Olivia giggled, elbowing him. "A baby, silly!"

"Oh," he said in surprise.

Em looked at him. "You're going to be an uncle!"

"I am?!" Aidan said in surprise.

She nodded and then Levi smiled at Liam. "And *you* are going to be a grandfather."

Liam pressed his lips together, his eyes glistening, and shook his head. "I guess life *can* change in a heartbeat."

COOP'S SOUL-WARMING CHILI

Ingredients

1 tablespoon canola or olive oil
1 onion, chopped
1 pound ground beef
4 garlic cloves, minced
2 teaspoon chili powder
2 teaspoons ground cumin
1 pinch cayenne
1 (28-ounce) can crushed tomatoes
3 medium tomatoes, chopped, or 2 (10-ounce) cans diced
   tomatoes
1 (15-ounce) can dark red kidney beans, rinsed
1 (15-ounce) can navy beans, rinsed
1 (15-ounce) can black beans, rinsed
1 small can mild green chopped chilies
2 cups water or chicken broth
½ teaspoon ground pepper

Directions

Heat oil in large pot; add onion and cook until lightly browned; remove onion and set aside; add beef or turkey to pan and cook until browned. Add garlic, chili powder, cumin, and cayenne to taste and stir constantly until fragrant—thirty seconds to a minute. Stir in canned tomatoes, beans (rinsed), green chilies, water or chicken broth, and pepper. Increase heat and bring to a boil. Reduce heat and simmer for two hours. Or, after the onion and meat have been browned, transfer to a Crock-Pot, add other ingredients, and cook on low for four hours.

Serve with shredded cheddar, sour cream, and corn bread or crusty rolls.

Sally's Lasagna

Ingredients

1 pound sweet Italian sausage
¾ pound lean ground beef
½ cup minced onion
2 cloves garlic, crushed
1 (28-ounce) can crushed tomatoes
2 (6-ounce) cans tomato paste
2 (6.5-ounce) cans canned tomato sauce
½ cup water
2 tablespoons white sugar
1½ teaspoons dried basil leaves
½ teaspoon fennel seeds
1 teaspoon Italian seasoning
1 tablespoon salt
¼ teaspoon ground black pepper
4 tablespoons chopped fresh parsley
12 lasagna noodles
15 ounces ricotta cheese
1 egg
½ teaspoon salt
1 pound mozzarella cheese, shredded
¾ cup grated Parmesan cheese

Directions

Cook sausage, ground beef, onion, and garlic over medium heat until browned. Stir in crushed tomatoes, tomato paste, tomato sauce, and water. Season with sugar, basil, fennel seeds, Italian seasoning, 1 tablespoon salt, pepper to taste, and 2 tablespoons parsley. Simmer, covered, for an hour, stirring occasionally.

Bring a large pot of lightly salted water to a boil. Cook lasagna noodles in boiling water for 8 minutes. (Sometimes I just soak the noodles in a pan of warm water while I'm getting the other ingredients ready!) Drain and rinse with cold water. In a mixing bowl, combine ricotta cheese with egg, and remaining parsley.

Preheat oven to 350°F (190°C).

To assemble lasagna, spread ⅓ of the meat sauce in the bottom of a 9 × 13-inch baking dish. Arrange four noodles over the sauce (three the long way; one across the end). On top of the noodles, spread ⅓ of the ricotta cheese mixture. Top the ricotta with ⅓ of the shredded mozzarella and sprinkle with ⅓ of the Parmesan. Repeat the layering two more times, ending with mozzarella and Parmesan. Cover tightly with foil that has been sprayed with a cooking spray or lightly wiped with oil to prevent sticking.

Bake in preheated oven for fifty minutes.

NANTUCKET

Nan Rossiter

ABOUT THIS GUIDE

The suggested questions that follow
are included to enhance your group's
reading of *Nantucket*.

Discussion Questions

1. Liam has lost more than his share of loved ones. How has this affected him? What is his life like?

2. The book is simply titled *Nantucket.* Is there a metaphor in this?

3. Describe Liam's relationship with Cooper. How does their relationship change over the years? In what ways are they similar? How do they each adjust to fatherhood?

4. Liam and Cadie share an intense, intimate relationship at a young age. If they had been allowed to see each other, do you think their relationship would have lasted?

5. Should Cadie have tried harder to get in touch with Liam? Are her reasons justified?

6. When a loved one is terminally ill, waiting for the end is heartbreaking. Levi tells Emma he "just wants it to be over," but at the same time he feels selfish because it will only be over when his mother dies. How does each character deal with Cadie's impending death? Do you think assisted death should be legal in terminally ill cases?

7. In the story, Liam considers how life can change in a heartbeat. *In a heartbeat* usually means "in a short time." In Liam's case *in a heartbeat* has more than one meaning. Explain.

8. Discuss the irony of Cadie's ultimate triumph over her father.

9. In real life, sorrow and joy often walk hand in hand. In what ways is this reflected in the story?

10. Do you think Liam and Tracey end up together?